The Bodyguard Series:

Book 2:

The
BODYGUARD
and the
Show Dog

by
Christy Tillery French

Behler™
PUBLICATIONS

California

Behler Publications
California

The Bodyguard Series
Book 2-The Bodyguard and the Show Dog
A Behler Publications Book

Library of Congress Cataloging-in-Publication Data is available
Control Number: 2005934855

FIRST PRINTING

ISBN 1-933016-37-X
Published by Behler Publications, LLC
Lake Forest, California
www.behlerpublications.com

Manufactured in the United States of America

For my brother, Charlie Tillery. I love ya, Twiggy.

Acknowledgments

Special thanks to the wonderful folks at Behler Publications. They are a professional, personable group, and truly an author's dream. I'd like to send a huge thank you to my editor, Karla Keffer, whose insight and expertise helped shape this into a much better book.

I would like to offer my thanks to Robert Satoloe, owner of Birchwood Kennels, Powell, Tennessee, for his patience in answering my numerous questions, as well as helping to make this project so much fun. As a dog lover, I cannot say enough about Rob's endeavors. Since 1982, under the Birchwood prefix, Rob has raised and shown English Springer Spaniels. He has received numerous awards, as dog breeder, owner and handler, and is highly respected in the dog show venue. He has become known for his considerable work with Heritable Genetic Defects for English Springer Spaniels, an area to which he has devoted his career and name.

For more information about Rob and his amazing ventures, visit his website at: www.hometown.aol.com/birchwoodess.

Another big thanks to my friend and fellow author, humorist (and nudist) Allen Parker. Allen shared much information with me regarding nudists and nudist resorts, and through conversations with him, I have developed a healthy respect for this lifestyle. I encourage everyone to read Allen's books *Nudist Among Us* and *Mouse Among Us*, two very funny books.

Thanks also to Gary Littman, private investigator, for answering my questions regarding the licensing process to become a bodyguard.

Special thanks to my core group of friends/authors whose encouragement and support are so much appreciated: Sherry Russell, Victoria Taylor Murray, Laurel Johnson, Lynn Barry, Kathy Bosworth, Beverly Scott, Evelyn Horan, Tammie Newby and Cyndi Hodges, who is also my sister.

As an author, I have taken the liberty to embellish certain circumstances, and any mistakes I have written regarding dog show terminology or descriptions, the nudist lifestyle and/or resorts, and the bodyguard profession are mine alone.

And to both, bee and flower, the giving
and the receiving of pleasure is a
need and an ecstasy.
- Kahlil Gibran

Chapter 1

Natasha leaned back in her chair, feet propped on the desk, lost in reliving the prior night's marathon with Striker. She was working herself into a fever and knew if she didn't stop, she'd be calling him within the next half-hour, finding some excuse to see him, using him to put out the fire. She had just gotten to the really good part, where Striker finally quit playing around and got down to serious business, when bright yellow light burst into her office, conquering the inner fluorescent murk.

Startled, Natasha tilted back and crashed to the floor, her legs in the air. "Ope!" she grunted, staring at the ceiling, thinking that was what she got for buying second-hand office furniture.

As awkward as a turtle on its back, she struggled to untangle from the chair. Aware of warm, moist air tickling her ear, she turned her head. Something wet and slimy rubbed across her lips, and she drew away with a "Phhtt." A small dog watched her, panting a smile. Was there a merry glimmer in the animal's eyes? Was it laughing at her? Her gaze followed the dog's leash to the person attached to the other end. Natasha rolled off the chair and lunged to her feet.

"Can I help you?"

"Oh, my dear, are you all right?" an elderly woman asked, one hand over her heart.

"I'm fine. I'm afraid I just overbalanced." Natasha snuck a glance at the dog. He was laughing at her. Talk about humiliating. After wrestling the chair into an upright position, she cleared her throat and repeated, "Can I help you?"

"Oh, dear, I hope so."

Natasha extended her hand, offering as warm a smile as she could manage under the circumstances. "I'm Natasha Chamberlain."

The woman transferred the leash to her left hand and gave Natasha a delicate handshake. "So pleased to meet you, Ms. Chamberlain. I'm Myrtle Galbreath."

Natasha stooped over to pat the dog's head but avoided looking into its eyes. She straightened and gestured toward one of the chairs beyond her desk. "Please."

Myrtle took slow, measured steps in that direction, the dog waddling along beside her, and gingerly sank into the seat. Seeing its mistress had collapsed, the pooch did likewise, emitting a small grunt when he landed.

Natasha lowered herself into her chair with caution. "Cute dog."

Myrtle's face brightened. "Thank you, dear. I think so."

Natasha regarded the small, wrinkled face staring lovingly into his mistress's beaming one. "What breed is he? Pug?"

"Yes, dear, Chumley's a Pug," Myrtle said, returning the dog's affectionate gaze.

Natasha nodded. This was the first of the breed she had ever seen up close.

Myrtle returned her attention to Natasha. "Are you, per chance, a dog lover, dear?"

"Oh, yes. I love dogs."

"Do you own any?"

"Well, my best friend Roger and I have a Weimaraner we share." Natasha eyed Chumley, thinking Brutus could eat him for lunch. "And my..." She paused, unsure how to refer to Striker. Boyfriend? He was more than that and definitely not a boy. Special other? That didn't fit either; it sounded too generic. She noticed Myrtle seemed confused by her hesitancy, so said, "My life mate and I have been talking about getting a dog together."

Myrtle gave her a concerned look. "Oh, my. That's a big commitment. I hope you're ready to take that step."

Wait a minute. They were only talking about a dog here, not a kid or anything. Commitment? *Yikes.* Natasha hadn't thought of it like that. She chased those thoughts away.

"What can I do for you, Ms. Galbreath?"

"Well, I saw your ad in our community newspaper."

"Yes?"

"And it says you offer private protection services."

"That's right."

"My attorney tells me that would mean something along the lines of a bodyguard."

"Yes."

"Well, I'm in need of one, I'm afraid."

Natasha tamped down the bubble of excitement threatening to overtake her. Oh, boy, here it was, her first client. She couldn't wait to tell Striker. Well, maybe not. He didn't want her to be a bodyguard. Not because his investigative firm provided private security and she would be competing with him, but because he thought it was too dangerous. Especially for Natasha, particularly after her first stint as bodyguard for her best friend, Roger. But that was another story. However, guarding an elderly lady shouldn't be dangerous in any — *hold it, back up.* What did it matter, how he felt about it? This was her life, not his —

"Ms. Chamberlain?"

"Oh. I'm sorry, my mind kind of wandered. Please, call me Natasha."

The older woman gave her a matronly smile. "And you must call me Myrtle."

"You're in need of a bodyguard? Might I ask the reason you would need one, Ms. Galbreath — excuse me, Myrtle?"

"Oh, my dear, it's not for me. It's for Chumley." Myrtle gave Natasha a look, as if she must be crazy if she thought Myrtle needed someone to guard her body.

Natasha tried not to let her disappointment show. Of course, her first official job as a protection specialist would be to guard a dog. Striker would get a kick out of this one; she'd never hear the end of it.

"Chumley's in danger?"

"Yes, dear, extreme danger."

"What kind of danger is he in?"

"Well, I'm afraid he's received a threatening letter."

Natasha's sympathetic look betrayed her inner concern that she just might have a nut case on her hands.

"Chumley's a show dog, a champion," Myrtle went on. "He's won Best in Show regionally for the past two years, and now he's received this terrible letter." She reached into her purse, withdrew a folded piece of white paper, and gave it to Natasha.

Natasha smoothed open the letter and read the typewritten statement out loud. "You show up at the Greater Tennessee Kennel Club Cluster this year, you're dead." She switched on her banker's lamp and held the paper toward the light. It was as ordinary as paper could be, with no linen look or embossing, no real heaviness. She rubbed her fingers over its smooth surface, concluding it was very much like the cheap paper she used in her printer for mundane matters.

"How do you know this letter was meant for Chumley? Maybe it was meant for you."

"Oh, no, dear. It's meant for Chumley. He's the champion. I'm simply his owner."

"How was it addressed?"

Myrtle retrieved a crumpled envelope from her pocketbook and handed it over.

Natasha examined the plain white mailer. Sure enough, it was addressed to Chumley at what she assumed was Myrtle's residence. Of course, there was no return address.

"Who would send a dog a letter? Dogs can't read."

"Whoever intends to kill him, of course."

"And do you have any idea whom that would be?"

"No, dear, I don't. But I would like to hire you to look into that for me as well."

Oh, man, to be offered the chance to do some actual, bona fide investigating. If only. "I'm sorry, Myrtle, but I'm not licensed as an investigator."

"Well, dear, surely it wouldn't require an investigator's license to try to find out who wrote a letter. Couldn't you be like one of those amateur sleuths so many people are writing about nowadays?"

Natasha thought about it. She supposed she could get Roger to help with a computer search. And if push came to shove, there was always Striker. "I could check around, maybe do some unofficial investigating."

"Certainly, dear. Whatever you think."

Natasha glanced back to the paper in her hand. "What exactly is a cluster?"

"It's a very large show, dear, lasting several days, usually with a different All Breed Dog Club sponsoring each day of the event."

"How many dog shows does Chumley participate in a year?"

"In the past, we've tried to do as many as one hundred."

Natasha looked at her. "That many?"

"Yes, but a regular show takes place over a weekend, which certainly makes it more convenient. However, this year, I've decided to be choosy about the shows Chumley attends. He won't be showing again until this cluster."

"Would the person who wrote the letter know that? Is that why they threatened him with this particular one?"

"No, dear, I wouldn't think so. I only recently decided to show Chumley at this cluster."

"Why this one?"

"Well, it's the largest in this area, the one with the most points, the one where Chumley attained championship status."

Natasha eased back in her chair. "As I understand it, once a champion, always a champion; isn't that true?"

"Yes, dear."

"So that wouldn't be a threat to Chumley if he misses the cluster this year."

"That's right."

Natasha nodded. "Then it would stand to reason whoever wrote this letter feels Chumley's participation will hinder or has hindered their dog's chances at Best in Show."

"Yes, or might possibly affect the dog's breed points."

"How does that work? The better the breed points, the greater interest by other dog owners or kennels for breeding; thus, the dog becomes more profitable? Kind of like with horses?"

"That's correct, dear."

Natasha returned her attention to the paper in her hand. "Did you take this letter to the police?"

"Yes, dear, first thing."

"And?"

"They said there was nothing they could do about it. Apparently they don't consider a dog's life as important as a person's." Myrtle gave Natasha an indignant look, as if she found this hard to believe.

Natasha shrugged. "Go figure."

"So I would like for you to check into this and try to find out who sent this terrible letter to my Chumley."

"I'll try my best."

"And be his bodyguard at the show."

"Certainly."

"Also, each day, I take Chumley for a walk around the block. He's put on a little weight recently and needs to be in shape for the cluster."

Natasha's eyes darted to the dog sprawled lazily on the floor. He reminded her of a short, plump Buddha.

"So I would like for you to accompany us on our daily walks in case the person who wrote that letter might be stalking Chumley," Myrtle continued.

Natasha wasn't so sure she wanted to take daily constitutionals with an elderly, arthritic woman and a miniature waddler. Shoot, it'd probably take an hour just to go twenty-five feet.

"I'll pay you for your time, of course," Myrtle said in a rush, seeing Natasha's look. "My attorney checked and said the going rate per hour for a bodyguard in this area would be one hundred ten dollars, but I'm willing to pay you one hundred fifty, and that would include traveling time to and from."

Natasha paper-clipped the envelope to the letter, engaged in a mental tug-of-war. The money was tempting but she didn't consider it ethical to perform a service that wasn't really needed and then charge for it.

"Natasha, dear?"

"I'm sorry. I was just thinking that since the threat involves Chumley attending this particular cluster, I'm fairly certain he won't need protecting for his daily walks. Are you sure you want to expend that much money?"

"Well, dear, as I always say, it's better to be safe than sorry, and I can certainly afford it. I'd feel much better if you escorted us."

Natasha grinned. A hundred fifty bucks an hour. That was more than Pit and Bigun made, and they had been bodyguards for years. She couldn't wait to tell her two Samoan friends. It took a little bit of the sting out of the fact that she was guarding a dog instead of a human.

"I'll draw up a contract," she said, opening her desk drawer.

After both had signed and dated the preprinted agreement, Natasha made a copy for herself. She handed the original to Myrtle, saying, "I've been thinking about the envelope, Myrtle. It's postmarked Valdosta, Georgia. Do you, by any chance, have the rosters listing the dogs and their owners from the last two years' shows? I was thinking I could check the addresses for anyone living in or near there."

"Yes, dear, I think I have the rosters, but the owners won't be listed there, they're in the catalogs."

"Do you have those as well?

"I believe I do."

"Could I have those?"

"Certainly, dear. I'll look for them this afternoon and have them ready for you tomorrow when you come for our walk."

"Great. I'll see you tomorrow, then."

Chapter 2

Natasha bypassed the ramp to Interstate 40, opting for a secondary, much longer route to Striker's house. After an eternal tour of strip malls, car lots, and fast-food restaurants, urbania gave way to open fields, with foliage abounding and horses and cows grazing on deep grass behind picturesque wooden fences.

She always enjoyed this part of the drive, the peaceful, bucolic atmosphere so different from inside the city proper, where commerce reigned and dirty air collected, coating the sky with a nasty haze on what would be an otherwise beautiful day.

Like most Knoxvillians, she loved the area but despaired over its chronic rank among the top ten cities with the dirtiest air in America. But Knoxville was not without its small-town charm. Nestled in the Tennessee Valley, flanked by the Smoky Mountains to the East and the Cumberland Plateau to the West, this was home to the Tennessee Volunteers, Lady Vols, Johnny Knoxville, and HGTV. Ideal for water enthusiasts, seven lakes surrounded the city, where the French Broad and Holston Rivers converged to form the headwaters of the Tennessee River.

In Natasha's eyes, there wasn't a more beautiful place in the world. If only the air quality level wasn't so poor. The fact that Knoxville formed the hub for three major interstates didn't help matters in that regard. She wondered who came up with that brilliant idea and decided it was probably a Republican.

Her mind shifted to Striker. Less than a year ago, she had been his employee, first as office manager, then bodyguard when Striker's good friend Roger Valentine needed a female protection specialist to pose as his girlfriend. At the conclusion of that case, she found herself unemployed and involved with Striker in an intimate relationship she could only consider intense. At which point, her whole world turned upside down.

The secret desire Natasha harbored for Jonce Striker during the three years she worked for him was minor compared to the present effect he had on her. She had never been so attracted to a man as she was Striker. Raven-black hair, obsidian eyes, and warm skin tone reflecting his Cherokee heritage, his broad shoulders, narrow hips, muscular arms, chest, abdomen and legs bore witness to a hard, powerful build. Awed by the enormity of her love for this man, she suspected it was more than physical chemistry that drew her to him, which frightened the hell out of her.

Although he claimed her for his life mate, a small part of her could not accept this. She kept waiting for the proverbial other shoe to drop. After all, she was well aware of Striker's prior reputation with the ladies, not to mention the women who used to hover around him like moths circling a spotlight, women with so much more to offer. Like looks and brains and, well, okay, maturity. She kept searching for that one fatal flaw in his character that would enable her to rationalize he was not worth her time, but she had yet to find one. Shoot. Why did he have to be so perfect?

Well, one minor flaw: his displeasure over her choice of career. Which brought her to the problem at hand — how to tell him about her first independent case.

Striker served as grillmeister while Natasha prepared a garden salad, baked potatoes, and roasted corn. The day's heat lingering into evening, they decided to eat dinner outdoors on the deck overlooking the Tennessee River, their preferred dining area.

The night air caressed her skin with velvety softness, the water gently splashing the nearby shore soothed her ears, and the enticing aroma of Striker's grilled steaks sent her stomach into growling spasms. Natasha, feeling damp and soft and feminine, her body tingling from Striker's earlier physical conquest, dug in with enthusiasm.

"See you decided to finally come home, Cat," Striker said, addressing the dark bundle of fur perched on the deck railing, staring at him.

Cat stretched and meowed hello.

Striker's eyes narrowed. "What's that around his neck?"

"I bought him a collar."

Striker looked at her with disbelief. "Pink? You put a pink collar on Cat?"

Natasha forked food into her mouth and gave an orgasmic sigh. No one could match Striker's skill when it came to grilling; the meat practically melted in her mouth.

Striker leaned toward her. "You put a pink collar on Cat."

"Sure. Pink looks pretty with black, don't you think?"

"He's a male cat, Natasha. You see those two dark, dangly objects between his back legs? Those are balls, you know."

"What are you, a sexist when it comes to animals?"

Striker glanced at the cat and shook his head.

"I thought it might help him get in touch with his feminine side," Natasha teased.

"Yeah? Well, let me tell you something. I don't have a feminine side, so don't go getting any ideas concerning me," Striker said, using his fork to point at himself.

Natasha's gaze was solemn.

"What?"

"You're perfect, Jonce. I wouldn't want to change one thing about you."

The heated look in his eyes sent shivers racing through her body. She gave him a wicked smile. "Besides, you already have a feminine side."

Striker's brow furrowed.

"You're very nurturing." Her expression grew serious. "No one takes better care of me when I'm sick." She hesitated, then added, "Or hurt."

Their eyes met, both flashing back to when Natasha had been injured while protecting Roger during her first stint as a bodyguard. Up to that point, Striker's and Natasha's relationship had been that of employer-employee, but shortly after she was kidnapped and assaulted by a computer nerd intent on forcing Roger to pay him a million dollars, things between them turned hot and serious.

Natasha smiled, back to teasing. "You know, darlin', I've seen men wear pink. It's a very becoming color."

"Males in my family do not wear pink. Pink's for girls."

Natasha resisted the urge to roll her eyes. "Striker, I'm not emasculating Cat by putting a pink collar on him. Come on."

Striker's raised eyebrows indicated he wasn't buying it.

"Speaking of which, when are you going to make that appointment?"

"She wants to have your balls cut off, Cat," Striker told the feline.

Cat gave out a cry of alarm.

"See?" Striker said. "He doesn't want his balls messed with. He likes them just fine the way they are."

"Oh, for Pete's sake. You don't know what the darn cat wants or doesn't want. As his owner, you should be responsible and have him fixed so he won't impregnate other cats or wander off."

"I'm not his owner. He just showed up here one day and decided he liked it well enough to live here, that's all."

"But you feed him and take him to the vet every year for his shots, so that makes you his owner."

"I simply maintain his physical health, and I'm not about to start messing with his psyche by getting him butchered."

Natasha couldn't understand why Striker was so adamant about this. Shoot, you'd think she was talking about having him neutered, the way he acted every time she brought up the subject.

"If you had him fixed, he'd hopefully stop killing poor defenseless animals and leaving them on the doorstep for you."

"Not to mention snakes," Striker said.

They had been landscaping near Striker's pool one weekend when Cat showed up with a dead garter snake hanging out each side of his mouth. Natasha didn't notice the cat until he rubbed against her and dropped his gift at her feet. In a panic, she scuttled backward and landed in the pool.

Striker laughed at the look on her face.

"It's not funny," she said, her lips curling up to belie her statement.

Striker gave Cat a grave look. "Okay, guy, it's your decision. If that's what you want, to become a eunuch, lie around all day and get fat, I'll make the appointment."

Cat rose up on all fours, arched his back, hissed at Natasha, and bounded off the deck.

"He says no," Striker said.

"He didn't say a thing."

"Take it from me, he doesn't want the operation."

"And who are you, Dr. Doolittle? You have this uncanny ability to communicate with animals?"

Striker shrugged. "Sure. I'm part Cherokee, it's my heritage." He leaned close. "Besides, there are times I know I'm communicating with you on a much more primitive level than merely as one human being to another."

Natasha tried to stop it, but the silly grin captured her lips. What was it about this man that got her all gooey and giggly inside, just with the way he looked at her sometimes?

"I love the heck out of you, you know that?"

"I have waited so long to hear you say those very words," he said in a dramatic voice.

After they finished doing the dishes together, Striker took her hand. "Let's go upstairs, get reacquainted."

Natasha smiled but didn't move.

"What?"

A pained expression crossed her face. "You might not want to take me upstairs after I tell you something."

He studied her for a moment, eyebrows raised. "Okay, what'd you do?"

Natasha drew in a breath. "I accepted my first client today."

A stormy look began to gather in Striker's eyes.

"It's not dangerous in any way, Striker, I swear," she said, and told him about Myrtle and Chumley.

"So she wants you to guard this dog on daily walks and at a dog show?"

"Yeah, and in the meantime check around, see if I can find out who's threatening the dog."

"I'll have my investigators do that. Don't worry with that part of it."

"I'd rather you didn't."

He cocked his head, as if he wasn't sure he had heard her right.

"This is my case, okay? I want to do the investigating, the private security, the whole bit. I don't need your help, Striker."

"Are you forgetting you're not licensed to be an investigator?"

"Not at all. When I explained that to Myrtle, she asked me to conduct an unofficial investigation. You know, check around, do a little research, that sort of thing."

His jaw muscles clenched.

"Let me do this on my own, okay? I'm ready to work, and I have to get my feet wet sometimes. Like I said, the danger aspect is *nada*, so —"

"It's never *nada*," Striker said in a firm voice.

"But a dog? Come on, Striker."

He looked away from her and ran his hand over his face, a sign he was becoming agitated.

"Maybe I should go, give you a chance to mull this over."

Striker returned his eyes to hers. "I'm just concerned for you."

"I know. But we've talked about this countless times." Natasha straightened her shoulders with resolve. "I've spent the better part of the past year training to be a protection specialist, obtaining my license, and getting federal and state approval. I've poured most of my savings into that and setting up my office, and I'm running out of money, sweetie. I need to do this."

Striker's mouth tightened into a thin line. "How many times do I have to tell you I'll take care of you, that you don't have to worry about a thing?"

"I can't do that and you know it."

"Why do you have to be so damn stubborn?" he said, wondering how many times now they had argued over this and how many more times they would.

Natasha gave Striker a beseeching look, and he felt himself soften when she reached out and touched his arm.

"This is something we agreed to disagree about, so let's just stick to that."

His disgruntled expression signaled he wasn't happy with that compromise.

She stepped back. "Are we going to fight over this? 'Cause I'm telling you if we do, we'll neither one win. This is what I've chosen to do with my life, even though I'm aware it's not what you want for me. But I've worked toward this for months and I'm ready to move forward. So, if you won't accept my decision, I'll go play bodyguard and cry myself to sleep every night and you'll do, well, whatever you do to get yourself through a traumatic time in your life."

Striker studied the woman standing before him, her sunny-blond hair pulled away from her face into a loose braid trailing down her back, drawing attention to green, almond-shaped eyes framed by long lashes and kissable lips with an upward tilt at each corner. His gaze traveled her body with a hunger he could not quench, noting that, as usual, her feet were bare and she was braless beneath the summer sweater she wore.

The most domesticated, independent, feisty, loving, sometimes downright ornery, generous-to-a-fault person he'd ever met, she remained an enigma to him. He couldn't seem to wrap his mind around his fascination for her, which only escalated with time. He noted the determined look on her face and knew there was no winning here. He had a choice—he could either support her decision and do what he could to protect her, or say no, he wouldn't agree to it and lose her.

"I don't like it, but I can't stop you, Natasha. Just promise me you'll be safe."

"I promise."

"And if you need help, don't feel like you can't ask for it."

"Of course."

"And above all, be careful. You may not think it's dangerous, but it is."

Natasha leaned into his chest. "Jonce?"

"Yeah?"

"You think I would do anything to endanger this?"

He didn't answer.

"My life is perfect with you. I'll be careful, I promise."

"Let's go upstairs," he said in a rough voice.

Chapter 3

Again leaning back in her chair with her feet resting on the desk, Natasha studied the postmark of the envelope that had contained the threatening letter. She had spent the past week, when she wasn't engaged in lengthy strolls with Myrtle and Chumley, cross-referencing the prior two years' rosters and catalogs, making a list of which owners went with which dogs, researching their addresses, phone numbers, and vocations. So far, her investigation had revealed zilch; none of the participants that she could detect lived near Valdosta, Georgia. And all seemed to be upstanding citizens.

She sighed, having trouble focusing on the task, her mind constantly finding its way back to Striker. Her thoughts turned to the prior evening's events and the only interest the envelope now held was to fan her flaming face. Whew. It could not get any better than this. But then, she had said that same thing to herself several times before. She shivered, visiting those memories, Striker taking control of the lovemaking, Natasha letting him, knowing from past experience she would not be disappointed, his large hands traveling her body, his tongue...

Her desk phone rang.

Natasha startled and over she went once more. "Damn it." Her gaze darted to the phone after another shrilling blare demanded her attention. She rolled off the chair, struggled to her knees, and snatched up the receiver. "Hello."

"Oh, dear, I hope I'm not interrupting anything," Myrtle said.

Natasha closed her eyes, resisting the urge to groan. "No, no. I'm afraid I was concentrating on something and, well, you know."

"Of course, dear, I understand." Myrtle's tone implied she wasn't buying that excuse. "Actually, I was calling to ask a favor, dear."

"Sure."

"Well, I forgot I have a doctor's appointment this afternoon and neglected to make arrangements for my sister to babysit Chumley. Since she already has plans, I was wondering if I could hire you to take care of him for me."

"No problem. What time's your appointment?"

"At two."

"I'll be there by one-fifteen. Then, if you don't mind, I'll take Chumley with me to my friend's house. Roger's a computer genius, knows how to find all sorts of information using the Internet, and I was going to see if he could help me research the owners whose dogs showed against Chumley."

Natasha chose not to mention that Roger was one hell of a hacker and could work miracles uncovering data not meant for John Q. Public.

"Don't worry, Chumley will be safe," Natasha said when Myrtle didn't respond. "I won't let anything happen to him. He does like to ride in a car, doesn't he?"

"Yes, dear, I take him in the car all the time. You will watch him closely? You won't let him out of your sight?"

You'd think they were talking about a kid or something. "Of course not. I promise, he'll be safe with me."

Myrtle's Tudor-style home was located in an old, moneyed part of Knoxville, the winding Tennessee River for a backdrop and the University of Tennessee campus within walking distance. Myrtle met Natasha at the door, holding Chumley in her arms. A large tote sat inside the foyer with a colorful picture of the Pug dominating the front. Natasha eyed the bag, which looked an awful lot like one of those cloth bags young mothers used to tote around diapers and bottles and all kinds of mysterious things. She leaned over and peeked inside the tote. It was stuffed with chewy treats, bottled water, a water bowl, and toys.

"We're only going to be gone a couple of hours."

Myrtle gave her an indulgent smile.

Natasha collected Chumley and the doggy bag while listening to instructions for the proper care and feeding of the little Buddha dog. After stuffing her file containing the rosters, catalogs, and her compiled list of owners inside the bag, she packed it into the small cargo space of her blue Jeep Wrangler. She placed Chumley in the front passenger seat and headed out, ignoring Myrtle's concerned look when she saw the vehicle in which her pet had been deposited.

Five minutes later, an evil smell permeated the inside of the jeep. Natasha glanced at Chumley, sprawled in the passenger seat with an innocent expression on his furry face.

"I know that wasn't me."

Chumley panted a doggy smile.

The odor seemed to gain momentum. "Dang." Natasha zipped down her window and leaned her head in that direction. She gave Chumley a disgusted look, but he didn't seem in the least concerned. "What the heck does that woman feed you?"

At Roger's mansion, Natasha hopped out of the jeep almost before it came to a complete stop. She gulped in fresh air and waved her hands around her head, wondering if an odor that pungent could attach itself to her hair or clothes, the way smoke could. She walked around to the passenger side of the jeep and opened the door.

"I'm going to have to go home and take a shower, thanks to you, you little gas bag," she said, attaching the leash to Chumley's collar. She picked up the dog, holding him as far away from her body as possible, and set him on the ground. She grabbed the doggy bag and started to close the door, but after some thought, decided to leave it open. Air the jeep out while she was inside.

Natasha inserted her key in Roger's front door, entered, and walked directly to Roger's office, but he wasn't there. She placed the doggy bag on the floor next to Roger's desk and returned to the foyer. Looking up the staircase, she yelled, "Roger. Hey, Rog, you here?"

Chumley collapsed beside her with a grunt.

Natasha, in a grouchy mood now, worried Roger would smell that terrible stench on her, frowned at the Pug. "Don't you do any extraneous moving around?"

Paws clicked against a marble floor. She turned to see Brutus padding toward her, wagging his nub tail and giving her a wide doggy smile. Chumley struggled to his feet to watch the monster dog approach.

Spying the miniature canine standing beside Natasha, Brutus came to a halt and gazed up at her with a hurt expression.

She held out her hands. "Hey, he's not mine. I'm just babysitting."

Brutus studied Natasha a moment, as if trying to make up his mind. Apparently deciding to believe her, he drew near and allowed her to bestow some loving attention while darting jealous looks at Chumley.

Unable to resist any longer, Brutus moved away from Natasha to begin an inspection of Chumley. Natasha watched, guessing the Pug was maybe one-fourth the size of the Weimaraner. When Brutus's nose darted toward Chumley's rear end, she warned, "I wouldn't do that if I were you."

Brutus ignored her, then drew back and sneezed.

"Try riding in a car with that," Natasha said.

Brutus backed away from the Pug. Natasha could have sworn his eyes were watering. Chumley waddled closer, panting and waving his tail. Reaching the large dog, he promptly wrapped his front paws around one of Brutus's back legs and began humping like mad. The Weimaraner sent Natasha a pained look.

"Stop it!" Natasha shrieked, yanking on the leash. "Get away from him." She pried Chumley's legs apart and peeled him off the other dog. "You pervert."

Chumley gazed lovingly at Brutus while squirming to escape Natasha's hold. The Weimaraner dashed away before the Pug could get free.

"Smart dog," Natasha called after him. She placed Chumley at her feet and held the leash snug to restrain him. After a couple of tugging efforts, Chumley gave up and collapsed on the floor.

Natasha yelled for Roger once more. Receiving no response, she decided to check the outdoor pool since the day was abnormally warm for early spring. When she entered the kitchen, Brutus was sprawled on his rug in front of the dishwasher, his favored spot. He left scratch marks on the kitchen floor in his haste to get away from the small dog.

It seemed to take forever to reach the pool deck with Chumley plodding along behind Natasha, puffing, sounding out of breath. She stopped and studied him.

"How in the world did you win Best in Show?"

Chumley ignored her.

"Okay, I know you've got that cute thing going on, but you're chubby and you stink, plus you're a pervert. Shoot, Myrtle must have paid a judge some pretty hefty bucks for you to win anything."

Chumley raised his nose toward the sky, added a strut to his walk. Natasha stepped onto the pool deck, wondering if dogs had evolved enough to be haughty.

Roger sat in a lounge chair, talking in a low voice to an attractive woman occupying the chair beside him.

Natasha cleared her throat. "Excuse me."

Roger startled and his face flushed when he saw Natasha standing there.

Natasha gave him a slight wave and smiled. "Hey, Roger."

"Nattie." Roger started to rise, seemed to remember something, and sat back down.

Natasha's eyes darted to his trunks, confirming what he was trying to hide. "Don't get up," she said, hoping to save him embarrassment. "I came by to see if you could help me with something. But that's okay, you have company."

The woman beside Roger was studying Natasha in a cool, detached, almost professional way. Huh, Natasha thought, staring back. The woman seemed very young, in her early twenties at the most, with chestnut-colored hair and pale-blue eyes. Her string bikini revealed a short, petite build, with the exception of her breasts, which just might win in a contest against Natasha's favorite celebrity, Dolly Parton.

"Nattie, I'd like you to meet Misty Bellows," Roger said.

Natasha almost snorted out loud. *Misty Bellows. Of course.*

"Misty, this is my good friend, Natasha Chamberlain," Roger continued.

Both women nodded at one another, still eyeing each other coolly.

"Roger, if you don't mind, can I use your computer?" Natasha said.

"Uh, sure. What's up?"

"I'm trying to get some information for that case I'm working on."

Roger studied the short Pug. "That has to be Chumley."

Natasha nodded with a grin.

Roger gave her a teasing smile. "How's Striker handling it?"

"He's fine. It was kind of shaky at first, but I think he's going to be okay with it."

They beamed at one another until Misty shifted, drawing Roger's attention.

Natasha got the message. "I'll be in your office, Roger." She turned around, tugging the Pug with her. As they slowly traversed the short journey back to the house, Natasha tried to be patient with Chumley and had to resist the urge to drag him. No way was she going to pick that stinky thing up and carry him.

Natasha settled in behind the desk in Roger's office. She didn't know the first thing about how to use his fancy computer equipment and knew it wouldn't be long before Roger showed up, curious about what sort of damage she might be inflicting upon his babies. Plus, she wasn't about to leave until she found out more about the woman on the pool deck. While waiting, she drew out the prior year's roster and catalog and checked her list against them, making sure she had matched the dogs that had shown against Chumley to their proper owners.

Ten minutes later, Roger stuck his head in the door, flashing white teeth. "I'll be down after I change."

He was back in a short while, wearing a smug look. Natasha leaned back in his chair and studied him. When she first met Roger, he had looked the part of the quintessential computer nerd or mad scientist, depending upon how involved he was with whatever project he was working on at the time. However, during the past year, thanks to the influence of Natasha and her two cohorts, Pit and Bigun, his appearance had changed considerably. Roger had morphed into a handsome, buff man. If she could get his self-confidence to a normal level, he would be perfect, she thought.

Roger blushed at her scrutiny.

"I think I'm jealous," she said with a smile.

His mouth tipped into a wide grin.

"Who, what, when, where, and why?" Natasha demanded in a friendly way.

Roger plopped into the seat across from her and shrugged his shoulders. "She's a grad student doing research."

Natasha nodded. Realizing he wasn't going to divulge anything else unless pushed, she said, "On what?"

Roger's expression was a happy one. "Me."

Natasha's eyebrows shot up. "Roger Valentine, computer genius extraordinaire, millionaire software king. That's a very interesting subject. Good for her. How long have you known her?"

"A few days."

"You didn't say anything when I was here a couple of days ago."

"I didn't know it would get to this point."

Natasha considered that. "This point. Uh-huh." She leaned toward him. "Roger, sweetie, she's awful young, isn't she?"

Roger's face changed. "Striker's several years older than you, and I don't see that that bothers either one of you."

"True, but I was almost twenty-five when I became involved with him. And it's not like he dropped out of nowhere. I worked for the guy for three years, remember? I knew him. But what do you know about Misty? She doesn't look like she's even out of her teens yet, much less a college graduate."

"She's old enough."

"It's just you're an extremely rich, intelligent, good-looking guy. You need to be wary of certain female critters out there waiting to prey on guys like you."

Roger frowned.

"Don't get mad. I'm only warning you, the way you warned me about Striker."

"Point taken," Roger said curtly.

"Roger, you're my best friend and I love you dearly. I don't want to see you hurt."

"I know. But it's my life, and sometimes you have to take a chance, Nattie." Roger looked at her, saying, with his eyes, *just like you did with Striker.*

Natasha grinned her agreement.

"So fill me in on the case so far," Roger said.

She had barely begun to tell him about the list of owners she had compiled when she smelled that terrible odor. Natasha shot to her feet.

"What?"

She hurried toward the door, waving her hand in front of her face. "He stinks to high heaven."

Roger stood, glancing around the room. "Who?"

"Chumley."

"Where is he?"

"Behind the desk," Natasha said with one hand over her nose.

Roger got a strong whiff of the sharp aroma and headed after Natasha. "Good gosh."

"He's worse than Brutus."

"He's even worse than Bigun."

They escaped to the foyer to wait for the room to air out. While they sat on the stairs, Natasha told Roger about what she was trying to discover, smiling with relief when he offered to utilize his computer skills to conduct a more in-depth investigation of the participants than she would be able to do.

"Thanks so much, Roger. I was hoping you could help me. I brought with me the list I've compiled of the owners' names and addresses for the cluster each of the past two years. I'll leave a copy with you, if that's okay."

"Sure, Nattie, no problem."

Misty's sudden appearance interrupted their discussion. "I'm going to go change," she told Roger as she passed, trailing her hand along his upper arm, ignoring Natasha.

Natasha pretended she didn't even notice her.

Roger's eyes followed Misty up the stairs and then returned to Natasha. "Why don't you make a copy of that list and I'll work on it for you"—his gaze traveled up the stairs once more—"this afternoon. I'll call you and let you know what I find." With reluctance, he turned back to her.

"Dang, Roger, you got it bad."

He looked away.

Natasha felt a little hurt by her best friend's rejection. "Okay, you want me out of here, all you have to do is tell me."

"Hey, Nattie, come on, it's not like that."

"No, really, I understand. I'll go get Chumley and we'll be off. Well, first I need to tell Brutus 'bye, if I can find him."

When Natasha returned from the kitchen, Roger was nowhere to be seen. In his office, she used his fax machine to make a copy of her list and placed it in the center of his desk. She returned the original to her file and stuffed it into the doggy bag. With a heavy sigh of disgust, she peeled a humping Chumley off one of the chair legs and walked back into the foyer, tugging the Pug behind on his leash and carrying the doggy bag.

She yelled, "Bye, Roger, I'll talk to you later." After waiting for the response she knew she would not receive, she left.

Natasha had to lift Chumley to put him in her jeep and, once more, she held him as far away from her body as she could get him. Before leaving, she rolled back the canvas top on her Wrangler, deciding if it got too chilly, she'd turn on the darn heater; she couldn't stand that smell.

~~~

Natasha watched Myrtle gather Chumley up in her arms, kiss his wrinkly little face, and speak baby talk to him. She handed her the doggy bag.

"Myrtle, if I were you, whatever it is you're feeding Chumley, I think I'd try something else."

"Why on earth would I want to do that, dear?"

"Well, he has this terrible gas problem. I could hardly stand being in the jeep with him, that's how bad it was."

Myrtle looked surprised. "Chumley? My Chumley never has gas."

Natasha mentally rolled her eyes. "Okay," she said, climbing in her jeep.

"Aren't you going to go with us for our walk, dear?"

Well, foot. Natasha wanted to get home and showered before Striker arrived.

"I didn't think you'd be up to that after a trip to the doctor's office, so I went ahead and walked him at Roger's house," she said, thinking of the short trip to the pool deck and back.

Myrtle gave her a relieved smile. "Oh, my dear Natasha, that was very thoughtful of you."

Natasha reached out and scratched behind Chumley's ear. "Bye-bye, Chumley." She smiled, thinking he really was cute. "I'll see you tomorrow, Myrtle." With a wave, she started the jeep and pulled away.

Chapter 4

Natasha called Roger at ten the next morning. He answered, sounding sleepy.

"Hey, guy, what's up?" She cringed when an image popped into her mind what could actually be up at the moment, with Misty now hanging around.

"Hey, Nattie," Roger said in a rough voice.

"You still in bed?"

"Yeah. We had a late night last night." Roger yawned into the phone.

"Did you get a chance to do anything with that list yesterday?"

"Ah, Nattie, I'm sorry. I forgot all about it. I'll do it today, I promise."

Natasha sighed. She understood but, dangit, she wanted to know. "That's okay, Rog. Don't worry about it. But when you do find time for it, can you begin with the owners from last year?"

"Sure, Nattie, whatever you want," Roger said in a muffled voice.

A female giggle sounded close to the phone.

Omigosh. Surely they weren't — "Um, just let me know when you get to it. Take care, Roger."

Roger hung up without saying goodbye.

Natasha stared at the phone for a moment, then pulled over a pad and wrote "Misty Bellows" on it, thinking maybe she ought to check this little chicky out.

Natasha drove to Myrtle's early that afternoon to accompany her for Chumley's daily walk. The elderly woman met her at the door, her face pale, sweat beading on her upper lip.

Natasha touched her arm with concern. "Myrtle, are you all right?"

Myrtle gave her an infirm smile. "Yes, dear. I seem to be having a minor reaction to some new medication, but I'll be all right." She sounded as though it was more like a major reaction.

"You should be in bed."

"No, no, I'm fine. Are you ready to walk Chumley, dear?"

"I'm ready, but I don't think you need to go." Natasha ushered Myrtle into her den, helped her onto the couch, and tucked an afghan around her.

"I do feel awfully weak," Myrtle said.

Natasha glanced at the Pug, asleep on an overstuffed chair. "I'll take Chumley, don't worry about it."

"Do you mind, dear?"

"Not at all," Natasha said, thinking she could probably get the chore done faster without Myrtle tagging along.

Myrtle lay back and closed her eyes. Natasha clipped Chumley's leash to his collar, tugged him up, and left as quietly as she could.

When they started down the drive, the dog was resistant at first and tried dragging his feet, whimpering and giving her a helpless look. Realizing Natasha wasn't going to pick him up, Chumley finally gave in and plodded along.

Natasha strolled slowly in order to give the laboring dog a chance to keep up with her. She turned her face to the sun, breathing in what she hoped was reasonably clean air, appreciating the day. After a long, cold winter, spring had finally settled in and the whole world felt vibrant and moist. She admired the colorful daffodils, tulips, and pansies flowerbeds in neighboring yards sported, spotting more than a few budding dogwood trees, their bark reminding her of snakeskin. She looked around for a marker indicating this neighborhood was part of the Dogwood Arts Trails but didn't see one.

Eventually her mind shifted to what it always did anymore, Striker and memories of him. A thrill ran up and down her spine and she shivered, losing all thoughts of Chumley.

Natasha didn't even miss the Pug until she had almost completed her circuit back to Myrtle's house. She glanced down, thinking how well Chumley had done keeping up with her; she hadn't had to tug at him once. Trailing along behind her was a leash attached to an empty dog collar.

"What the..."

She scanned the street but didn't see any sign of Chumley. "Damn it." She ran back the way she had come.

She found Chumley a block from home, wrapped around a small tree trunk in someone's yard.

"Chumley. What is wrong with you? Dang, guy, quit acting so perverted." She buckled the collar around the dog's neck and tried to pull him away.

But Chumley wouldn't have it and hung on for all he was worth.

Natasha didn't want to pick up the Pug, afraid he'd get that nasty smell on her, but what could she do? She reached down and tried to pry him off the tree once more. A menacing growl sounded behind her. She rose up and was staring into dark, black marbles ensconced within the face of a Rottweiler. She didn't like the look on the dog's face, not to mention the exposed fangs and drool escaping its blackened lips. Remembering one rule of thumb was not to look a dog directly in the eyes—they considered that a challenge—she turned her side to the drooling canine.

"Come on, Chum, or you're going to be that guy's dinner," Natasha coaxed, pulling harder.

When she peeled him away from the tree, Chumley squealed in protest. This sound, for some reason, angered the Rottweiler. He lunged at Natasha, snarling and biting air.

"Oh, shit." Holding Chumley to her chest, she raced away with the Rottweiler close behind.

~~~

Striker was in a meeting with the firm's office manager and his friend and business partner, Scott Thomas, when his cellphone bleeped. He plucked it from its casing, read the display, and keyed it to phone mode. Holding one finger up to Scott, meaning, *this won't take long*, he rose from the conference table and walked toward the bank of windows along the far wall, saying, in a low voice, "Hey, gorgeous, what's up?"

He listened for a moment. "What?"

Scott and the office manager turned their attention to him.

"You did what?" Striker yelled.

"He did what?" Roaring now.

"Where the hell are you?" He exited the door without glancing at the other two.

"Wonder what she did this time," Scott said, with resignation.

Striker rushed through the hospital emergency room entrance, stopping at the glassed-in reception area long enough to ask the clerk where he could find Natasha Chamberlain. He strode down the hall at a fast pace, found the room, and opened the door.

Natasha lay on her stomach on an examining table, a rounded portion of one naked hip peeking from beneath a paper sheet. A male resident worked over her, applying antibiotic ointment to the right buttock.

Natasha looked over her shoulder and sent Striker a sickly smile. He grinned.

"It's not funny," she said.

He walked over to inspect the area. "That had to hurt."

Natasha shrugged. "Yeah, well."

"You do any damage to the dog that bit you?"

She ignored that.

Striker watched the resident, making sure he wasn't taking more time than needed to dress the wound. After all, this was his love's shapely butt the man was tending.

"They catch the dog?" Striker asked, after assuring himself the resident was being professional.

Natasha made a face.

"Uh-oh."

"I know."

Unable to resist taking a jab, he said, "Those rabies shots hurt."

"I know," she said, with a tearful look.

Feeling bad for upsetting her, Striker leaned down and kissed her temple. "I'm sorry, baby." He pulled over an examining stool and placed it at the head of the bed. Holding her hand, he said, "Okay, tell me what happened," and tried not to laugh out loud when she did. Exchanging grins with the resident, Striker said, "How'd you get here?"

Natasha gave him a grumpy look. "I drove. How else do you think I got here?"

He raised his eyebrows, knowing her dislike of hospitals.

"Myrtle called that ask-a-nurse thingy, and they told her I better hightail it to the emergency room and have it seen. Dog bites are nothing to sneeze at, apparently."

"That's true," Striker said.

Natasha grimaced. "This guy said I was pretty lucky. The Rottweiler could have taken out a really big chunk, but instead, he mostly got hold of the shirt and jeans I was wearing."

Striker squeezed her hand. "Thank God."

Natasha gave a weary sigh. "I have got to lose weight."

"Lose weight?" Striker said, with a startled look on his face.

"Yeah, if that dog was able to grab hold of my butt, then it's way too flabby, no firmness to it at all."

"What?"

"I was running, Striker. How can you take a chunk out of a running butt?"

"What?"

"Why didn't you tell me I was getting fat?"

The resident, placing gauze over the wound, shot Striker a sympathetic smile.

"Natasha, you're not fat, for Pete's sake. Get hold of yourself. I like your butt just fine the way it is, so leave it alone."

Natasha glanced over her shoulder to track the resident's progress.

Striker watched him place tape over the bandage. "What about stitches? Don't you think she needs stitches?"

"Stitches?" Natasha said with an alarmed look.

The resident shook his head. "Wasn't deep enough. More a superficial gash than anything."

"Can she sit on that side? What about medication? How often should we change the dressing?"

"I'm pretty sure she'll be placed on oral antibiotics in case of infection, and I'll give you an instruction sheet about caring for the wound before you leave."

"What about the dog that bit her? How soon before she has to go through the series of rabies shots if they can't find it?"

Natasha moaned at that thought.

The resident stepped back from Natasha, peeling off his rubber gloves. "Once Animal Control locates the dog, they'll ascertain whether or not his rabies shots are up-to-date. They'll probably place him in quarantine for fourteen days just to make sure he's healthy. If the dog can't be found or if his shots aren't current, she'll have to be treated."

Natasha sent a silent prayer upward that the dog had an owner who wouldn't let something like that slide.

Striker leaned close to her. "Who was the one, Natasha, dear, who told me this case was not dangerous?"

She shook her head. "I knew it. I knew you'd throw that in my face." Her gaze met his and she grinned. "Guess I'm on top for awhile."

Striker's eyes, climbing toward the ceiling, caught the resident smiling at this.

Chapter 5

Natasha sat in Myrtle's living room, going over with her the participants of the cluster for the past two years. When Myrtle let it slip she used a handler to show Chumley, Natasha gave herself a mental slap on the forehead. *D'oh.* Why didn't she think of that?

"Whom do you use?" Natasha said, shifting around, trying to find a comfortable sitting position.

"Brad Aungst. He's a sweet, sweet man, dear. Brad's an entrepreneur who raises Afghan Hounds."

Natasha grew interested. "Does he show them?"

"Oh, yes, and usually wins. He's done amazing things with his animals."

Natasha leaned on her left buttock, overbalanced, and fell off the couch with an "Oomph."

"Oh, dear, are you all right?" Myrtle asked.

Natasha rose to her knees. "I'm fine, Myrtle. Sorry about that." She eased back on the couch, trying not to let her embarrassment show. "Um, where were we?"

"We were talking about Brad, dear."

"Oh, right. His Afghans wouldn't be in Chumley's class, right?"

"Right, dear. They're in the hound division."

"So he's not competing with you?"

"Well, only in regards to Best in Show."

"And you beat him the last two years?"

"That's true, dear. But Brad shows Chumley, so that's in his favor."

Natasha frowned as if she didn't understand.

"Handlers are a little like horse jockeys, dear. If he shows a dog that continues to win, it raises his status as a handler and gains him more business."

Natasha considered this while trying to resist scratching her butt. The dog bite may have been healing, but it hurt like the very dickens and had one mother of an itch. The only pleasurable thing to come out of the whole mess was Striker's efforts at playing doctor.

"You don't think Brad could be the one who sent you the letter?"

"Oh, dear, no, not Brad. He's such a sweet man."

"Maybe I ought to talk to him anyway. He might have a clue who did this or remember something from the last two years that could lead us to the person who threatened Chumley."

"Certainly, dear. I'll get you his card."

As Natasha expected, as soon as his owner was out of sight, Chumley heaved his heavy body up, plodded over, and began molesting the coffee table leg. Rolling her eyes, Natasha stood to take pressure off her butt. Blood seemed to rush to that area, causing her hip to throb.

"Ow, ow, ow," she said, hobbling around. She stepped within range of the mirror above the fireplace to gauge how swollen her right buttock looked. Her jeans had felt too snug that morning, so she was wearing loose-fitting cotton pants. Well, loose on one side, tight on the other. Shoot, she had one hell of a ghetto butt going on that one cheek, she thought with despair.

She heard Myrtle's footsteps and glanced at Chumley. As soon as the Pug perceived his mistress's return, he plopped down, raised his head, and gave Myrtle a loving look when she entered the room. Natasha shook her head with disgust.

Myrtle handed Natasha the card and spoke in a conspiratorial voice. "There's something I should probably tell you about Brad, dear, just so you'll be prepared."

"Really? What?"

"Well dear, I'm afraid he's not — oh, what is the term you young ones use nowadays?"

Natasha shrugged. She had no idea what Myrtle could be talking about and wasn't so sure she wanted to go there anyway.

"He's — well, he..." Myrtle leaned closer to Natasha. "He likes men," she whispered.

"Oh, he's gay."

"Yes, dear, he's a gay man."

"Do you know if he's hooked up with anyone?"

Myrtle frowned. "I'm afraid I don't know what that means, dear."

"Does he have a boyfriend? Is he dating anyone? Is he committed?"

"Oh. Well, I don't know, but I don't think so. He doesn't discuss his social life with me."

Natasha nodded.

"Why in the world do you want to know, dear?" Myrtle's eyes widened and she put her fingers to her lips. "Oh, dear. I hope I haven't offended you."

"Shoot, no. But I've got a cousin who's gay and looking around. So I was thinking maybe I'd take Cameron with me and introduce him to Brad." She shrugged. "You never know."

Myrtle gave her a forced smile.

~~~

Natasha paced the kitchen, holding the cordless phone over her head, a signal to Striker her mother was on the other end and they were having an argument.

He kissed her hello and drew back with a grin. "What'd you do this time?"

Natasha shook her head, brought the phone back to her mouth, and shouted, "Mom, Striker's here, gotta go, love you." She disconnected with a disgruntled look.

"Well?"

"For one, she found out I took a job." Natasha sent a glare Striker's way.

"Hey, I didn't tell her."

"I tell you what, it is pure hell being an only child. Mom and Dad won't stop with this overprotective crap, and if that's not bad enough, Mom won't go to the doctor and start that friggin' hormone replacement therapy so she can quit with all the different personalities she's developed since she hit perimenopause. Damn." She shook her head with frustration.

Her parents, high school sweethearts, had married at a young age. Natasha occasionally flirted with the notion that she had been an unexpected surprise, prompting their rush to the altar, although the date of her birth and the date of their marriage weren't within the requisite nine-month period. But it was close.

As their sole child and center of their universe, she bore the full brunt of their overprotectiveness, although there were subtle hints lately that things were changing. All of a sudden, her mom and dad were having fun without her, which was a little disconcerting. She caught Striker's eye and gave him a contrite look, thinking how insensitive she was. Orphaned at a young age,

Striker didn't have the luxury of complaining about too-involved parents.

"Oh, baby, I'm sorry," she said, touching his face.

Striker shrugged as if it didn't matter. "Don't worry about it. Instead of experiencing that kind of hell, I get to watch you go through it. And that makes it more fun." He grinned.

Her eyes changed. "Cameron must have told her. I'm gonna kill him."

"Why would Cameron tell your mom?"

"He probably told my aunt, who told Mom when she called to bitch about me. Aunt Irene's pissed because I'm trying to set Cam up with Chumley's handler, who's gay. She thinks that only encourages him to be gayer, if that's even possible, and that I should be trying to hook him up with a woman. But why in the heck would I do that when he isn't interested in being with a woman and would rather be with a man?"

Striker shrugged.

"Okay, I know Cameron's a slut. But maybe this guy will be different. Maybe this will be the one that will settle him down a little."

"Darlin', Cameron goes way beyond the word 'slut'."

"You're just jealous because you think he's prettier than you," Natasha teased. "Although to be honest, I think you have Cameron beat all to heck and back."

Striker, on his way to the refrigerator, took the time to send her a scowl.

"In a manly sort of way, of course."

He opened the refrigerator door, ignoring her.

"You're beautiful, Jonce, you know that?" she said in a soft voice, walking toward him. "Your pulchritude surpasses any member of the male species I've ever seen. I've thought that since I first noticed you."

"Get off the subject," he growled.

She shut the refrigerator door, leaned into him. "I love your face." She reached up on tiptoes to kiss his forehead, his eyes, and his nose before she found his lips. She unbuttoned his shirt, her mouth on his. "I love your body, I adore your body, I worship your body," she murmured, her tongue following her hands.

In the Jacuzzi, surrounded by bubbles, Striker leaned against the back of the tub with Natasha between his legs, her back supported by his chest. She was driving him crazy, squirming around, trying to get comfortable, rubbing areas that tended to harden with contact.

Natasha finally found a position that didn't put pressure on her wound and sighed with content. She lazily glanced around Striker's bathroom and smiled. The room was spacious, with a large skylight above them, an oversized shower chamber sporting four well-placed nozzles lending the ambience of standing under a waterfall, the huge bathtub with whirlpool jets that they occupied at the moment, a toilet and bidet, and large vanity with two sinks.

Candles were arranged around the tub and along the vanity, which Striker thought gave the room a cozy warmth, while Natasha felt it added a romantic touch. She had placed a ficus tree near the window, hung spider plants and ferns around the room, and recently had begun an African violet menagerie on a glass etagere, sprouting bright pink, violet and white flowers.

She sighed. "I really love this bathroom."

"Kind of makes me feel like I'm peeing in a jungle," Striker drawled.

She tilted her head back and smiled at him. "Good for your primitive soul."

He leaned down and grazed her lips with his own.

"Speaking of which." She turned around and straddled him.

The chiming doorbell drew her attention away from an intense exploration of Striker's muscular torso. "Well, shoot," she said with disappointment. "That's got to be Cameron. I forgot all about him." She gave Striker a quick kiss, carefully climbed out of the tub, pulled her robe off the hook on the back of the door, and limped out of the room.

Cameron was tall and slender, with a model's build and looks—bright-white teeth, dark-blue eyes, sandy-blond hair streaked with highlights, wide shoulders, and no hips. Natasha loved him like a brother and could not understand why her aunt had such a hard time accepting him as he was. She kissed him hello and invited him in.

Cameron's eyes floated up the stairs. "Why aren't you dressed?"

Following his gaze, Natasha suspected he was hoping to catch a glimpse of Striker. "Suffer, damn you."

He grinned.

"I'll get dressed and be right back. You know where the kitchen is if you're hungry, the bar if you're thirsty."

"Oh, my," Cameron said, watching her stiff gait as she walked away from him.

She glanced at him over her shoulders. "What?"

"You know what."

Her face reddened. "Like I said, Cameron, suffer, damn you," Natasha said in an arrogant manner and flaunted upstairs. She didn't bother to explain the stiffness was from an injury, not what he suspected. But then, again...

Striker declined Natasha's invitation to visit Brad. "You want to play matchmaker, go ahead. I'm staying out of it," he said, rummaging in the refrigerator.

"Coward," she said, and left.

Brad Aungst could have been a darker version of Cameron. He was also tall, with a slender build, bright-white teeth, chocolate-colored eyes, wide shoulders, no hips, and dark-brown hair highlighted blond. Brad owned a bookstore in the Old City called the Book Schnook. Natasha wondered if he knew what schnook meant or was just going for the rhyme effect.

Following introductions, Brad led them to a table in a far corner of the café in the back of the building, away from the customer noise. After an employee took orders for drinks, Brad and Cameron began conversing with one another and ignored Natasha. Finding it difficult to get either one to pay attention to her, she irritably waved her hand between the two men.

"Excuse me, Brad, Cameron, there is another person present at this table."

Cameron glanced at her and smiled. Brad turned his attention to her with reluctance.

"Listen, I just want to ask a few questions, then I'm out of here and you two can go on to whatever you want to go on to."

Cameron leaned back in his chair, his eyes on Natasha. Brad did the same.

"Okay, Brad, Myrtle tells me you've been the handler for Chumley both times he's won Best in Show."

Brad nodded as his eyes wandered in Cameron's direction.

Natasha leaned forward, into his field of vision, and almost screamed when the developing scab on her wound pulled against skin. She eased back with care. "And I'm sure she's told you about the letter Chumley received."

With an annoyed look, Brad nodded once more.

"So, what's your take on that?"

Brad shrugged. "Those shows are full of weirdoes, darling."

Natasha thought he sounded just like Cary Grant.

"It's a very political arena, very competitive," Brad went on. "There's a lot of backstabbing, a lot of threatening gestures."

"What kind of threats?"

"Well, darling, to exemplify, last year, we had to hire people to guard our dogs when we weren't with them because there was this crazy competitor, and I don't need to tell you who, darling —"

"Why not?"

"Why not what, darling?"

"Tell me who."

"I would have thought Myrtle would have told you."

"Told me what?"

"There's this woman who shows every year..." He took the time to dramatically roll his eyes and glance at Cameron. "Poodles, darling."

Cameron snorted.

Brad smiled and turned back to Natasha. "Last year, as she would go by a dog's station, if no one was there, she would reach out and snip fur to spoil the dog's look."

"You're serious?"

"As a dead cat, darling. People were very upset. But what could we do? No one could prove it."

Natasha wondered if all these people who showed dogs used terms of endearment, what with Myrtle and her "dears" and Brad and his "darlings." "Who was this person?"

"Hermione Googendorf, darling."

Natasha's brow furrowed. "What kind of name is that?"

"It's her stage name, darling. I have no idea what her real name is."

"Now that's what I call competitive."

"Actually, darling, that's what I call weird."

Natasha glanced at Cameron, who hadn't taken his eyes off Brad. "And Chumley won against her dog?"

"Yes, Best in Show for two years now."

"Do you think she could have sent the letter?"

"Oh, I doubt it. Her dog didn't even place."

"But Chumley also won against your dogs."

"Right, darling."

"That didn't bother you?"

Brad shook his head. "It would be nice to win Best in Show, but as Chumley's handler, it got me some attention."

Natasha gave him a skeptical look. "You're okay with that?"

"Certainly, darling."

Natasha watched Brad and Cameron smile at one another. Damn, her hip hurt. Her lengthy stay in the Jacuzzi had seemed to make matters worse, softening the scab and stimulating blood flow in that cheek, which throbbed with each heartbeat. She winced and tilted further to the left. Her elbow slipped off the arm of her chair and she almost hit her chin on the table. She glanced at Brad and Cameron, relieved they hadn't noticed.

"You got any idea who would be so crazy to send that letter, threaten Chumley's life?"

Brad reluctantly returned his attention to her. "There are some crazy competitors out there, darling, but no, I don't have a clue."

Brad's gaze wandered back to Cameron. Natasha could almost see a current vibrating between the two men. *Geez Louise.* She wasn't going to make much progress the way those two were looking at one another. Besides, Striker was at home and her butt needed some of his loving attention. She picked up her purse, drew out a business card, and placed it on the table in front of Brad, tapping it with her fingernails to gain his attention.

He glanced at her.

"In case you remember anything."

"Of course, darling."

She stood, carefully leaned over, and pecked Cameron on the cheek. He didn't even look her way.

Annoyed with her cousin for ignoring her, Natasha said, "Oh, Brad, something you might want to know. Cameron's a slut."

Brad kept his eyes on Cameron. "Really, darling? What a coincidence. So am I."

Natasha rolled her eyes and left.

Chapter 6

Natasha didn't feel like going for a walk with Chumley, so she talked Myrtle into accompanying her to Roger's place instead. She wanted to personally nudge her friend to do what he had promised, utilize his hacking skills to uncover any illegalities among the people on the list. When they arrived, Roger was nowhere to be found, but Pit and Bigun were in the kitchen scrounging around.

"Hey, guys." Natasha noticed Myrtle and Chumley staring in awe at her two friends, who could be intimidating with their broad stature and shaved heads. She made introductions all around, explaining, "Pit and Bigun also live here."

"You gonna stay tonight, Nattie?" Pit asked.

"I hadn't planned on it. Why?"

"Man, we're tired of nuked food. We were hoping you'd cook dinner."

"Oh, you poor dears," Myrtle said. "I'll fix you something to eat if you want."

"Myrtle, you don't need to do that," Natasha said, but she hoped Myrtle would; she wasn't in the mood to stand over a stove.

"Oh, but I insist, dear," Myrtle said. "I'm a good country cook and I've missed preparing large meals since my husband died. I'd love to do it."

"Well," Natasha said.

Myrtle smiled at the two male bodyguards. "How about fried chicken, mashed potatoes, green beans, biscuits, and a big apple pie?"

Pit licked his lips. "Oh, man."

"Hey, dudette, you got a nice friend here," Bigun said.

Myrtle patted Natasha's arm. "You go find your friend, dear, and I'll start dinner for these two strong young men."

"We'll help," Pit and Bigun told Myrtle as Natasha left.

Natasha searched the mansion but couldn't find Roger anywhere. Afraid that Myrtle and the boys might involve her in some sort of domestic chore, such as cleaning up the mess she was sure they were making, she elected to take Brutus for a run in order to get out of the house. Besides, she needed to try to work the stiffness out of her hip.

When they returned, Striker was standing in the drive beside his Hummer, looking toward the street. Natasha smiled and a thrill swept through her body at the sight of him. She unhooked Brutus from his leash and watched him lope toward Striker, resisting the urge to try to outrun the large dog.

When she reached her lover, she gently nudged Brutus aside, saying, "My turn now." She stepped into Striker's arms and kissed him hungrily. "I have missed you so," she said against his mouth.

"Me too, baby."

Natasha eyed his attire. Striker was dressed in what she called his mercenary uniform, black from head to toe—fatigues, boots, flak vest, sleeveless T-shirt, billed cap, with dark shades covering his eyes. With his tall, muscular build, he appeared powerful, ominous. Beautiful.

"You going or coming?"

"Going."

She wanted to ask him where exactly, but knew from the past that when Striker dressed like this, he never divulged anything, which drove her nuts but attracted her even more, this mysterious life he led.

She cocked her head. "How much time have I got?"

He grinned. "I need to leave by seven."

"I'm all sweaty. I need to shower."

He gave her a lecherous look. "I like you sweaty."

"Then come with me." She took his hand and led him into the house.

Chumley was in the foyer, banging away at a chair leg.

"What the hell?" Striker said with an amused look.

"Chumley," Natasha said.

The Pug glanced around. He spied Brutus standing next to Striker, unwrapped his legs from the chair leg, and waddled his way. Brutus gave Natasha a panicked look before racing upstairs.

"What is wrong with you?" Natasha scolded Chumley.

Ignoring Natasha, the little dog focused on Striker.

"You try doing that to me, you're going flying," Striker said.

Natasha intertwined her fingers with Striker's. "Come on, darlin'."

Growling noises sounded behind them and something latched on to Striker's boot. He looked down to see Chumley tearing away at the leather.

"What the hell?"

Natasha yanked on the Pug. "Get off him, Chumley."

Chumley sunk his teeth in deeper and growled, shaking his head from side to side.

"Myrtle," Natasha yelled, knowing Chumley never acted out in front of his mistress.

"Yes, dear," they heard from the kitchen.

"Call Chumley, please."

"Chumley. Here, boy," Myrtle said, her voice growing louder as she neared the kitchen door.

Chumley released Striker's boot and bared his teeth at him before waddling off in the direction of Myrtle.

"You see what I have to contend with?" Natasha said.

Striker shook his head. He couldn't understand it; he got along with most dogs and had always been proud of that fact, his theory being canines were better judges of character than their owners were. He forgot that concern rather quickly when they reached Natasha's bedroom.

Natasha talked Striker into having dinner with the others, enticing him with Myrtle's fried chicken, mashed potatoes, and biscuits.

"That's awful heavy food," he said. "I don't need something that's going to lay in my stomach all night."

"Well, then, just eat small portions. Come on, darlin', at least sit down with us. I want to show you off, let Myrtle see how absolutely gorgeous you are."

They sat around the table, sharing the country meal Myrtle had prepared, everyone exclaiming over the dishes. Natasha calculated in her mind how long dinner would take, trying to think of a way to get out of helping with the cleanup and get in some Striker time before he had to leave. Her eyes wandered to Misty, sitting beside Roger, ignoring everyone but him, occasionally shooting a curious glance in Striker's direction. Resisting the impulse to send her a smug look, Natasha straightened when an idea occurred.

"Hey, Misty, you ever worked as a stripper?"

"Ah, Jesus," Striker groaned, knowing what was coming.

Misty frowned at Natasha. "I beg your pardon."

"It's just...Misty Bellows, no offense, but that sounds like a name an exotic dancer would use. Plus you have that great body with those —"

Striker nudged Natasha with his knee.

"What? Well, it's true."

All eyes turned to Misty, who was busy glaring at Natasha. "No, I've never worked as a stripper."

"I only meant it as a compliment." Natasha was quiet for a moment, then said, "I wonder if you'd be interested in applying as one."

Roger huffed an exasperated sigh. Misty glared some more. Striker nudged Natasha again.

"What? Okay, I apologize if I've said anything to offend anyone." Natasha glanced around the table and focused her gaze on Myrtle. "The owner of the dog who placed second in Best in Show last year owns a strip club outside Knoxville. I was trying to figure out a way to get to him, to find out if he knows anything about that letter to Chumley. And Misty has that great body, so I figured if I could talk her into going with me on the pretense of applying as a —"

"Why don't you apply yourself, dear?" Myrtle said.

Natasha's eyes grew wide.

"Forget it," Striker said.

"Actually, the dudette would make a great stripper," Bigun said.

Striker glowered.

"What? Well, she would. Look at the way she dances, dude, plus she's got great le..." He hesitated when Striker's expression grew stormier.

"Yeah, but my breasts are too small," Natasha said.

Striker glanced heavenward. *Here we go.*

Pit snorted.

"What?" Natasha said.

"You ever been in a strip club? Hell, man, they got dancers in there all shapes and sizes."

"He's right, dear," Myrtle said.

Everyone looked at Myrtle.

Natasha caught Striker staring at her. "What?"

"Did it not occur to you to simply call the guy up, make an appointment to discuss this case with him, and go talk to him? Why the hell do you have to act like you're applying for a job?"

"Well, if he knows something and I introduce myself to him as the person investigating the case, he's not going to want to tell me anything. Geez, Striker, you should know that."

Striker bristled.

"But if he thinks I'm applying for a job..."

"Yeah? What if he asks you to dance for him, do a strip, what are you going to do then?"

Natasha made a face. "I didn't think about that."

"Of course not."

"Hey."

Striker gave Natasha an intense look. "Let's drop the stripper thing. Those clubs aren't the safest places in the world, you know."

She responded with a noncommittal shrug.

Natasha made sure she got Striker upstairs before seven. After she walked him to his vehicle and kissed him in a way that promised more where that came from upon his return, she headed to the kitchen, feeling guilty that she had left Myrtle and the others to clean up the mess from dinner.

Myrtle, Pit, and Bigun were sitting around the table, drinking coffee. Each gave her a sullen look, but no one said anything.

Natasha tried to act surprised. "Oh, shoot, you've already done the dishes. I'm sorry. I wanted to do that but needed to talk to Striker about something first."

Their identical expressions seemed to say, *Yeah, right.*

Ignoring this, Natasha busied herself putting away pots and pans. She noticed Chumley sitting passively at Myrtle's feet, acting like a gentleman, and shook her head, unable to understand the difference in the dog sans Myrtle.

Natasha poured a glass of iced tea, sat down at the table, and glanced around. "Where's Roger?"

Three sets of eyes traveled to the ceiling.

"I'd say he had something he needs to discuss with his young lady, much like you did with your young man," Myrtle said.

Natasha's face grew red. "I'm in love, okay? I can't help myself. Surely you guys understand that."

This fell on deaf ears.

Natasha gave up trying to defend her actions. "Myrtle, you think if you went with me to that strip club, you'd recognize this guy?"

"Hey, man, you're not gonna go, are you?" Pit asked. "You heard what Striker said."

"Yeah, dudette, the Strikester made it clear he doesn't want you to go there," Bigun added.

"Hey, Striker doesn't tell me what to do, okay? I need to talk to this guy, and since Myrtle, in a way, knows him, I figured we'd go there together and see if we can find out anything."

They stared at her.

"What? I was thinking Myrtle could act like she remembers him from last year, introduce me to him, tell him I'm her niece, looking for a job as an exotic dancer."

Pit gave her a warning look. "Striker's gonna find out, man. You know that."

"Yeah? You gonna tell him?"

Pit's eyebrows drew together.

"Hey, Pit, I got an idea. Why don't you and Bigun go with us, kind of act as our bodyguards, just in case something happens?"

"Shoot, dudette, if you're involved, you know something's gonna happen," Bigun said.

"Well, there you go," Natasha said.

Pit and Bigun looked at one another.

"I'll pay the cover price," Natasha said.

They gave a collective shrug.

Natasha turned to Myrtle.

"Well, I suppose, dear, but what about Chumley?"

"Can your sister babysit for an hour or so?"

"I'll call her and see."

Chapter 7

On the way to the club, Natasha reminded Myrtle of the owner's name. "We'll ask for him, and I'm sure once you see him, you'll recognize him."

"Oh, dear, I hope so," Myrtle said, with a worried look. "You're sure you've got the right man? You're sure he owns the dog who placed second?"

Natasha tried to sound more confident than she felt. "Don't worry, Myrtle. I've got the right man."

When they walked into the club, Natasha had to resist the urge to cover her eyes. Some of the women were in glass cages, rubbing paint all over their bodies, pressing their bulbous breasts and globulous buttocks against the glass.

"That is so nasty," she said. When no one responded, she glanced at Pit and Bigun, looking around like kids in a candy store. "Big mistake," Natasha told herself, grabbing Myrtle's arm and guiding her toward the bar.

Natasha told the bartender they wanted to speak with the owner, Mr. Myers. When he inquired what business they had with him, she told him she was there to apply for a job.

While they waited for Myers, Natasha tried keeping her eyes on the floor, the bar, the drinks, anything but the naked women scattered around the room. Her mouth dropped open at one young woman sitting on a chair on an elevated platform, explaining her genitalia to a group of men gathered around watching with lewd fascination.

"Men are such pigs," Natasha said. Again, no response. She looked around for Pit and Bigun, who seemed to have disappeared. So had Myrtle. *What the...* Natasha frantically scanned the room, finding Myrtle further down the bar, drinking what appeared to be whiskey.

"Myrtle, I thought I lost you," Natasha said, joining her.

Myrtle gave her a glassy smile.

Natasha grew alarmed. "How many of those have you had?"

"Just the one, dear, but I'm afraid I don't hold my liquor too well."

"Well, don't drink anymore. You need to be alert for this guy so you can play your part."

Myrtle picked up her drink. "Certainly, dear. Don't worry about me. I can handle it."

Natasha shook her head and resumed searching the room for her two long-lost bodyguards.

A man of average height and build with fiery red hair and a mustache to match approached them. He introduced himself as Mickey Myers, club owner, as he shook hands with Natasha and Myrtle.

Natasha nudged Myrtle, who had missed her cue; this was where she was supposed to recognize the dude.

Myrtle gave her a drunken look. "Yes, dear?"

Resisting the urge to put her hands around Myrtle's chicken neck and squeeze, Natasha forced a smile on her face. "I'm Nattie and this is my aunt, Myrtle Galbreath."

Myers nodded at Myrtle. He turned to study Natasha, his eyes callously roaming her body. "You danced in clubs like this?"

Natasha waited for Myrtle to say something, but Myrtle seemed to like her drink too much to do anything but take another sip. Shoot. Natasha tried to figure a way around that.

"Hey, you look familiar. Doesn't he look familiar, Aunt Myrtle?" she said, poking her cohort.

Myrtle gave her a foggy smile. "Familiar? Why, yes, dear, he does."

Natasha waited, but apparently Myrtle didn't feel the need to expound. "Are you involved in anything else other than this club?"

Myers gave her a suspicious look.

"It's just—it drives me crazy recognizing someone but not remembering where I've met them," Natasha said.

"Take your top off."

A stunned look crossed Natasha's face. "What?"

"Let me see what you got."

Natasha glanced at Myrtle, busy ordering another drink. She turned back to Myers. "But I'm not wearing a bra."

"So?"

"Well, you know, I don't take my top off for just anybody."

Myers frowned. "What the hell you think this is, girl? Not one dancer in here has a top on, or anything else for that matter."

Natasha glanced around, desperate for something to say to get her out of this mess.

Myers reared back. "What's your angle? Shy schoolgirl? Virgin nun?"

Natasha shrugged. "Take your pick. Hey, I remember where I saw you. You were at a dog show my aunt was at last year."

Myers seemed to be contemplating while studying her.

Growing uncomfortable at his scrutiny, Natasha looked to Myrtle for support, but her elderly friend was concentrating on sipping her liquor and didn't notice. Natasha forced herself not to knock the whiskey glass out of her hand.

Myers nodded. "Might work. We've never had either one of those in here before."

Natasha tried once more. "She has a Pug. His name's Chumley; he won Best in Show. I believe your dog placed second."

Myers rubbed his chin. "Put you in one of those schoolgirl uniforms. You know, pleated skirt, sweater, knee socks, ribbon in your hair."

Was he even hearing her? "Surely you remember that cluster."

"Better yet, I like that virgin nun idea. You kind of got that innocent, shocked look about you. Yeah, I can see you in one of those outfits. You come onstage, acting all surprised and horrified." He stepped back and nodded some more. "That could work. Get the music going, get you slowly into it, dancing a little, the guys encouraging you on, then you start taking off that — what's that thing they wear on their head?"

"I don't know. I'm not Catholic. Wait, wait. Is it a habit? No, that's what they call the robe, isn't it?"

"Whatever. Take it off, let that long, blond hair down, strut around, shaking your hair loose, then remove that big collar thing they wear, then the robe. Nothing on underneath. Well, maybe thongs. Take those off. Maybe wear a wooden cross but keep that on. Yeah, I can see that."

"Actually, you know what might work better? If I wore, like, white cotton panties, not thongs. Something ultraconservative. And maybe a white cotton bra. Or better yet, a white T-shirt, no bra." Natasha hesitated. Wait a minute. *What* had she just said?

Liking that, Myers nodded in agreement. "Okay, you're hired."

Her mouth dropped open. "You're kidding."

"You got one of those outfits?"

"Not on me, no."

"Don't worry about it, I can get you one. When can you start?"

"But you haven't seen me do anything," Natasha sputtered.

His eyes traveling over her body, Myers reached out and skimmed his fingers along her left breast.

Natasha smacked his hand away. "Hey."

"You're a little on the skinny side, but that's okay. Those legs of yours will more than make up for whatever else is missing."

Her eyes narrowed. "What?"

"Okay, we'll let you do the nun bit, but you got to go into the cages at least once a night." Myers waved in the direction of the women painting the glass with their naked bodies.

Natasha gaped. "Cages?"

"It's mandatory."

She was beginning to panic that he'd somehow maneuver her into one of those things. "First, can I ask you something?"

Myers shot her a lewd look. "Sure, baby, ask me anything. After all, you're gonna get to know me a whole lot better than this."

"I don't think so. But I was wondering, at that dog show, did you see or meet anyone acting suspicious? Someone who maybe got upset over Chumley winning Best in Show?"

Myers's brow furrowed. "What's it to you?"

"Well, it's just, he's my aunt's dog and he's gotten this threatening letter."

Myers's scowl deepened. "Did you come here about a job or to ask questions about some dog?"

"I'd like to talk about the dog, but we can discuss the job later." *Like, yeah.*

Myers's face was beginning to match his mustache. "You want the job or not?"

"Well, actually, to be honest about it, we're trying to find out who sent the dog that note."

Myers waved the bartender over. "Get her out of here."

Natasha looked around the room for Pit and Bigun. They were standing in front of the table with the woman who had been explaining her genitalia, watching in awe as she inserted what looked to be one huge dildo.

The bartender put one beefy paw on her arm.

"Wait," Natasha screeched.

The bar grew quiet.

"Come on, Myrtle, we're leaving," Natasha said.

Myrtle gave Natasha a drunken smile. "You go ahead, dear. I'll wait for the boys."

Natasha wrenched her arm out of the bartender's hold and stomped over to Myers. "Hey, I gave you one hell of an idea, you doofus. The least you can do is answer my question."

Myers gave her an amused look. "Okay. Did I see anyone upset or acting suspicious? Hell, girl, just about everybody at those shows acts suspicious. There're always a few nuts that think their darling little mutt should be the one to carry away the grand prize. Shit, some of those people are vicious. They'll do anything to win."

"Which puts you in the same category, since your dog placed second behind Chumley."

Myers snorted a laugh. "It doesn't surprise me one bit your aunt got that threatening letter. I'm sure I would have if my dog had won."

"Did you or did you not send the letter?" Natasha said, watching his eyes.

Myers gave her an annoyed look. "No, I didn't send any kind of a letter to anybody. Why should I care? I don't do those shows anymore, takes up too much of my time." His eyes darted toward the bartender. "Get her out of here." He turned his back on Natasha.

"Pit! Bigun!" Natasha yelled, while being dragged toward the door.

The two men apparently didn't hear her; all their senses but one having gone to hell as they watched the woman slowly move the dildo in and out.

The bartender shoved Natasha out the door and watched as she stumbled around, barely managing to keep her balance. She glared at the tapster until he went back inside and then looked around helplessly. What was she going to do? Pit had driven and he had the keys. She had no way home.

Natasha found Pit's SUV and tried the doors, but they were all locked. Growing frustrated, she yanked on the door handles. She was kicking the tires when her phone bleeped. She dug it out of her purse and leaned back against the SUV, out of breath.

"Yeah?"

"Have you eaten yet?" her mom asked.

"Oh, hey, Mom. Yeah, Striker and I ate at Roger's."

"Well, come on over and have dessert with your dad and me. I made banana pudding."

Although her mom wasn't a particularly good cook, no one could top her banana pudding. But how in the world could Natasha get there?

"It'll have to be later, Mom. I'm kind of in the middle of something," she said, disappointment in her voice.

"Oh? What's going on?"

Natasha rolled her eyes, wondering when her mom's world would expand beyond her daughter's doings. "I'm investigating," she said.

Stevie huffed into the phone. "Nattie, don't you think it's time you got serious and found a real job?"

When would her mom ever respect her choice of profession? What would it take? Natasha decided to push buttons, just to get her back. "Well, actually, Mom, to tell you the truth, that's what I'm doing, applying for a new job."

Stevie's voice perked up. "You are? Well, that's wonderful. What job are you applying for?"

"I'm at this strip club outside Knoxville. I thought it'd be fun to try my luck as an exotic dancer."

There was shocked silence on the other end. Natasha's phone twirped.

"Oops, gotta go, Mom, they're calling me in for my audition," Natasha said and clicked over. "Hello."

"I'm heading home," Striker said. "You still at Roger's?"

Well, shoot.

"You there?"

"Yeah, sweetie, I'm here," she said, trying to make her voice sound chipper.

"Where are you?"

She gazed heavenward, wondering why she couldn't be a liar like everybody else on earth. "I'm at that strip club."

"You're what?"

"Yeah, and I — well, I kind of need a ride home. They kicked me out."

"They what?" Striker said in an amused voice.

"You think you could swing by here? Pit's got the SUV locked and he's still inside and I'm standing out here in the parking lot."

"I'll be there in ten."

Natasha's phone trilled and she glanced at the display. Stevie. She debated answering, putting her mom's mind at rest. Instead, she turned off her phone, deciding to let Stevie suffer a little. She'd call her back tomorrow.

Striker pulled into the parking lot, located Natasha with his headlights. He braked to a stop beside Pit's SUV and waited for her to climb into his Hummer.

Natasha turned to face him after closing the door. "I know, I know. You do not have to say it."

"Where's Myrtle?"

"Inside."

A small smile played across Striker's lips. "What?"

"Yeah. She got drunk. Can you believe that? Had this whole little scenario worked out and what does she do? Starts drinking, leaving me to wing it on my own."

"Where're Pit and Bigun?"

"Watching some woman insert a monster of a dildo into her vagina," Natasha said, staring out the window.

Striker chuckled.

She frowned at him.

"Okay, tell me what happened."

He laughed at her disgust over the women smudging the glass with their bodies, even more so when Natasha told him the owner had offered her a job as a stripping nun.

"It's not funny," she said.

Striker leaned toward her and said in a lewd voice, "Baby, you can strip for me anytime."

Natasha pouted.

"Well?" Striker said.

"Well what?"

"Did you find out what you came here for?"

"Yeah, which was nothing, right before he had the bartender throw me out."

Striker's eyes darkened and his jaw muscles clenched. "What?"

"You couldn't listen to me, could you? Couldn't just once take my advice, do what I ask?"

Yikes. But Natasha knew a way to divert him. She leaned toward him and put her hand on his thigh.

"Why don't we go home and I'll pretend I'm a stripper looking for a job and you pretend you're the man that's thinking about hiring me, and I promise I'll take my top off for you."

Striker frowned.

She smiled. "I can promise you a really good time."

Without saying a word, he started the Hummer.

Chapter 8

Natasha sat at her desk, trying to get a handle on this Chumley deal. Irritated with Roger, who hadn't come through with the detailed owner research, she reminded herself she still hadn't checked into his diversion: Misty. She picked up her list of participants and continued cross-referencing names against the latest City Directory, smiling when she noticed one of the judges owned a kennel on the outskirts of West Knoxville. It shouldn't take too long to pay a visit, meet the judge if she was there, and prod her for information.

Natasha stepped out of her jeep to the music of dogs yapping, studying three rectangular block buildings neatly painted white and trimmed in yellow. The signs before each indicated a training area, toy house, and kennel. Behind the kennel were gated runners; she estimated a dozen, each containing at least one dog. A sign pointed to an exercise field, another to hiking trails leading into a wooded area flanked by a wide creek bed. A cantilevered barn with attached paddock occupied the greater portion of a clearing across from the kennel. She watched two horses frolicking about, admiring their grace and beautiful design.

A middle-aged woman wearing jeans, western boots, and a T-shirt that said "Death to Animal Abusers" joined her, smiling at Natasha's veneration.

"This is just beautiful," Natasha said, thinking if she ever needed a temporary place for Brutus to stay, this would be it.

"We like it," the woman answered.

"This yours?"

"Mine and my partner's." She held out her hand. "Windy, with an I, Carstain."

Natasha returned her handshake. "Are you the Windy Carstain that judges dog shows?"

"That's me."

Natasha offered Windy her business card and introduced herself.

Windy stepped back, eyeing her. "A female bodyguard? I've never met one before."

Natasha explained her reason for being there, adding, "So, I wanted to talk to you about a show you judged last year, the Greater Tennessee Kennel Club Cluster, the one in which Chumley won Best in Show."

Windy nodded, smiling. "Chumley. He's a real character."

"He is that." Natasha watched the horses once more. "Can we walk around while we talk?"

"Sure."

"Do you mind if I take pictures of your barn? It's kind of a hobby of mine. So many seem to be disappearing from this area and you don't see many cantilevered nowadays."

"Feel free."

Natasha retrieved her camera from the jeep. While they walked toward the barn, she questioned Windy about the show, trying to ferret information she could provide concerning any unstable contestants who might have held a grudge against Chumley. Windy didn't have anything to offer but volunteered to think about it and call if she remembered anything.

Natasha walked around the structure, snapping pictures from all angles, marveling at the barn's weathered beauty. "Mind if I look around inside?" she asked.

Windy's smile conveyed her pleasure at Natasha's interest. "Sure."

They stepped into the dark, cool confines of the barn, breathing in the comforting smell of horse. Natasha walked around, noting most of the area had been converted to stalls. All were vacant save one, the horse's Roman nose marking him for a Holsteiner. Natasha stroked down its regal length, speaking softly to the gelding, enjoying the velvety sensation against her hand. She gently touched the scarred flesh around his eyes, which had a milky haze.

"What happened?"

Windy ran her hand beneath the horse's mane. "One of our neighbors was recently arrested for abusing animals. Ben here got more than his share. The sick prick blinded him with battery acid."

Natasha stepped back, shocked. "What kind of person would do that to an animal?"

"The kind that ought to be paying a visit to the electric chair."

"I hope he's in prison."

"Nope. They arrested him but his trial hasn't come up yet. He's out on bail."

"You said a neighbor?"

"Yes."

"What's his name?"

"Barry Dugan."

"And you're sure he did it?"

"The whole community has been calling the humane department on Barry for years. I can't tell you how many animals we've rescued from his cruelty. The day he blinded Ben, I could hear his screams all the way over here."

"Where does he live?"

Windy studied her for a moment. She gave a knowing smile. "Turn right at the end of our drive. He's the second house on the left, about a mile down."

Natasha returned to stroking Ben's muzzle. "So how come you ended up with Ben?"

"We try to rescue as many animals as we can, to keep them away from the shelter. They take in more than they have room for and euthanize almost a hundred a day there."

Natasha gave a sad sigh. "That is so terrible."

"Anyway, we run a pet foster program here. We adopt these animals out, but in the meantime, we act as their foster parents or find foster homes for them."

"So, Ben's up for adoption?"

"Yes. Or fostering."

"What kind of special needs does he have?"

"Well, he's blind, he's been abused, he doesn't hold much trust for people. In fact, you're the first person I've seen that he's allowed to touch him around his eyes."

Natasha reached out to open the half-gate but hesitated. "May I?" she asked.

"Go ahead."

Natasha entered the stall and walked around the horse, trailing her hand over his flank. "Say I wanted to adopt him or foster him. What would that take?"

"You're interested?"

"Definitely."

"Well, he's not much trouble. Of course, we can't let him into the fields; he can't see the electric fencing. He'd keep running into it."

Natasha stepped behind Ben and studied him from that angle. "What about a small area, fenced in? Would he do okay there? I'm talking wooden fence, not barbed wire or electric."

"He should. Just walk him around it a few times, get him used to the layout. He should do well."

"Okay. Where do I sign up?"

"Have you owned a horse before?"

"I have a Quarter Horse I keep at my mom's and dad's place, with their two Walkers and a friend's Quarter Horse. They own about twenty acres in Heiskell, most of it pasture. Our barn has six stalls, so there's plenty of room."

"Okay. You'll need to fill out an application, then we'll inspect the area you'll stall him, make sure you don't have a record for abusing animals, that sort of thing."

"Great."

"It will take a few days."

"That's fine. Can we get started?"

"Let's go."

After completing the paperwork, Natasha paid another visit to Ben. Assuming a nonchalant attitude, she asked Windy if they sold horse manure. "I like to garden and it's great for my bedding plants," she said.

Windy smiled that knowing grin again. "Sure. I'll bag you up some."

Natasha packed the large bag of manure into her jeep and headed out. She turned right at the end of the drive, left two houses down. She sat in the driveway leading to a ramshackle rancher-style home, studying the small, barren yard, wondering where in the world this idiot had kept a horse. Surely not in that horrible garage-like structure sitting in the back corner of the yard that looked ready to fall down if someone so much as breathed on it.

A small, blond dog appearing to be at least half Lab sat miserably at the base of a tree, watching her. The rope used to tie the dog couldn't have been much longer than ten feet. There wasn't a water bowl Natasha could detect, or food of any kind.

She picked up her cellphone and called Windy. After telling her where she was, she said, "If he's been arrested for animal abuse, what the hell is he doing with a dog tied to a tree?"

Windy uttered several curses. "I'll be right there to get it. He's been enjoined from owning any animals."

Natasha watched the pathetic-looking dog, feeling sorry for it. "That's okay, I'll take it." She climbed out of the jeep and crossed over to the dog to pet it, noting its lethargic response, dirt-encrusted fur, and the way its ribs bulged against skin. The poor thing couldn't have been more than six months old. She walked up the front steps of the house and rang the bell. When no one answered, she returned to the car, retrieved the bag of horse manure, and dumped the contents on the front porch. She swung by the tree, untied the dog, picked it up in her arms, and left.

Chapter 9

Striker turned off the lights behind him as he walked in the direction of his bedroom, dog-tired from driving to Atlanta and back in one day. But not too tired for Natasha, as proven by one part of his anatomy beginning to stir, knowing she was in the house. Like a missile locked onto a heat source.

Climbing the stairs, he contemplated how things had changed since Natasha had come into his life. Before, he would have simply stayed overnight and driven back the next day, not in any great hurry to return home. Now, he counted the moments until he saw her.

He stopped moving, his hand on the rail, his head tilted to the side. What was it about this woman that intrigued him so? What drew him to her; what was it about her that had gotten under his skin like no one before? And just when the hell had his feelings gotten so damned out of control?

Before, he had lived the life of a loner, a confirmed bachelor, relegating his interest in women to a superficial level. But then along came Natasha, with her cocky, badass attitude, who would not allow anyone to intimidate her, whose impulsivity kept landing her in all kinds of crazy situations. Although she possessed an explosive temperament, he understood the reason behind that.

The victim of a date rape several years before, Natasha now channeled the resultant anger into her efforts to protect those she deemed worthy, even if it meant getting hurt or possibly killed in the process. Ah, but to counter all this was the domesticated nester hidden inside this woman who loved him without inhibition, whose passion matched his, whose soul was twin to his own.

Stepping into the bedroom, he caught sight of Natasha asleep on the bed, dressed in one of his T-shirts, her body curled around his pillow. Papers were strewn about her, several cascading off the mattress and onto the floor. Cat, nestled against the backs of her knees, raised his head and began purring at his master's presence.

Striker sidestepped the debris littering the bed, reached down, and picked up the feline. Holding him close to his face, he said, "She's mine now. Get lost," and put the pet on the floor.

Cat gave him an indignant look before trotting off.

Striker looked around for the pup, Natasha having called earlier and told him about the dog and horse. He spotted the Lab mix laying on the lounge, watching him. He crossed over to the dog, knelt down and ran his hand over its spine, feeling the sharp protrusions. Although Natasha had bathed the pup, its fur felt bristly, unhealthy. Rubbing the mutt behind the ears, he said, in a low voice, "We got you now, you're safe." The dog stared at him in a somber manner.

Natasha stirred, gaining his attention. Striker walked over to the bed and lightly stroked her cheek, watching her lips turn up in response while she slept. An answering smile appeared on his face when she arched her back and gave a contented sigh. He leaned down to kiss her temple. He began to straighten up, but her hand was at the back of his neck, forcing him to remain close.

Natasha's kiss relayed a fierce hunger that had the tendency to nearly drive him mad with desire. She pulled him onto her, one hand remaining at the back of his neck, the other fumbling with his belt buckle while he tugged at her panties.

They made an ingress and egress and fused together with a force that was mind shattering, working each other, not saying a word, losing themselves in the physical world into which they had escaped.

Afterwards, Striker shifted his body into a more comfortable position. He lifted his head at crackling noises and noticed the crumpled paper around them.

"What's this?"

Natasha made a face. "Shoot. I had that all sorted out. Now look at the mess."

Striker picked up one of the sheets of paper. "Chumley," he said, putting it down.

Natasha nodded. She tried to crawl under the covers, but the papers were in the way. She swept them off the bed. "I'll clean this up tomorrow."

Striker followed suit until something caught his attention. He picked up a sheet of paper on which Natasha had written a name followed by a large question mark.

"What's this about Senator Goodman?"

"I've been researching the judges at that cluster show the past couple of years, and he was there both times. I was wondering if you know him."

"Yeah. In fact, I bought a couple of tickets to his fundraiser next Saturday night."

Natasha perked up. "With the intention of attending?"

"Hadn't planned on it."

"I'd like to go."

He slanted a sideways glance at her. "He's a Republican."

She shrugged. "I promise not to hold that against him."

Striker grinned.

"You know him or just know of him?"

He lay back and closed his eyes. "I've known him for a few years now."

"Let's go," Natasha said excitedly.

Striker gave her a suspicious look through slitted eyes. "Wait a minute. I thought you hated political functions."

"Well, yeah, you try going to those supercilious things and getting glared at by all those cat-women jealous 'cause I took such a gorgeous man out of the running."

Striker smiled at that; he didn't believe her but liked what she said. A thought entered his mind. "Uh-uh."

"What?"

"If we go, you're not planning on doing something like cornering him, asking questions, working yourself into another crazy situation?"

Natasha rolled her eyes.

"'Cause that seems to be your specialty, you know."

"Yeah, right."

He raised his eyebrows.

"Okay. How about I have you introduce me to him. And later, not that evening, but in the next week or so, I'll call him up, reintroduce myself, tell him I'm investigating this thing with Chumley, ask him if he can give me any kind of information. Feel him out, so to speak."

Striker thought about it.

"Please, Striker. I won't say a word at the fundraiser, I swear."

"Uh-huh."

"Cross my heart, hope to die, stick a needle in my eye," Natasha said, sounding like a kid.

"Well, in that case."

She kissed him her thanks.

Striker settled back, tucking her against his side. "So, you thought of a name for the dog?"

Natasha rose up to make sure the Lab was doing okay. "Hey, baby," she said, in a soft voice.

The pup watched her with a sad look.

"Uh-oh."

"What?"

"I think we may have just offended Emma."

Striker smiled. "Emma? I like that. It fits her."

Natasha nestled her head against his neck, placed an arm over his chest. "I think Mom wants her."

If the dog lived with him, that might encourage Natasha to stay more often. "You can keep her here. I don't mind."

"Thank you, sweetie, but I promised to take her over there tomorrow, see what Mom thinks about her."

"Like I said, she can stay here, Natasha. I've got room."

"We'll see."

"What'd you decide about the horse? You know I've been planning on building stables for our horses. I can speed that up if you want to keep him here."

"He can stay at Mom's and Dad's with the others." She relaxed into him. "Remind me tomorrow to talk to you about making a substantial donation to the animal shelter," she said, her voice trailing off as she drifted into sleep.

Striker placed a kiss on top of her head. This was his Natasha, protector of the innocent.

In the bedroom, wearing string bikini panties and a tank top, holding the cordless phone in the air, Natasha glimpsed a grinning Striker standing in the doorway. She brought the phone to her mouth, said, "Striker's home, Mom. I'll talk to you later, love you," and flipped it over her shoulder.

Striker dropped a large box onto the chaise. "What'd you do this time?"

She shook her head, rummaging through clothing piled on the bed. "Cameron's in love."

"Oh, my."

She frowned at him. "Yeah, that Brad guy. Aunt Irene's blaming me for the whole mess."

"You did take Cameron to meet Brad, you know."

Her eyes shot daggers his way.

Striker glanced around the room at clothes strewn everywhere. "Where's Emma?"

"Mom fell in love with her, so she took her. Which made Cat a happy kitty."

Striker raised his eyebrows when Natasha threw a pair of jeans on the floor and stomped on them. "Okay, what's wrong?"

She turned to show him her profile, cupping her rounded abdomen. "Look at this."

He leaned against the doorjamb and crossed his arms. "Looks beautiful to me."

"Sometimes I absolutely hate being a woman. I mean, okay, maybe Eve should have been punished for fooling around with the snake, but for Pete's sake, Striker, what women have to endure goes beyond redemption."

A smile played across his lips. "What the hell are you talking about?"

"Look how bloated I am," she said, waving her hand in the direction of her stomach. "I swear, I finally get my butt to go down and my stomach explodes. All my jeans are too tight, nothing fits, and if that's not bad enough, my face is breaking out. On top of which, I have resisted the urge all day to do somebody some kind of heavy harm. Next, I'll start to bleed like a stuck pig and have headaches every day and cramp like the very dickens. I hate being a woman."

Striker caught her as she passed. "But baby, I'm so glad you are."

Natasha lay on the bed, eyes closed, face flushed, her body thrumming, with a smile on her lips. Something cool touched her skin and she reluctantly opened her eyes. A large, white box tied with a mauve silk ribbon rested against her abdomen.

"What's this?"

Striker sat beside her on the bed. "Don't get mad."

"Mad?"

"I bought you a present." He held up his hands at her look. "Natasha, I know you don't like wearing the same evening dress every time we go formal. I know that bothers you. Today, Scott and I were at a strip mall in Farragut looking at some office space, and I noticed this in the window of a boutique there."

Natasha sat up and opened the box. She folded back dusky-pink tissue paper to reveal a satiny material so dark-green it appeared black in shadow.

"The color reminds me of your eyes," Striker said, thinking how dark they became when she was passionate, or angry. "I had to buy it because of that."

She gave him a pained look. "But darlin', this is too much. I can't accept this."

"Why not?" he said, trying to keep the irritation out of his voice.

"Well, it's expensive. I can tell just by the box it came in, not to mention the fabric."

"So?"

"So, I can't afford it and I can't let you —"

He placed two fingers on her lips. "You are my life mate, Natasha, you are my destiny. What's mine is yours. How many times do I have to tell you that?"

She drew her head back and opened her mouth.

Striker shook his head to silence her. "If I choose to buy you expensive gifts from time to time, I don't understand why you have a problem with that. Women in my past have appreciated that from me."

Natasha leaned toward him. "But I can't afford to buy you expensive gifts, and it makes me uncomfortable when you do that for me. It's not fair to you."

"Baby, you give me a gift every time you look at me, don't you know that? Every time you kiss me, when we make love. That's the best gift you could ever give me, your love."

She smiled. "It's the same for me with you."

"Take it, Natasha. It'll look beautiful on you."

She drew the gown from the box and held it up, admiring it.

"Try it on," Striker said.

Natasha stood to pull the gown over her head. It was simple in style, but when she filled it, the dress assumed elegance, as if it were meant for her. Her eyes met his, and Striker thought he could lose himself in those dark depths.

Natasha walked over to the cheval mirror to study her reflection. "It's beautiful," she said, running her hands down the length of her torso.

Striker stepped up behind her, stared at her reflection in the mirror. "You're beautiful."

Chapter 10

Natasha stood beside Striker while he introduced her to Senator Goodman, who was without a doubt the most popular man in the state. A former lawyer turned politician, he wasn't an exceptionally handsome man. Of average height and build, his once dark-brown hair was heavily streaked with gray. His face reminded her of a hound dog, with coffee-colored eyes half-hidden behind heavy lids and large, droopy ears and jowls. But there was a charismatic air and down-home sense about him that she and the majority of voters in Tennessee found charming enough to keep him in Washington, D.C.

"Senator Goodman," Natasha gushed. "It's so nice to meet you."

Striker stepped back and scowled.

The senator smiled with delight, showing bright-white teeth. "Well, it's certainly nice to meet you, my dear."

The two of them beamed at one another.

"Have you met my wife?" Goodman asked.

"No, sir. I'm afraid I haven't had the pleasure."

Goodman tucked her hand into his arm. "Well, let's go find her. I'm sure she'll be tickled pink to meet the beautiful young lady that caught Striker's attention."

Striker watched the senator disappear into the crowd with Natasha, irritated they had walked away from him, seeming absorbed in one another. After a moment of indecision, he gave a slight shrug and decided to go find the bar.

"Is she upstairs?" Natasha asked, when they reached the elevators.

"I believe she's still in our suite, yes." Goodman stepped back, eyeing Natasha.

She glanced over her shoulder. "Where's Striker?"

Goodman gave her an indulgent smile. "I'm sure he's not too far behind." He turned his attention to the elevator doors when they slid open, nodded at the people stepping off, and herded Natasha on. Punching the Close Door button, he gave her that look again.

Natasha wasn't too surprised to find they were alone when they entered Goodman's suite.

The senator walked toward the bar. "How about some champagne?"

"I don't know if that's such a good idea," Natasha said, beginning to feel apprehensive.

Goodman gave her the puppy-dog eyes.

"Well, maybe one drink."

"Why don't you take your shoes off, stay awhile," he drawled, shooting her a toothy grin.

Natasha moved to the sofa and sat down but made sure her shoes stayed on.

Goodman drew two glasses toward him and poured champagne into one. "So what do you do when you're not hanging around Striker?"

Natasha explained she was also in the private security field.

Goodman downed his drink in one swallow before filling Natasha's glass. "That's interesting. Are you employed by Striker?"

"Well, I was, but when we became involved, I left and started my own firm." Natasha forgot all about one certain promise to Striker, adding, "Which is one reason I was hoping to meet you tonight."

Goodman refilled his drink before joining Natasha. He carried both glasses to the couch and sat on the opposite end after offering one to her.

Placing it on the coffee table, Natasha explained about Chumley and his threatening letter.

While she talked, Goodman rose, crossed over to the bar, and retrieved the champagne bottle. He returned and poured more of the pale fluid into his glass.

Natasha grew concerned that he was drinking so much so quickly. Giving him a skeptical look, she finished by saying, "So, I was wondering if you could offer me any information, you know, something you might have picked up on, regarding who could possibly be threatening Chumley to stay away from this year's cluster."

She watched Goodman down yet another glass, remove a bottle of pills from a pocket, shake one out, and pop it into his mouth. She wondered what kind of pill was blue in color.

Goodman refilled his drink and held it toward Natasha. "To women."

"Ditto." Natasha picked up her glass, clicked it against his, took a sip, and set it down.

"Well now, sugar, let me think a minute," the Senator drawled, his accent looser, more Southern. He finished his champagne while he supposedly contemplated. He turned glazed eyes upon her, murmuring in that heavy accent, "I tell you what, darlin', you are, without a doubt, one fine-lookin' woman."

Uh-oh. "Thank you." Natasha averted her gaze from his. Finally unable to resist, she turned to look at him.

Goodman flashed a wicked grin. "Why don't you come on over here and let me show you something big."

Natasha's mouth formed a shocked oval. "Senator, you're old enough to be my father. You should be ashamed of yourself."

He gave her a lecherous giggle, as if she had somehow complimented him.

Natasha stood, giving him a haughty look. "I think you've drunk way too much and it would be best if I just leave."

"Oh, now, darlin', don't go gettin' your panties in a bind." Goodman struggled to his feet, swaying slightly, trying to maintain his balance.

Natasha warily watched him, unsure what to do, half-afraid he was going to fall.

"'Course, I myself would like to accomplish that certain feat, if you get my gist." He lunged toward her, his hands in front of him, groping for her breasts.

Natasha shoved him away. "Get off me, you jerk."

Goodman stumbled back against the couch. Losing his balance, he sat down abruptly before tumbling off. He landed facedown on the carpet, where he stayed.

Natasha waited for him to move, but he remained still. *Omigod.* What was she going to do? "I can't be caught like this; he can't be caught like this," she said out loud. She began pacing. "Why do these things always happen to me? I'm not a bad person; I don't hurt people. Well, not deliberately." She knelt beside Goodman, reached out, and gingerly touched his shoulder. "Senator?"

Goodman remained motionless.

Natasha straightened. "Please, dear God, don't let him be dead," she prayed. "Please don't let this be a heart attack. Please don't make me have to put my mouth on his and breathe for him. What if he's wearing false teeth, they're too perfect not to be, or maybe capped, and wouldn't I have to remove them first if they're false? Oh, please, don't make me have to do that. Please don't let him die and me have to call the cops and Lord knows who all else, and this get in the paper. And oh, yeah, God, please don't make me have to explain this to Striker."

Natasha tugged on his shoulder, trying to turn him over. Damn, he felt like he weighed a ton. When she managed to wrestle him onto his back, one arm flung limply out, slapping her leg in the process. She squealed and jumped back.

Natasha watched for signs of breathing, wishing she had paid more attention during CPR class. Remembering the bottle of pills, she fished in the pocket from which she had seen him retrieve them and pulled the bottle free. Holding it up, her eyes opened wide when she read the word "Viagra".

She punched his shoulder. "You idiot." She jumped when someone banged on the door.

Natasha glanced from the senator to the door and back again. Another series of knocks, these quite a bit louder than the previous ones, motivated her to rise to her feet.

"Just a minute," she called. She stuffed the bottle into Goodman's pocket, picked up both his feet, and tried dragging him toward the bedroom. He was so heavy she could hardly budge him.

The pounding on the door was insistent now. Natasha's eyes darted around the room. When the knocks grew thunderous, she shoved the senator against the sofa, grabbed an afghan from a chair, and draped it over the cushions and toward the floor to cover him.

It sounded like whoever was on the other side of the door was trying to knock it down. Natasha hurried into the small foyer and flung the door open. Striker stood in the hallway with his fist in the air. She reached out, grabbed his arm, and pulled him into the room.

"Thank God you're here. I think I killed Senator Goodman."

"You what?"

Natasha stuck her head into the hallway and glanced to the right and left, hoping no one had heard him. Seeing an empty corridor, she shut the door. "He tried to, you know, and I — "

"He what? Where's the son-of-a-bitch? I'm gonna fuckin' kill him."

Striker stormed past her, into the room. It didn't take him long to find Goodman. Natasha guessed it was one of the senator's well-polished shoes peeking out from beneath the afghan that did it.

Striker yanked the afghan off, kneeled down beside Goodman, grabbed his shirtfront, and pulled him up. The senator made a loud, snorting sound and smiled drunkenly. With a disgusted look, Striker released his shirt. Goodman's head bounced against the carpet and he became still once more.

"Well, thank goodness," Natasha said. "I thought he was dead."

Striker stood and gave her a dark look.

Uh-oh.

"You want to tell me what the hell you're doing in his suite, alone with him?"

"He said his wife was here and he wanted her to meet me, so what else could I do?"

Striker shook his head. "You are way too gullible, Natasha, you know that?"

"Well, he's a senator, for goodness' sake. He's supposed to be moralistic and scrupulous, not some lecherous old fart making advances at me, trying to get me to, you know — "

Striker's eyes roamed the ceiling while she said this. "He's a politician, Natasha. They don't even know how to spell words like 'moralistic' and 'scrupulous', much less enact them."

"Now you tell me," she said, giving Striker her own indignant look.

"What's that supposed to mean?"

"You let me go off with him. You didn't follow us; you didn't try to stop him. You at least could have warned me about him if you were going to entrust me to him."

"Oh, so it's my fault you didn't have sense enough to — "

"Hell, yeah, it's your fault. I trusted the man. After all, no one bothered to tell me what a lech he was."

They exchanged angry glares.

Striker couldn't stop himself from asking, "Did he touch you?"

Natasha shrugged with a pout. "He tried, but I pushed him away and he landed on the couch and somehow ended up on the floor."

Striker gave her a look.

"What?"

"What caused him to pass out? You didn't shoot him or do anything drastic, did you?"

"Wish I had. The stupid idiot was downing champagne like you wouldn't believe, on top of which he took a Viagra."

"He what?"

"Yeah."

"I'll kill that son-of-a-bitch."

"You think maybe the Viagra interacted with the alcohol? You think that could be fatal or something?"

Striker studied the man to make sure he was still breathing. "I hope to hell it does."

"Don't you think we ought to get out of here?" Natasha said, glancing around. "In case his wife does actually show up here?"

Striker reached down, snatched up the afghan, and threw it on the couch. "Come on." He grabbed Natasha's hand and led her into the hallway. He stopped just before closing the door. "I'll be right back."

Natasha watched Striker reenter the room, approach Goodman, draw his foot back, and kick him in the rear. The senator didn't even seem to feel it. Ouch, she thought, knowing one certain politician would have a nasty bruise there tomorrow.

Striker grabbed her hand, slammed the door after them, and strode toward the elevator. She went along willingly.

As the cart descended, Natasha glanced at her lover, caught him studying her. "What?"

Striker looked away. "Nothing."

Natasha smiled; she knew what the look meant. She stepped closer to him, leaned into his chest. "What?"

Striker put his hand on the back of her neck and, his mouth against hers, said, "You know what."

The next morning, Goodman called to tell Natasha what a wonderful evening he had enjoyed with her. She wondered if he noticed the bruise on his butt but didn't dare ask. His side of the conversation indicated he was under the impression they had made love. She couldn't figure out how to set him straight, so decided to leave that to Striker next time the two met. She steered the conversation to the cluster the past two years but learned nothing of interest. When Goodman offered to call her if he thought of anything, she readily agreed, although doubted his intentions would be good. That afternoon, Goodman sent roses and a card with his private phone number on it. She threw away the card but kept the roses. Well, until Striker showed up. Then the roses went in the trash, too.

Chapter 11

Outside Striker's bedroom, on the deck overlooking the Tennessee River, Striker reclined in a lounge chair with Natasha cuddled up in his lap, in the dark, in the nude. This was something they often did in the aftermath of love; coming down, their bodies cooling, admiring the stars in the sky while enjoying the warm night.

Natasha tilted her head back and gazed at him.

Striker brushed her lips with his, thinking he had never been so contented as he was at this moment. "What?"

"Can I talk to you?"

"Sure, baby. What's on your mind?"

She glanced away but he did not miss her slight frown.

"I want to talk about us," she said quietly.

Striker, not sure he wanted to have the conversation, tried to make his voice even. "Go ahead."

Natasha straightened so they were eye to eye and gave him a serious look. "I think we can both agree this relationship would be considered intensely sexual."

Striker considered for a moment. "I'd call it that, yeah."

"I've never been in this sort of relationship before."

"Neither have I."

"It worries me sometimes."

"Yeah? Why's that?"

She sighed and folded her bottom lip between her teeth. "It's just, when we're together, the thing we do the most is this, engage in sexual liaisons together. I mean, darlin', we make love a lot. In all my other relationships, what few there were, it was never this way. Not two, three times every time we see each other, or the sexual marathons we have from time to time."

Striker shot her a lewd grin in an effort at levity. "I'm not complaining."

"Neither am I. I love the way we are together. It's perfect. Scary perfect, you know? But what I was wondering —"

"Am I going to like this?"

"What I was wondering is if that's the way you were with other women, if that's normal for you. If, before me, you were one of those guys who happens to be very sexually active, with an extremely high sex drive."

"You're serious?"

She nodded.

"Natasha," he said in that gravelly way of his that made her stomach clench and sent a tingling sensation to her toes and back, "it's never been this way before. I just told you that."

She studied his face. "It's just, you're so masculine, and maybe you're one of those guys who has an overabundance of testosterone, who has to have sex frequently, who can't go without sex for any length of time —"

"No, I'm not one of those guys," he interrupted.

Their gazes met.

"Okay, remember when we were working on Roger's case, back in the good old days when you worked for me and I at least had the luxury of believing I could control your somewhat wacky ways —"

"Oh, for the love of Myrtle," she said with frustration.

"Okay, I'll skip that part. I'm talking about the second time we went to meet the extortionist, when you stopped that woman from paddling her kid, and we got into it, there in the parking lot at Wal-Mart. Remember that?"

Natasha nodded while giving him a curious look.

"And you called me that night?"

"I remember."

"And the next day, you wouldn't talk to me because you said you felt like you were interrupting my being with a woman."

Natasha glanced away. "I don't know if I want to hear this."

"No, wait. Just hear me out. I was with another woman, and we were planning to make love. But then you called, and when I got off the phone with you, I looked at her and she…well, she didn't appeal to me. I wanted you there instead, so I took her home. And from that point on, I committed myself to you. I didn't sleep with another woman. I waited to see what was going to happen with you."

Natasha smiled. "Really?"

"Swear to God. I have never felt such passion for another woman as I do for you." He gave her a wicked grin. "I guess you bring out the animal in me, baby. That's the only explanation I've been able to come up with."

"So you've thought about this, too?"

"You caught me."

She rested her head against his neck and looked out at the still, black water. "What happens after this?"

"After what?"

"When this starts to wane, when the physical need isn't so important, not like it is now. What happens then?"

Striker drew back and studied her, could see this really had her worried. He gently tucked her hair behind her ear, his hand lingering on her neck.

"I mean, from everything I've ever read on the subject, the passion will eventually fade. Although I have to tell you, Jonce, I don't want it to. I love what I feel for you, the way you are with me, the things we do together. But when it does start to fade, are we going to be looking at each other, wondering what the attraction had been, wish we were with someone else? Is that going to happen to us?" There were tears in her eyes.

Shit. "Does this feel real to you?"

"More real than anything before, ever."

"For me, too. And like you, I don't want this to fade, but you're overlooking one important fact here, darlin'."

"Yeah?"

"We were friends before we were lovers," Striker said. "And if our passion does start to fade, diminish, whatever, I guess that will give us more time to focus on the other interests we share."

"You think so?"

"Sure. We both love animals, horseback riding, boating, working on this house. And eventually, if I can ever talk you into it, start a family, have a couple of kids together, raise them, invest all the time and energy that takes."

"Well, see, that's what worries me."

"What?"

"I wonder if you haven't reached that point in life most guys get to, where they've sown all their wild oats and are ready to settle down, and I just happened to come along at the right time in your life, wrong time in mine."

"What?"

"Sure. It makes sense, doesn't it? You're in your thirties, and from what I've been told, you've done a hell of a lot of sowing —"

"Oh, for Christ's sake."

"My point is, I worked for you for three years before we became involved and I saw the women you dated. I'm realistic enough to know I don't hold a candle to most of them, so it's logical that I came along right about the time you —"

Striker put his fingers under her chin and pushed, clicking her mouth shut. "Look at me. Listen to what I'm saying. You're the most beautiful woman I've ever known, ever *will* know, ever want to know, mentally, physically, spiritually. You fit me, baby, here," he said, touching his temple, "here", touching his heart, "and here," he finished, gesturing toward his body.

"It's the same for me. You know that, don't you?"

"I pray so."

"But in all honesty, I'm not ready to settle down. I'm not ready to have babies and start a family. I've just started my own business, I haven't had time to even get it off the —"

"Will you shut up?"

She drew back from him. "What?"

"Did I say start a family now? Did those words come out of my mouth? I said eventually. Big difference there, babe."

"Oh, right."

"I'm not asking you to marry me or anything," he said with a disgruntled look.

She gave him am impish grin, relaxing against his chest. "But eventually you will, right?"

"Who knows what the future holds," he said with an aloofness he did not feel. After all, her silky, bare ass kept shifting in his lap, eliciting responsive movements in the nether region.

"So there's a chance you won't ask me to marry you?" Her voice harbored disappointment.

"How the hell did we get to this point? I thought you didn't want to get married. I thought you didn't want to settle down —"

She put her lips on his, gave him a lingering kiss. "Yeah, but there's another problem."

"God help me, what is that?"

"You're starting to change my perspective."

"Damn, Natasha, I was thinking that very thing not too long ago about you," Striker said, his hands moving over her body hungrily, his mouth seeking hers once more.

Chapter 12

Back to the City Directory, Natasha smiled when she recognized the name of a judge from the prior year's Best in Show division, one Mr. Arnold Butler. The past summer, she and Roger had played a foursome with Butler and his wife, Annie, at Roger's country club. Her smile widened, thinking about that. Annie, a short, heavyset woman with sparkly blue eyes and close-cropped gray hair, had a witty sense of humor that kept everyone in stitches the eighteen rounds they played. Reaching the point she was afraid she'd pee her pants if Annie's jokes didn't stop, Natasha would cross her legs and clinch every time she laughed, expecting a flood.

She picked up the phone, called Roger, and asked him to set up another golf game, explaining Butler's involvement with the dog show and her hopes of interviewing him. Roger's eager agreement surprised her. Maybe things were winding down with Miss Misty. Then again, Roger was a real golf nut.

Roger called back with the news they were set for the next morning at ten. "I'll pick you up," Natasha told him.

Natasha stepped into the mansion, calling for Roger, but was greeted by Brutus. While she waited for her friend, she played fetch with the Weimaraner. The dog drove her nuts playing the game; he never would release the stick and expected her to chase him all over the grounds to try to take it away from him. Brutus was fast on his feet and could do a ninety-degree turn on a dime, it seemed. After falling on her face more times than she could count, Natasha gave up. She returned to her jeep, collected a plastic grocery bag and large scoop, and went hunting with Brutus.

Roger was placing his golf bag in the back of her jeep when they returned. Natasha hugged Brutus bye and shooed him inside. She placed the plastic bag on the back floorboard, climbed in her vehicle, waited for Roger to take his seat, and headed out.

Roger looked around and made a face. "Is Chumley in here?"

"No. Why?"

He sniffed the air. "Good gosh, what's that awful stench?"

"Oh. It's a bag of dog poop. We have to make a pit stop before we go to the club."

"Pit stop? With a bag of dog poop? Why?"

"You'll see."

On Dugan's street, Natasha drove down the road at a snail's pace, studying the house and yard. "You see anyone?"

Roger craned his neck to look past her. "No. Who lives here anyway?"

"You know Ben, that blind horse I adopted?"

"Yeah."

"This is the guy that blinded him."

"Oh, no. What are you gonna do, Nattie?"

"Just leave a little present."

"Oh, man," Roger whined.

She parked two houses down and stared at the wooden structure behind the house. The door was closed, so she couldn't see what was inside. Surely he wouldn't put a vehicle in there, as unstable as it appeared.

"Okay, Roger, when I get out, you slide over into my seat. If anything happens — I'm not saying it's going to," she hurried on, at his look, "but if it does, take off."

Natasha climbed out of the jeep, reached behind the front seat, and grabbed the plastic bag. Crossing the street, she had a funny feeling about this place. That building in back had been open and empty when she visited before. She quietly crept to the front porch, opened the bag, and was tilting it over when the front door banged open. She jumped back, dropping the sack.

"What the hell?" a short, overweight, balding man wearing sweat pants and nothing else roared. "What are you doing trespassing on my property?" He stepped toward her and tripped over the bag of manure. "Shit. It's you." His eyes hardened. "I knew it was a woman trashing my house." He turned back inside. "Where's my gun? I'm gonna —"

Natasha didn't wait to hear the rest. She kicked the bag into the house, slammed the door, and took off down the driveway, yelling, "Go!"

Roger scrambled into her front seat, slammed the jeep in gear, and squealed tires down the street.

Natasha stopped in surprise. "What the hell are you doing? You're supposed to take me with you."

The jeep turned the corner and passed out of sight.

Natasha glanced behind her. The man was in the doorway, kicking his way past the plastic bag. Was that a rifle in his hand? "Shit." She ran after Roger.

She had watched countless movies where the person being chased always ran down the middle of the road, out in the open, and her one thought invariably was how stupid they were for making themselves an easy target. Why didn't they veer off into the grass or run between buildings? And here she was, running down the middle of the road just like the stupid victims. But she seemed frozen to the asphalt; she could not make her legs veer over into a yard.

She turned the corner and there sat her jeep idling at a stop sign. She waved her arms. "Roger." He gunned the engine, shot onto the next street. "Dammit to friggin' hell, will you stop?"

Footsteps thundered behind her. She glanced over her shoulder. Dugan was coming up fast, one hand holding his rifle, the other hanging onto his drawstring pants, which were slipping down around his hips. "Oh, please, fall down," she prayed and found the strength to go onto the grass.

She ran across a front yard, veered along the side and into the back. She ducked into the next yard and jumped over a fence. Looking behind her, she was shocked to see Dugan keeping pace. How in the world was he keeping up, as fat as he was? She tried to think where Roger could be. He had turned right, so she ran in that direction, angling across yards, hopping over bushes, and dodging trees.

Natasha sprinted past an elderly woman toddling to her mailbox behind a walker. "'Morning, ma'am," she said, as she blew past. The woman gave her a puzzled look. "Might want to go back inside," Natasha called over her shoulder. "There's a crazy man with a gun."

The woman raised the walker in front of her, legs extended, and turned around.

"Yes," Natasha said, hearing the crash behind her. She ran a few steps more, then stopped. What if the woman was hurt? What if, God forbid, Dugan shot her?

She wheeled around. Dugan was sprawled on his back in the driveway, panting. The elderly woman stood over him, leaning against her walker, pointing his rifle at his head.

Natasha sauntered over to them with a smile. "Thank you."

The elderly woman looked up. "You're that girl put shit on his front porch, ain't you? The one that adopted that poor horse he blinded."

Natasha nodded. How'd she know that?

"The whole neighborhood's been hoping you'd come back," the woman said with a toothless grin. "We don't cotton to animal abusers around here."

"Me either."

"Now, you go on. I'll hold him off till you're out of sight."

Natasha started to turn, then paused. "But what if he does something to you in retaliation? I can't let that happen."

The woman glanced up. "You hear that?"

Natasha cocked her head. "I don't hear a thing."

"Them's sirens. The cops are coming. We got us a watch in this neighborhood. I reckon my neighbors called 911 they seen him running down the road with his rifle."

Dugan struggled to sit up. The woman poked his stomach hard with the rifle. He collapsed with a weak, "Shit."

Two police cars fishtailed onto the street at the end of the block.

"You better git afore he gets a chance to tell 'em who you are," the old woman said.

Natasha leaned over, kissed her on the cheek. "Thanks, ma'am." She crossed the street, ambled along the sidewalk and onto the grass of the only two-story house on that block, trying not to appear conspicuous as the police cars roared past. She headed for the back yard, breaking into a run when the house hid her from view.

Natasha meandered from street to street, lost, wondering what in the heck had happened to Roger. And would she ever get out of this maze? And why in hell hadn't she clipped her cellphone to her belt instead of leaving it in the jeep? She finally came upon a stream and stopped to throw water over her sweaty face. Didn't Windy's place have a brook running through it? She followed the creek bed, hoping she was going in the right direction.

The houses were further apart and she could see fields in front of her, so she knew she had to be close to the kennel. She walked another mile, smiling with relief when she saw the three block buildings.

Windy was waiting on her at the barn, her eyes dancing with humor. "I figured you'd find your way back here. You all right?"

"I'll live." Natasha trudged to the water trough and plunged her head in. God, she didn't think she had ever sweated this much. The humidity hung in the air like a wet blanket, draping her body with moisture, soaking her clothing with perspiration.

Windy handed her a towel when she came up for air. "Beulah called. Said the cops arrested Dugan for drunk and disorderly, along with indecent exposure."

"Indecent exposure?"

"Seems he lost his drawers when they stood him up."

Natasha winced. "I am so glad I didn't see that."

Windy offered her a water bottle. "Beulah said they didn't believe his story about you. Thought he was having hallucinations from DTs or something. 'Course she probably helped them arrive at that conclusion."

Natasha grinned around the lip of the bottle. "I do like that woman. She's got some oomph to her."

"That's Beulah all right."

"You don't think he'd hurt her, do you, since she helped me?"

"He knows better than that. All those old geezers in that neighborhood keep a lookout. They won't let anything happen. Don't worry, he won't tangle with them."

"Thank goodness. Do you mind if I use your phone? I lost my ride."

Natasha followed Windy into the main building and called Roger's cellphone.

He answered on the first ring. "Nattie? Is that you?"

"What the hell did you think you were doing? I didn't mean leave without me."

"You said take off. You didn't say wait."

"For Pete's sake, Roger, why would I want to be stranded?"

"Oh. Well, I guess I panicked."

Sometimes she had a real hard time understanding how someone so dense could have such a high IQ. "Where are you?"

"I'm at the country club, playing golf."

"Are you *serious*?"

"Well, yes. We didn't want to lose the tee-off time."

"You're playing golf while a two-hundred pound gorilla is chasing me down the street with a rifle? What the hell is wrong with you, Roger?"

"I didn't know he had a rifle."

"Well, he did."

"I'm sorry, Nattie."

"Quit playing and come pick me up."

"Can it wait? We're on the eighth — "

"You don't come and get me, I'm gonna find you, Roger, and pound your head into the eighteenth hole."

"I'm coming."

"Now."

"Now."

Thirty minutes later, Roger drove onto the complex. Natasha had taken the time to visit with the cats and dogs Windy fostered while telling her about the love affair going on between her mom and Emma and how well Ben was doing in his new home. She decided she admired this woman a lot and signed up to become a foster parent for Weimaraners and disabled animals looking for homes.

Roger hurried out of the jeep, giving Natasha a concerned look. "Are you all right? You look kind of — "

"Just get in the jeep, Roger." Natasha waved goodbye to Windy and climbed in the driver's seat.

Roger sniffed the air. "Good gosh. What's that smell?"

She gave him a look.

"What?"

After showering at Roger's place, Natasha changed into jeans and a sleeveless T-shirt. She found Roger in his office, working on his laptop, and had him call Arnold Butler's cellphone. Butler, at the country club eating lunch with his wife, didn't seem too happy with the intrusion but agreed to speak to Natasha. She made her apologies for the canceled game and sought his permission to interview him about the prior year's cluster. Like Windy, Butler had nothing to offer. She asked him to call her if he remembered anything and hung up. It frustrated her that no one seemed to know anything.

Natasha ate lunch with the boys and then headed for Striker's. All that excitement had gotten her in a bawdy mood, so she decided to surprise her love with spinach lasagna, his favorite, and dessert—meaning herself, of course. Striker usually arrived home around six, and by that time, she planned to be in the kitchen, wearing a baker's apron and chopping salad, appearing domestic. To counter the nester mode, she would be nude beneath the apron. So as soon as Striker walked through the kitchen door, she'd flash a smile his way, turn around, bend over the lower oven and...*Bingo*. She gave him maybe ten seconds.

Fully clothed, she placed the lasagna in the oven and keyed in the cooking time and temp. The front door banged opened and Striker bellowed, "Natasha," startling her.

She hesitated, her hand in the air. Damn it, Roger must have called Striker and told on her.

Striker loomed in the kitchen doorway, giving her a dark look.

She tried to ignore that. "Hey, baby, you're home early. Guess what? I'm making spinach lasagna, your fav —"

"What the hell are you doing throwing shit on some guy's porch, then getting chased all over the damn neighborhood with a rifle?"

"He's the one that blinded Ben."

"And?"

"Well, the legal system hasn't done anything to him yet, so I was just doing my part."

"By dumping crap on his porch."

"Sure, my own form of harassment, you might say. Making a statement on behalf of all animals."

"Shit. Will you grow up?"

"Grow up? Hey, if I had done what I wanted to, he'd be hanging upside down from a lamppost, covered in syrup, where the animals could get to him and do their own kind of damage. He blinded a horse, Striker. He abuses animals."

"That's why we have laws, Natasha. He'll be punished."

"Maybe once his case gets to court, which will probably be months, if not years."

Striker stepped toward her. "So you risk your life playing passive-aggressive with this guy?"

"Well, actually, I didn't think he was home and I for sure didn't know he had a rifle."

He studied her for a moment. His eyes widened with awareness. "How many times have you done this?"

She shrugged. "I don't know. A couple."

"A couple? What the hell is wrong with you?"

"Hey, it's the least I can do."

"So what's next? Rolling his lawn with toilet paper?"

"Gee, I hadn't thought of that."

His jaw clenched. "You're going to stop."

"No, I'm not."

"Today, that's it. No more of this crazy shit. He could have killed you."

"Nah, he was too busy running and trying to hold up his pants."

"Natasha, I'm serious. Promise me this is it, that you'll stop playing around with this guy."

"I'm not going to promise you anything."

"Natasha."

"No."

Their gazes clashed and held.

After several long moments, Striker said, "Okay, let's take it to the mats."

She thought about it. "Let's go."

Striker stepped aside and with a sweep of his arm indicated for her to precede him to the basement.

In the downstairs gym, Natasha and Striker claimed separate corners of the mats to remove their shoes and socks. They stood and faced one another.

Natasha punched at the air. "So, what are we fighting for?"

Striker stripped off his shirt. "I win, you stop acting like a nut and quit dumping crap at this guy's house."

"And I win, I do whatever I want, with no comments from you."

Striker glared at that.

She stepped into the center. "Let's go."

Striker was a fair man after all. With a grudging look, he said, "Okay, a pin constitutes full body contact with the mat. Since you're a *girl*, I'll spot you two."

Natasha tried to ignore his effort to make her angry enough to become careless. Usually she wouldn't accept free points but this time she intended to win. "Two it is," she said, butting fists with him.

Thirty minutes later, they circled one another, sweat glistening on their bodies, both breathing heavily. The mutual taunting had now ceased, each focusing on the match and their effort to claim victory. It had become serious now, the score four to four with the fifth pin claiming the loser.

Striker tracked Natasha's moves, thinking she was the most beautiful woman he had ever known, even red-faced and sweaty, doing her damnedest to kick his ass. Her sunny-blond hair was pulled back into a ponytail; those incredible eyes stared fiercely into his. Her tall, slender, athletic frame enticed him in sweat-dampened T-shirt and jeans.

Natasha watched Striker, his glistening, hardened body creating slithering sensations throughout her abdomen. Angry like this, he intimidated the hell out of her, which only served to strengthen her attraction for him. Go figure. She made sure to stay out of arm's reach, knowing if he got his hands on her, she was a goner. She waited for the moment to make her move, the one she had been saving for the time when winning against him meant something more than being homaged by his body.

Striker, used to the offensive position, stepped closer and reached for her. She ducked, spun behind him, and knocked into the backs of his knees with her shoulder. He stumbled but quickly began to right himself. Clearing his body, she swept out with her right foot. Striker faltered, fighting for balance. She tangled her feet with his, a smile forming as he crashed toward the mat.

"Hoo-wah," she yelled, jumping up and racing around, fists in the air.

Striker watched her with a disgruntled expression.

After her victory dance, she collapsed beside him. "Take me, darlin', I'm yours."

With an exasperated huff, Striker straddled her and yanked her jeans down.

Afterward, he smoothed her hair back, giving her an intense look. "Promise me, Natasha, you'll stop dumping dog crap at this guy's house. If he abuses animals, he's one step away from seriously hurting a human."

She noted the concern in his eyes and decided to appease him. "Okay, I'll stop dumping dog crap, I promise."

But, now, horse manure was a different matter altogether.

Chapter 13

Natasha had convinced Myrtle to stay inside while she took Chumley for his daily constitutionals. She worried about her friend being out in the heat, noting that the elderly woman was an even slower stroller than her pet. It didn't surprise her that Myrtle quickly gave into her suggestion.

Natasha decided to change their route, away from the direction of the house with the Rottweiler. Although the owner had been instructed by the City to chain the canine, he lunged for her every time she went past with Chumley. Even worse, the dog's owner would stand in the yard, glaring, looking ready to lunge, too. Her right buttock throbbed in anticipation of forthcoming harm every time she passed them. Relieved to learn the owner had sense enough to keep the dog's shots updated, she wondered what would happen if he chose to bite her himself.

Strolling along with Chumley trailing behind, Natasha's mind dwelt on her victory the prior evening, replaying that final pin, memorizing exactly how she had accomplished it.

A small boy jumped in front of her, waving a toy rifle in the air. Natasha stepped back, startled. He pointed the rifle at her and yelled, "Bang, you're dead."

Playing along, Natasha clutched her stomach, staggered around, and collapsed in the yard. She spread her arms and pretended to be dead. Chumley lay down beside her with a grunt.

The little boy leaned over her prone body to peer into her face. "It's just make-believe."

Natasha hid her smile, giving the child a surprised look. "Really? Shoot, I thought I was dead."

His grin revealed a missing front tooth.

What a cutie. Natasha sat up. "What's your name?"

"Nathan."

"What kind of a gun are you playing with, Nathan?" Natasha said, thinking it looked almost real.

"It's a BB gun," Nathan said in a proud way.

"Is it yours?"

"Yep. I got it for Christmas."

"You don't shoot anything with that, do you?"

Nathan shrugged.

"Where are your parents?"

"My daddy's at work and my mommy's in the house taking a nap."

"They let you play outside by yourself?"

"My mommy likes it quiet when she takes a nap."

Natasha wondered what kind of parents these were, giving a little kid a BB gun, letting him play outside by himself in this day and age. There should be a test for people contemplating parenthood. They should be required to attend classes to learn about parenting and then have to take an exam. If they passed, they could procreate, but if they failed —

"Hey."

"What?" Natasha followed the little boy's gaze. Chumley was molesting a plastic gnome. "Chumley."

Nathan raised his BB gun. "You better make him get off there or I'm gonna have to shoot him. That's my daddy's, and he don't like his things messed with."

"I'll get him." Natasha hurried over to Chumley and tried to peel him off the yard decoration. "Come on, Chum, let go."

The little dog bit into the gnome's felt hat and growled, shaking his head from side to side.

Natasha yanked on the cap. "Quit it, Chumley."

Nathan took aim with his toy gun. "You better make him stop that."

Natasha grew alarmed. This kid looked like he meant business. "Put that gun down. You can't shoot him; he's just a small dog."

"My daddy told me not to let nothing mess with his things," Nathan said, with a grim look on his face. Squinting one eye, he sighted down the barrel of the gun.

"Hey, put the rifle down. I'll get him; don't worry about it."

Natasha tugged harder on Chumley and finally pulled him off the gnome. She forced the dog's mouth open to retrieve the hat. Holding it up, she noticed it was full of ragged, chewed holes.

Nathan's face turned red. "Look what your dog did."

Natasha wadded the cap up so Nathan couldn't see the damage. "It's okay. Tell your dad I'll pay for it." She put the hat back on the gnome and tried patting it into place so it wouldn't look so shredded.

A spitting noise sounded behind her and she watched a BB slide into the ground beside her right foot. When she turned around, Nathan had the BB gun pointed at Chumley. She picked up the dog and held him behind her back. "Put the gun down, Nathan. You could hurt someone with that thing," she said, trying to sound parental.

Nathan ran around Natasha, the gun at eye level, aiming for the dog.

"Shi— shoot." Natasha placed Chumley against her chest and sprinted away.

~~~

Striker was talking to his secretary at her desk when the receptionist alerted him he had a call from a Ms. Myrtle Galbreath. He picked up Gloria's phone and said, "Striker," into the mouthpiece. He quickly looked upset. "What?" he said, in a loud voice. "She did what?" he yelled. "He did what?"

Gloria stared at him.

"Where is she?" He slammed the phone down and rushed away.

"Where are you going?" Gloria called after him.

Striker ignored her.

He didn't have to ask which room Natasha Chamberlain was in this time; he could hear her yells out in the waiting area. Striker hurried toward that sound and opened the door to find his love once more on her stomach, an eclipsed portion of one naked buttock peeking from a paper sheet and a male resident attending to same.

Striker entered the room and glanced at him. Recognizing him from the last time Natasha was there, he nodded.

The resident smiled at Striker. "How's it going, man?"

Natasha stopped yowling and looked over her shoulder.

"Pretty good." Striker inspected her bare bottom. He raised his eyebrows.

She gave him a miserable look. "You don't have to say it."

"Heard you tangled with a BB-toting five-year-old," Striker said.

The resident laughed.

Natasha's face flushed. "Yeah, well, he looked a hell of a lot older than five."

Striker leaned closer to peer at the red pockmark on her left hip, surrounded by Betadine stain. "So, what's the problem this time?"

The resident held up a medical contraption resembling a large pair of tweezers. "Trying to get the BB pellet out. It's shallow enough, I think I can get it if she'd hold still long enough."

"Hold still, Natasha. Let him do his job."

"It hurts."

"Of course it does, but he needs to get that thing out of there. Lead poisoning could set up, you know."

Her eyes widened with alarm. "Really? Omigosh. That could be fatal."

Striker watched the resident plunge the tweezers in while Natasha squirmed around and did some more yelling.

He withdrew the instrument with a sigh of resignation.

"Stop being a baby," Striker scolded.

Natasha gave him an indignant look. "Okay, let me shoot you in the butt with a BB gun, then dig around in the hole with a huge foreign object. You tell me how that feels to you."

"I offered to deaden the area with an injection, but she refused that," the resident said.

Striker looked at Natasha. "Why don't you let him give you the shot?"

"I hate shots. You know that. I practically faint at the sight of a needle."

"So you'd rather endure minutes of him digging around in your ass instead of the seconds it will take to give you the shot?"

"I don't want the shot," Natasha said between gritted teeth.

Striker turned to the resident. "What if you can't get it out?"

"She goes to surgery. They'll take it out there."

"You want that?" Striker asked Natasha.

"Shoot, no, I don't want that."

Striker stepped closer and placed his hands on her hips to hold her steady. "Okay, get ready."

Natasha gritted her teeth and put her face into the paper sheet. The tweezers plunged and she immediately yelped and started wiggling. The young doctor gave Striker an aggravated look.

Striker said, "Keep going. That thing's been in there too long as it is."

After a couple of minutes of digging and Natasha yelling and Striker leaning into her, trying to keep her hips as steady as he could, the resident withdrew a bloody BB. "Got it."

"Thank God." Natasha moved to sit up.

"We're not done yet," he said, dropping the pellet into a metal container. It made a pinging sound when it landed.

She gave him a skeptical look. "What other kind of torture have you got planned for me?"

"I've got to put an antibiotic on it, then dress it."

"Oh, yeah. Sorry."

"You don't think she needs stitches?" Striker asked with a worried look.

"Will you quit with the stitches?" Natasha said.

The resident shook his head. "It should heal well enough on its own without them."

Striker watched the doctor pick up Betadine and a gauze pad. He focused on Natasha. "What's with you and this dog, and you ending up in the emergency room with a naked ass twice now?"

Natasha chose not to answer.

After the wound was bandaged, Natasha said, "Can I get dressed now?"

"Not yet," the resident said.

"Why not?"

"I've got to give you a shot of penicillin to kick-start the antibiotic we're going to put you on."

Natasha's eyes grew round. "Shot?"

Striker grinned.

"I'm glad you think this is funny," she said caustically. She gritted her teeth and waited for the needle, digging into the paper sheet with her hands and grasping at it.

Her loud expulsion of breath told Striker it hurt.

The resident properly disposed of the contaminated needle and syringe. "I'll go write up your instructions and be right back. You can put your pants on now."

"I hope you're happy," Natasha said, snatching her jeans out of Striker's hands.

He gave her a wicked grin. "Baby, you have made my day."

When the young doctor returned, Striker said, "What about a tetanus shot?"

Natasha fought the urge to tackle Striker and wrap a bandage around his mouth to shut him up.

The resident checked the chart. "She told me when she was bitten by the dog that she's had a tetanus shot within the past couple of years." Handing Natasha a yellow sheet of paper, he explained the instructions for caring for the wound.

Striker walked toward the door, keying in a number on his cellphone. He held a brief conversation in the hallway. "She lied," he said, reentering the room.

"What the hell are you doing?" Natasha fumed.

"Your mom says it's been over ten years since your last one."

"She'd say that just to get me poked."

The doctor gave Natasha a serious look. "How long since your last tetanus shot?"

"I'm not sure. But I know it's been sooner than ten years ago." This was said with a glare toward Striker.

"Looks like tetanus is next," he said.

"What?" Natasha said.

He made a notation on his chart. "I'll be right back."

After he left, Striker grinned at Natasha. "Guess you're back on top."

Chapter 14

The next morning, Natasha forced herself to get out of bed. Her hip protested movement of any sort, but she knew it would only be harder to maneuver the longer she procrastinated. She groaned with pain as she shuffled into the bathroom to shower. Sitting on a pillow, she drove to Dugan's house to dump more manure — back to the horsey stuff — but a rusting, red Toyota sedan sat in his driveway. She stopped at the curb, hauled the bag out, and hurled it into his yard. She jumped back into the jeep and drove away, hunkering low over the steering wheel, in case a bullet slammed through the back window.

Sitting at a traffic light, she spied a Toyota two cars back similar to the one she had seen in Dugan's driveway. She sped away when the light turned green, watching in her rear-view mirror. The Toyota stayed with her for a mile or so, but she lost it once she hit the interstate. By the time she reached Myrtle's house, she was beginning to wonder if she wasn't being paranoid.

On their usual route, Natasha stopped while the Pug took care of business as he did every day in the same corner of the same yard. She patiently waited, debating whether or not that Toyota had been following her. Her thoughts were interrupted by a shrill female voice demanding she get that damn dog out of her yard.

Natasha looked around, surprised to see a portly woman in a quilted housecoat barreling toward her, wagging her finger and shouting at the top of her lungs.

"I been watching you and every day you let that friggin' animal take a dump in my yard, lady, and you do that one more time, I'm gonna call the cops."

"Excuse me?"

"Clean that mess up," she shouted, drawing closer.

"I'm sorry. I didn't realize this bothered you."

"This is my yard and I don't want no dog taking a crap on my lawn."

"Oh. Well, actually, I believe the county retains a fifteen foot right-of-way from the street."

The woman's face turned crimson. "It's still my yard."

"Okay, I apologize. It won't happen again."

"You bet your sweet ass it won't. Now clean it up."

Natasha looked around. "But I don't have anything to clean it up with."

"Lick it up for all I care, but I want that crap out of my yard."

Natasha didn't like the glazed look in the woman's eyes. "Okay, tell you what. I'll take Chumley back home and get a scoop and some paper towels and be right back to take care of this."

Crossing her arms, the woman gave Natasha a defiant look. "Ain't gonna happen."

Natasha pointed at Chumley's mess. "Hey, I'm not licking that up, for one, and I'm certainly not gonna pick it up with my bare hands."

The woman placed her hands on hips. "Who's to say you don't hightail it home and never come back?"

Natasha gave her an offended look. "Like I'd do that."

"Clean it up."

"Okay. Have you got any paper towels I can use?"

"I ain't giving you paper towels, I ain't giving you nothing."

"Fine, then, I'll go get some." Natasha picked up Chumley and walked away. Hearing what sounded like a herd of buffalo behind her, she glanced back to see the enraged woman charging her, closing the gap fast.

The woman outweighed Natasha by, she guessed, a good fifty pounds, so Natasha easily outran her to Myrtle's home. Injury and all, Natasha was surprised she could move so well when harm loomed close. She banged on the door for Myrtle to let her in, looking over her shoulder to track where her nemesis was.

Myrtle eyes widened at the sight of her panting neighbor stomping up the driveway, waving her arms in the air, and trying to yell at Natasha but only managing soft grunting noises.

Natasha quickly explained what had happened.

Myrtle brought her hand to her mouth. "Oh, dear," she said, looking with alarm from Natasha to the huffing woman and back.

Natasha and Myrtle waited for the neighbor to catch her breath. Both gasped in horror when she clutched her chest and fell to the ground.

"Call 911." Natasha rushed over to the woman, who was sprawled on the grass, breathing erratically. "Is it your heart? Are you having pain?"

The woman shook her head as she struggled to sit up. She lay back down with a weak moan.

Chumley plodded over to inspect her body. Apparently deciding her prone leg would do just fine, he darted a quick glimpse at the house before he began humping away.

"Chumley!" Natasha yelled.

Chumley went willingly enough when Myrtle stepped outside.

"The ambulance is on its way," Myrtle said, joining them.

"Do you know her?" Natasha asked.

Myrtle shook her head. "No, dear. They haven't been in the neighborhood long."

Natasha felt helpless. "You think it's her heart? Should we perform CPR or something?"

They listened to the woman's wheezing breaths. Both sighed with relief when Chumley began howling in answer to a shrieking siren wielding its way toward them.

"Thank goodness," Natasha said, watching the fire truck rumble up the street.

"It's a good thing the station isn't far away," Myrtle said.

Two paramedics jumped out of the truck and strode toward them at a fast pace. Natasha and Myrtle backed away, clutching one another. They watched the EMTs hover over the woman on the ground.

One of the paramedics glanced up and noticed their worried expressions. "It's okay. She's having an asthma attack, but she'll be fine."

"Thank God," Natasha murmured.

A police car pulled into the drive, followed by an ambulance. After the woman's breathing had returned to normal, the paramedics from the fire department and the ambulance packed up their equipment and left.

The policeman knelt beside the woman, now sitting up, taking slow breaths, with her hand on her throat. It wasn't long before she began ranting about Chumley and the mess in her yard. The young officer rose to his feet, mouthing something into the radio mounted on his shoulder. He approached Natasha and asked for her explanation.

"Listen, I offered to clean it up, but she wouldn't give me any paper towels. So I came back here to fetch some, and she started chasing me."

The policeman glanced at the woman, struggling to stand. He looked to Myrtle for confirmation.

"She's telling the truth, Officer," Myrtle said.

A truck from the city's Humane Department swung into the drive.

"What's that for?" Natasha said.

"The dog," the policeman said.

"What about the dog?"

"He's been involved in an altercation. I'm going to have the humane officer take him in until we get this cleared up."

"Altercation? Excuse me, but the only one involved in the altercation was that lady there. She was the one yelling and running. Chumley didn't do anything but use the bathroom in her yard, and I was only trying to get back here to find something to clean it up with."

The officer bristled at her objection. "According to her, that dog was loose and roaming the neighborhood. And the law is we take it in. There's a leash law inside the city, you know."

"But the dog was on a leash. You can see I'm holding it in my hand."

"He wasn't on a leash when I got here."

"This is his house, his yard. He can go without a leash in his yard, can't he?"

"Just following procedure," the policeman said, stepping around Natasha.

Myrtle backed away with a panicked look, clutching Chumley to her chest.

"Run, Myrtle," Natasha said, placing herself between the officer and Myrtle.

The officer tried to shoulder past Natasha. She pretended to trip, landed against him, and both went down. Natasha made sure to stay on top.

"Run, Myrtle, run," Natasha yelled. She kept herself tangled with the policeman until Myrtle and Chumley were safely inside the house with the door closed.

The officer stood, yanking Natasha up with him. His reddened face and glaring eyes gave her pause. Still, that didn't give him the right to be so rough with her.

"Hey," she said, trying to escape his grasp.

He pulled her over to the police car and shoved her into the back.

"Yeow," she screamed when her injured hip came in contact with the seat.

He slammed the door. She tried to open it, but the locks were engaged. She pounded on the window and demanded he let her out. He walked away, pretending not to hear her. She yelled and cursed, slamming her hands against the grill between the front and back seats.

She calmed down when a red Toyota slowly cruised by. The windows were tinted, so it was impossible to see who was inside the vehicle. Did that car in Dugan's driveway have tinted windows? Damn it, why didn't she take down the license plate number? The car turned onto the main thoroughfare at the end of the street and passed out of sight.

Natasha returned her attention to the action in Myrtle's yard, watching the humane officer confer with the policeman, the woman in the housecoat, and several neighbors who had gathered around to see what the ruckus was about. Apparently, someone told the humane officer the dog had been on a leash, because after yelling profane insults toward the policeman, in addition to thanking him for wasting his time, the humane officer jumped in his truck and left.

The red-faced cop stalked back to his car and climbed inside. Ignoring Natasha, shouting at him from the back, he drove to the police station.

Chapter 15

Striker and Scott were meeting with the firm's financial adviser, debating whether the funds were available for an expansion of their office space or if it would be cheaper to rent a larger space elsewhere or invest in buying their own building, when Striker's cellphone bleeped. He plucked it out of the casing attached to his belt, read the display, opened the handset, and keyed it to Phone Ready for privacy.

"Hey, darlin'," he said.

Natasha hesitated just long enough for Striker to think, *ah, shit.* He rose from the conference table and walked to the farthest corner of the room, away from the other two men.

"I was wondering if I could ask a huge favor of you," Natasha said in a small voice.

Striker turned his back on the others. "Sure, baby, you can ask me anything."

There was another pause.

With a sense of foreboding, Striker said, "Okay, what happened?"

"I got arrested," Natasha whispered.

"You what?" Remembering Scott and their adviser were in the room, Striker tried to control his temper by taking the time to count to ten. If he turned around, he would have caught Scott grinning widely, which wouldn't have helped matters. He lowered his voice. "What the hell happened, Natasha?"

"I — well, they're accusing me of assaulting a police officer."

"You what?"

"I need you to come bail me out," she said, on the verge of tears.

Striker ran his hand over his face. He hated it when she cried; it upset him when she did.

"Please, Striker, don't let them keep me in this place. It's — well, it's scary."

"Where are you?"

"At the jail downtown."

"On my way." He disconnected and left in a hurry, ignoring the others.

The adviser gave Scott a questioning look.
"That was Striker's destiny," Scott answered with a sigh.

After her promised phone call, two jailers, one male, one female, sandwiched Natasha between them and led her to a steel door. They waited for another officer, hidden somewhere undetectable, to disengage the lock. The three stepped through into a large, rectangular room divided by cells lining each wall, sporting iron bars across the fronts and sides. All looked filled to capacity.

Natasha drew back at the door. Each jailer took an arm and silently urged her to walk forward with them. Natasha remained where she was, looking around with alarm.

The woman jailer's eyes flashed the message *don't mess with me,* as she said, "You can make this easy or you can make this hard."

"But I didn't do anything," Natasha said. "I'm not supposed to be here. I don't deserve to be put in a jail cell."

"Honey, they all didn't do anything." The male jailer placed one beefy hand around Natasha's upper arm and pulled her along behind him.

Natasha dug her feet in, but they only slid on the concrete floor. He dragged her to a cell near the end, the one with the least amount of bodies in it, and waited for the female jailer to insert her key into a lock. She opened the door, stepped back, and callously watched while he shoved Natasha inside. Natasha turned and tried to dart out the door, but it was rudely slammed shut right in her face.

Natasha put her hands on the bars and tried to shake them, but there wasn't much give. "I don't deserve this. This isn't right. I didn't do anything. Let me out of here." She was shouting, unaware of the laughs and jeers from the other inmates.

Her gendarmes strolled to the door at the end of the aisle, waited for the invisible jailer to release the lock, and stepped through. The door closed behind them with an unsettling loud bang.

Natasha kicked at the bars in anger. Understanding her temper tantrum wasn't going to gain her freedom, she leaned her head against the door, hoping Striker got there soon.

It had quieted down some, and Natasha darted her eyes sideways at the scores of bodies around her in this cell and the one beside it. All were watching her as if waiting to see what she would do next. She raised her head, stared into the cells across the aisle, noticed women over there studying her in the same way. Wasn't this supposed to be a holding area? Why were there so many women here?

Natasha knew she could play this one of two ways: continue to act like a baby and have a hissy fit and probably get beaten up for it, or, worse, raped; or she could act like a hardened criminal, like this was nothing to her. She gave the inmates across the aisle a sardonic grin, turned around, and stared back at the women in her cell. A large black woman claimed one corner, arms crossed, sending Natasha a sullen look. *Yikes.* That woman could kill her with one finger.

Natasha took her time making eye contact. She drew back, assuming an attitude. "Who died?" No one seemed to understand her effort at levity. Switching tactics, she tried to keep the desperation out of her voice. "Anybody in here know how to hip-hop?"

To Natasha's relief, this was met with grins. She boldly looked at the black woman, said, "Show us your stuff, girl," and grinned at the smile that broke across the woman's face, moving away from the corner and into their midst.

~~~

Striker drove like a maniac to Natasha's rescue, arriving in less than ten minutes. He knew the head jailer and was granted a huge favor by being allowed into the inner sanctum to collect his love himself after he posted the predetermined bail. Striker felt heroic when the steel door boomed open, already anticipating how thankful she would be and what she would do to show him how much she appreciated him. Stepping through with the two jailers who had escorted Natasha in, all three hesitated, surprised at the sounds of women singing and clapping and yelling out words of encouragement.

What the hell? Striker walked down the aisle with the officers, watching the inmates having a fine time with one another, ignoring Striker and the jailers. Some moved their bodies to a song being belted out by an Aretha Franklin voice, others danced the hip-hop that Natasha liked so well and Striker liked to watch her

do so well, some clapped their hands to the music, while others
sang along.

Another voice rose above the fray, one that sounded a lot like
Stevie Nicks, only throatier, one Striker recognized. He frowned.

All three stopped at Natasha's barred cubicle. She sang in
harmony with a large black woman, the one with the Aretha voice,
dancing back-to-back with her, their bodies grazing as they
performed the strangely erotic dance. Natasha put her arms above
her head and the black woman did the same, both moving in
synch, so much unlike each other yet so much alike. Dancing in
that sexy way, hips swaying, bodies flowing, turning to face each
other, arms gliding toward one another...

Striker glanced at the officers, wondering why they didn't put
a stop to this jailhouse party. The male jailer watched the dancers,
open-mouthed with eyes glazed over. Striker was pretty sure he
was going to start drooling before long. The female jailer bopped
her head to the music with a grin on her face. *Shit.*

Striker stepped closer to the cell. "Natasha." She was now
moving her arms down her body in a seductive way. He resisted
the primordial urge to get in there, put his arms around her, let her
dance around him like that, pull her down to the floor and rut
away, whoever saw them be damned. Another, more buried part
resisted the urge to haul her out of that cell and soundly throttle
her. Thinking he was one sick puppy, Striker boomed, "Natasha!"

This seemed to bring the male and female jailers out of their
lost little worlds. They stepped up to the bars and began to bang
away with their billy clubs.

Smiles faded from the inmates' faces at this rather rude
interruption and all looked in the direction of the harsh sound.
Natasha and the black woman stopped dancing and turned
toward the grating noise.

Striker scowled at Natasha, upset because he had rushed over
here, thinking she was in big trouble. All kinds of images had
played in his mind, the worst of which was his love being
buggered by a gang of rough women before he could come to her
rescue. And what did he find? Natasha partying.

Natasha drew back from the stormy expression on Striker's
face. Deciding she'd worry about that later, she hurried to the
door. "Oh, darlin', thank you so much for coming." She turned to
the other women, mainly so she wouldn't have to see the look

Striker was giving her. "Ladies, meet my man, Striker," she said proudly.

All of the inmates stared at Striker, whose eyes remained on Natasha.

Natasha wasn't sure what to do; she was afraid she'd say something that might make the situation worse. Shoot, it probably would have been better if he'd found her beaten up or raped, then he'd feel sorry for her.

The female jailer inserted her key into the lock and slid the door back. Striker folded his arms and watched Natasha step up to the threshold.

She started to smile but thought better of it. "I'm glad you came."

He pretended he didn't hear her. "You gonna tell me how come you're in here?"

Natasha could not only see his anger, she could sense it. Casting her eyes around, she said, "Can we talk about this later? Like outside? Like anywhere but here?"

"This is because of Chumley, isn't it?"

She thought it in her best interests not to go there, knowing Striker's feelings about that dang dog.

"Well?"

Since Striker was barring her exit from the cell, she figured it might be a good idea to offer an explanation. "The policeman I've been accused of assaulting, which I didn't do, by the way, in case anyone is interested in that fact—" Natasha took the time to glare at each of the jailers, both of whom pretended not to notice, before turning back to Striker "—was going to take him. I couldn't let him do that, Striker. I couldn't let him take Chumley away."

Striker's eyes roamed toward the ceiling.

A woman strutted over to the bars and positioned herself next to Natasha, staring at her. She reeked of cheap wine and cigarette smoke. Her skirt rode high on her thighs and her blouse dropped low enough to reveal an amazing cleavage.

"What?" Natasha said.

"You mean to tell me you got a fine-looking man like that," the woman slurred, loosely waving her arm in Striker's direction, "and you're going around with some other dude, getting put in jail because of some other dude?"

"Chumley's not a man," Natasha said.

"Chumley's a dog," Striker said.

The inmate put her hands on hips and gave Natasha a look of disbelief. "You going around with some ugly dude, when you got this guy at home?"

"No, Chumley's a real dog," Natasha said.

"Short, fat, all wrinkled, with bug-eyes," Striker added.

The woman's eyes danced between the two of them before returning to Natasha. "You going around with some short, fat, ugly, old dude, getting yourself arrested over him, when you could have this? Damn, girl, no wonder he's so mad at you."

The women prisoners took a moment to study Striker.

Natasha turned to face her. "Do you not understand what the word 'dog' means?"

The woman nodded. "Oh, I get it. You mean Chumley's your friend, right?"

"No, that's not what I mean."

"Well, then, what is it? He no good in bed? Is that why you like this Chumley dude better?"

All eyes were on Striker now while the inmates contemplated this. Striker shifted restlessly and wished he were anywhere but there.

"That's not it at all," Natasha said.

"Shit, girlfriend, you can teach him, you know. Damn, what you doing fuckin' some old, wrinkled, fat dude when you can have this big, muscular guy in bed with you? Teach him how to be a good lover, then you won't want that Chumley."

"I don't need to teach him anything," Natasha said, gesturing in Striker's direction. "In fact, to be honest about it, he's taught me a few things."

The prisoners' eyes were back on Striker, some sending him lewd grins.

"Then what the hell are you wanting with this Chumley dude?" the woman said.

Several voices agreed with this.

"Because Chumley's my job, that's why."

The woman narrowed her eyes and nodded.

"What?"

She looked around at the others. "See? I told you she was a ho."

Natasha's mouth fell open in astonishment. Striker grinned.

"I'm not a hooker," Natasha said.

The woman leaned toward Natasha and almost lost her balance. She grabbed the bars to remain upright. "This Chumley's your pimp, right? Hell, girl, what you doing working for a fat, ugly pimp when you got that?" She turned to Striker and gave him a lecherous smile. "I'd come work in your stables anytime, big man."

Natasha pointed at Striker. "He's not a pimp. And I'm not a hooker. And Chumley's not a pimp, either. He's a bow-wow, barking dog, all right? A Pug dog, walks on all fours, drinks water with his tongue, cocks his leg to pee, likes to hump anything vertical. You get it?"

The woman's eyebrows shot up.

"What?"

"You're into that kind of shit? Damn, girl, you're worse than a pervert."

"Pervert?" Natasha said, voice rising, "What? Are you accusing me of doing dogs?"

"Well, if the shoe fits."

"Don't you have another bottle of wine you need to finish off?" Natasha turned her back and stepped closer to Striker. "Can we go now?"

Striker had had enough of this. He stood firm. "First I want an answer."

"An answer?"

"This is it, Natasha. I'm tired of coming to your rescue when you get into these crazy situations involving Chumley. So take your pick. Him or me."

"Coming to my rescue? Hey, it's not my fault I got bit by a dog, then shot with a BB gun. Nor did I ask to get thrown out of that strip joint. And if you're thinking of Senator Goodman, nothing would have happened if you had warned me about the lech. Besides which, I didn't actually kill him, you know. So I don't see that you rescued me from anything."

Both jailers perked up at the word "kill."

"You don't want to know," Striker told them.

"Striker, you know you're not being fair. I can't pick between the two of you, not at this point. Come on."

The Hispanic woman shook her head with disgust. "I give up." She turned to Striker. "You want a real woman, come see me."

Natasha glared at her. "Hey. This is my man. Keep your friggin' hands off him."

The woman fluttered her hand at Natasha dismissively and seemed to melt into the crowd of inmates standing around the cell.

Natasha turned back to Striker.

"Well?" he said.

She looked away.

"Close the door," he told the jailers.

"What?" Natasha shrieked.

"Keep her here. Let Chumley come bail her out."

"Striker."

The female jailer pushed Natasha back into the throng of women and slammed the door shut. Natasha clutched the bars with tears in her eyes. Striker turned around so he wouldn't see, knowing how vulnerable he was to that, and walked away. The two jailers trailed behind, smiling at one another, enjoying this turn of events.

"Striker, please, don't leave me here." Natasha yelled. "Come on, Striker, let's talk about this. Striker. Please, plea—" Her voice cut off when the steel door clanged shut.

Striker turned to the female guard. "Let her stew for a few minutes, then let her out."

The woman nodded.

He pulled out his wallet and handed over a fifty. "Can someone drive her home? Make sure she gets there safely?"

She checked the wall clock. "I go off duty in fifteen minutes. I'll give her a ride."

"Fifteen minutes in there ought to do it," Striker said, and left.

Natasha turned back to her cellmates and noticed the looks they were giving her. "What?"

No one answered.

"And just to set the record straight, I am not, nor have I ever been, a hooker." Furrowed brows motivated her to add, "Not that I have anything against hooking, you see. I mean, whatever turns you on, baby, but I'm not one, you know, at least at this point in time." Thinking she better shut up before she got beat up, she said, "Hey, where'd my dance partner go to?"

The party was once more in full swing when the woman jailer returned. Natasha, trying to get back into it but having a hard time, was relieved to hear that she was being released. She turned and waved to her colleagues when she left, calling goodbye to them.

The woman jailer led Natasha out of the cellblock, trying not to shake her head with disdain at this ditzy blond. She handed Natasha a large envelope with her personal belongings and told her Striker had posted her bail, she was free to leave, and she'd take her home if she needed her to.

Natasha thanked her and, when asked for her address, gave Striker's without even thinking about it.

After being dropped off in Striker's driveway, Natasha's cellphone rang. She debated whether or not to answer it, thinking it was probably Striker wondering where she was. Curiosity got the best of her, so she dug it out of her purse. She checked to see who was calling and emitted a small "Oh," when she realized the call was from Myrtle. Without any preliminaries, Natasha said, "Chumley's home with you, right? They didn't take Chumley, did they?"

"Yes, dear, we're both here."

"Oh, thank God," Natasha said, relieved.

She was on the verge of telling Myrtle about the arrest and spending half the day in jail, but Myrtle didn't give her the chance.

"I'm afraid I have some bad news, dear."

Natasha grew worried. "Chumley's okay, isn't he? Nothing happened to Chumley, did it?"

"Chumley's just fine."

Whew. "Oh, well, okay. What?"

Myrtle paused before answering, and when she spoke, there was disappointment in her voice. "Well, dear, I'm afraid I'm going to have to fire you."

Natasha looked around with disbelief. *What the...* She had just gotten arrested over that darn dog, risked her life for that little runt, could have gotten beaten up, could have gotten raped, no telling what could have happened to her, and here Myrtle was firing her for —

Her angry thoughts were interrupted by Myrtle, who was saying, "I've come to the conclusion you're a little too reckless for Chumley and me."

"Reckless?"

"Yes, dear. You seem to keep getting yourself into situations that don't seem ordinary by any means."

Natasha looked around. *Situations?* Didn't Striker use that word?

"And well, dear, to be honest, Chumley and I both led a much safer life before you came along."

"Came along. Hey, lady, who hired whom here?"

Myrtle was silent.

Natasha felt terrible for raising her voice. "I'm sorry. I didn't mean to yell at you."

"That's perfectly understandable, dear. Send me a statement for your services to date and I'll mail you a check. I hope you understand my reasoning."

"Well, actually, Myrtle, dear, I don't have a freaking clue what your reasoning could be." Natasha stopped talking when she realized no one was on the other end of the phone line. She pulled the cell away from her ear and looked at it with frustration. Here she had probably bungled things with Striker by picking that little mutt over him, for nothing, only to get fired because she kept getting herself into *situations*.

"Situations? What the hell do they mean by situations?" she asked the air, then remembered where she was.

~~~

Striker was tearing down the wall between the two guest bedrooms upstairs with the intention of turning the space into a large office or study, whichever Natasha wanted. Maybe even a nursery one day if he could talk her into it and they were lucky enough. He banged away, trying to rid himself of Natasha-induced stress and a growing sense of frustration, wishing, in a way, that wall was her body. He was mad at her, mad at himself. He hoped she'd do what he wanted her to, but knew she wouldn't. He wondered which home she would go to, where she was, what she was thinking, was she mad. He paused to wipe sweat from his brow and the front doorbell rang.

Striker dropped the hammer and ran his hands down his clothes to get off as much sheet rock dust as he could so he wouldn't track up the other floors in the house. He stepped into the hallway and hurried down the stairs. The doorbell repeated its chime, insistently this time. He yelled out, "Coming," and opened the door.

Natasha stood on the porch. "Can I come in?"

"You have a key. Why didn't you use it?"

"I didn't know if I'd be welcome."

"Oh, Natasha, for Christ's sake. You know you're always welcome here. This is your home as much as mine."

Natasha stepped uncertainly into the foyer.

Striker closed the door.

She studied his clothes. "What are you beating up on that represents me in a metaphorical way?"

He blinked, surprised she understood this about his behavior. "I'm tearing down the wall between the guest bedrooms upstairs."

She nodded.

"I figured you'd go home."

Without even thinking about it, she said, "This is home."

He was glad she felt that way.

"I was really mad at you when I thought you were leaving me there," she said.

"Yeah? Well, I was really pissed at you for not picking me."

"The lady jailer gave me a ride."

She better have, Striker thought, but didn't say.

"I'm not mad at you now, you know," Natasha said.

"That's good."

"Are you mad at me?"

"A little."

"You understand why I couldn't choose, don't you?"

"No."

"It's my job, Striker."

He stared at her, refusing to give.

She sighed. "It doesn't matter anymore anyway."

He raised his eyebrows.

"Myrtle fired me. She thinks I'm too reckless."

He smiled.

"It's not funny," she said with tears in her eyes.

Now he sighed, reaching out and pulling her into his arms.

Chapter 16

Striker leaned back in his executive chair, his feet resting on the credenza beneath the windowsill of his office. He appeared to be staring at the scenery outside but was actually reliving images in his mind.

The past two weeks had been two of the best weeks of his life. Natasha and he were back to playing house, he was sole center of her universe once more, and all was right with the world. She had spent each night with him and hadn't gone home to her cottage or even to Roger's place to spend time with the boys. This was a pleasant surprise for Striker, who had grown accustomed to Natasha doing this at least three or four times a week in the past.

He picked up a framed picture from his desk, his favorite, taken on a weekend trip to Hilton Head, South Carolina. Natasha was on the beach in the early morning, walking toward the camera, wearing a neon-pink tankini top and a long, colorful, beach sarong tied low at one side, exposing a tanned bare abdomen and one shapely leg. Her sunny-blonde hair was blowing around her in the wind. The sky was ablaze with pastels behind her, the ocean ranging from a foamy algae color to aquamarine. But Striker didn't notice these extraneous details; his eyes were focused on the expression on his love's face. Scott had once told Striker he envied him the look Natasha was giving in that picture; you could practically feel the heat in her gaze as she stared at Striker behind the camera. Her lips were curled into a secret smile, one that conveyed sated content mixed with yearning desire. Striker put his finger on her picture lips, remembering the effect that look had on him then, and still had on him, and what had occurred after the picture had been snapped.

His expression sobered. Pursued by females since the age of fourteen, Striker had readily and quite happily accepted his fate. But now, the tide had turned and he found himself chasing Natasha with surprising diligence and fortitude, something he wasn't used to. In the past, he had never encountered problems getting his way with women, but this one kept throwing obstacles into his path, thwarting his efforts, another thing he wasn't used to.

She frustrated the hell out of him. If he wasn't resisting the urge to put his hands around that elegant neck of hers and strangle the life out of her, he was resisting the urge to drag her by the hair into a cave and rut away like a damned Neanderthal.

Why the hell did he have to fall in love with a woman who aspired to be a kick-ass bodyguard? Of all the women who had come into his life, there had never been a question whether or not they would let him take care of them. With Natasha, there was. And, he feared, there always would be.

He was wondering how in the world he could talk Natasha into marrying him when his office door opened, interrupting his musings. He glanced over his shoulder, hoping it was his love, disappointed to see his business partner's scowling face.

~~~

In bed, titillating herself with erotic scenes involving Striker, Natasha stretched her body and sighed with content. She told herself she needed to get up, but she didn't want to get up, not yet. She turned over, buried her face in her partner's pillow, and breathed in his scent, thinking her world was perfect. Her hip had healed nicely, she and Striker were playing house, and the last couple of weeks had been fantastic. There was nothing more she could ask for.

Except a job, maybe.

Her eyes opened wide. She turned onto her back and stared at the ceiling. She was in big trouble and didn't know what in the world she was going to do about it. Why did Striker have to be so right for her? Why did he have to be so perfect? God, he was so smart, so achingly good-looking. And the way his body fit hers with unsettling precision, like two pieces of a puzzle, was an exhilarating bonus. He was her life mate, definitely, no doubt about that. But why did he have to come along at this particular time in her life, when she was just starting a new career and needed to focus more on her vocation than her relationship with him? But that was impossible; he intruded on every thought, every moment. Well, okay, so she had been in love with him first; she had encouraged the relationship, but she never imagined it could be this intense, or beautiful.

She now found herself constantly engaged in a mental battle over this predicament. Part of her wanted to concentrate on building her business and making her niche in the field, while the other was content to play housemate to Striker, which was all she had done the past two weeks. Damn, she was practically living with the man. That wasn't what she had planned this early in her li—

The phone rang, and she rolled over and snatched it out of its holder, glad for the interruption. "Hello."

"Natasha, is that you, dear? I didn't wake you, did I?"

Natasha made a face at the ceiling. *Not Myrtle.*

"Are you there, dear?"

"Yes, I'm here, Myrtle. I'm sorry, I was kind of busy with something."

"Oh. Well, dear, I don't mean to interrupt, but I'm afraid I'm in need of your services once more."

Natasha opened her eyes. "My services?"

"Yes, dear, it — well, it seems Chumley has disappeared," Myrtle said, sounding tearful.

Natasha sat up. "Disappeared? When? What happened?"

"Well, dear, I was getting ready to take him ouside for his morning poop. The phone rang, so I went inside to answer it, and by the time I got back to check on Chumley, he was gone."

"Did you search the neighborhood?"

"Yes, dear. I've walked the entire neighborhood, asked everyone I know, but no one has seen him."

"You don't think it could be that woman, you know, who chased me?"

Myrtle sighed. "No, dear. I think they're on vacation. I haven't seen anyone at that house for over a week now."

"Have you noticed anyone suspicious hanging around or gotten any other threatening letters, anything like that?"

"No, dear, it's been very quiet."

They were silent for a moment, each wondering where Chumley could be. Dugan crept into Natasha's mind. No, it couldn't be. His beef was with Natasha, not Myrtle.

"Anyway, dear, I was hoping I could hire you to find Chumley for me," Myrtle said.

Natasha grimaced. How was she going to tell Striker?

"Please, dear. I'm so afraid for Chumley. I'm terrified that whoever wrote that nasty letter has taken him."

"I wouldn't worry too much about that, Myrtle. If the person who wrote that note was going to do anything about Chumley, I

think they would have done it long before now. He probably just
wandered off or something. He'll come home soon, I'm sure."

Myrtle began to sniffle.

"Ah, please, don't do that," Natasha said.

Myrtle continued to cry into the phone.

Natasha sighed. "Okay, Myrtle, I'll find him."

"Oh, thank you, dear. Thank you so much," Myrtle said, in a
chipper voice.

Natasha pulled the phone away and stared at it, surprised at
Myrtle's quick change of mood. When she put the phone back to
her ear, Myrtle was speaking.

"Why don't you come over for an early lunch, and we can
discuss what you think should be done?"

"Sure, but in the meantime, you need to call the animal shelter
and make sure he wasn't picked up by a humane officer."

"Oh, my. I hadn't thought about that. Thank you, dear. I'll do
that right now and expect you here by eleven."

Natasha put the phone into its holder and sat there a moment,
thinking about Striker. She climbed out of bed and headed for the
shower.

~~~

Natasha handed a box to Striker's secretary. "You're probably
going to need these."

Gloria opened the plastic case and smiled at the earplugs
nestled inside. "Uh-oh."

Nodding, Natasha tightened her lips grimly.

Gloria flashed a mischievous grin. "It's been a little boring
around here lately. We've gone awhile without hearing Striker yell,
'You did what?' and go running out the door. I think he's getting
restless."

"Yeah, well, he won't be after he hears what I've come to tell
him."

"How long before he starts yelling?"

"First I'm going to try to put him in a mellow frame of mind,
so give me maybe twenty minutes. Then put those earplugs in,
'cause it ain't gonna be pretty."

Striker sat behind his desk, nodding at something Scott was saying. When Natasha opened his office door, he glanced in that direction. His eyes brightened and a smile broke across his face.

"Hey, baby," he said in his gravelly way, which caused a lightning bolt of sensation to shoot from her stomach to her toes and back. He stood when she entered, being the Southern gentleman he was.

Natasha grinned as she stepped inside the room. "Hey, darlin'. Hey, Scott."

Scott rose from the chair across from Striker's desk with an aggravated look. He gave Natasha a curt nod when he passed.

After he closed the door, she turned to Striker. "What'd I do?"

Striker grinned. "Scotty thinks you're keeping me up too late."

"Let me guess. You're not here at eight every morning, and Scotty thinks that sends the wrong message to the employees, even though you do own the firm."

"You got it."

Striker watched her stride toward him, appreciating the way she moved in her low-riding jeans and sleeveless mock turtleneck, her hair down and long and her legs looking like they went on forever. Natasha gently pushed him into his seat, straddled him, and settled her mouth on his.

"Jonce, I swear, I cannot get you out of my mind. I think I could make love to you every hour of every day and never grow tired of it."

Striker put his hands around her waist. "I've been thinking about taking some time off. See if we can't go away by ourselves for a month or so, try to work this thing out."

She smiled. "To the mountains?"

"I missed my yearly visit, so I figured I'd take you with me."

"I've been wondering why you didn't go."

"I guess because I was too busy falling in love with you," he said, and kissed her.

"That would be paradise, darlin'. Only problem is, I don't think I'd ever want to come home again, having you to myself for that long. But in the meantime..."

Gloria was taking the earplugs out of the box when Scott walked by, heading for Striker's office. "Nattie's still in there," Gloria warned, stopping his progress.

Scott noticed the earplugs. "What are those for?"

Behind the door, Striker roared, "You what?"

Shaking his head, Scott turned around and returned to his office.

"Striker, I don't want to do this, really I don't, but Chumley's missing," Natasha said, climbing off his lap. "I have to find him. I love that dog; don't ask me why. I know he's ornery and perverted and stinks to high heaven, but there's something about him that just… well, appeals to me."

Striker stood, shoving his chair away. "You like getting yourself into crazy situations, that's what appeals to you."

"Honest, that's not it. You think I like getting myself into trouble all the time? You think I like having to call you to come bail me out of trouble?"

The arrest flashed into both of their minds.

"Hell, yes, I think you like getting into trouble and I think you like having me come to your rescue."

Natasha gave him a stubborn look. "Well, then, I won't call you next time."

"That's not what I mean, Natasha."

"I have to do this, Striker. Chumley may be in trouble. He may be hurt or something even worse than that."

"Shit."

"These past two weeks have been absolutely the best of my life," she said in a soft voice.

He drew back, remembering that he had been thinking the same thing earlier.

"What I'd give if my life could be nothing but what it has been the past two weeks. But that's living in a fantasy world, darlin', and you know it."

"What the hell's fantastical about it? It's two people living together, sharing their lives together, loving each other. What the hell is wrong with that?"

"Because one of the people is living her life solely for the other person, that's why. And even though I want to do that, I can't continue to or somewhere along the line I'm going to get lost in you and forget me. Don't you see that?"

"No, Natasha. I do not see that."

She sighed. "Okay, look at it this way. What if our roles were reversed and you were the one at home, unemployed, cooking, cleaning, gardening, planning romantic liaisons with me when I came home? How would you feel about that?"

"I'd probably enjoy the hell out of it," he said petulantly.

"Sure you would, for a while. Then you'd start to realize you couldn't live the rest of your life doing that."

"I could live the rest of my life doing nothing but loving you and never grow tired of it."

"Well, I feel the same way about you, but I wonder if you wouldn't get tired of me doing that to you, or I wouldn't get tired of you doing that to me."

Striker's brow creased.

"I'm not making sense, I know." Natasha paused, considering this predicament. "Okay, let's compromise. Why don't you help me find Chumley, and after that's over with and he's back with Myrtle and you clear up what you need to here, we go away like you suggested? Just you and me, alone, no one around, no phones, no people; spend time together and figure out how to solve this problem that keeps popping up with us."

Striker walked away, rubbing his face.

"I'm asking for your help, in case that hasn't hit you," Natasha said, watching him.

He turned and looked at her. He wanted that time away with her badly. But he did not want her to get back into that Chumley mess; it was almost as if that damn dog had her jinxed. However, she had asked for his help and he was more than aware how hard that was for her. Up to this point, Natasha had been adamant she could do this on her own, without his assistance. He knew she felt she had something to prove to herself. That thought stopped him.

"Striker."

He held up his hand. "Let me think."

Natasha dropped into a chair and waited.

Striker paced, glancing at her from time to time. He realized he was at a crossroads with Natasha. If he stepped in and helped her, would she appreciate it or resent him for it, simply because she had not accomplished what she had set out to do on her own? If he backed off once more, would she be able to find the dog, find the person who had taken him, along with the person who had threatened him? Could she protect the dog without getting hurt? God, he couldn't bear it if he lost her. He stopped moving, noting the worried look on her face. Did she have any idea how much he truly loved her? Deciding he would give her the one true gift he knew he should, Striker settled into the chair beside Natasha.

"Do what you need to do."

A look of relief crossed her face. "You'll help me?"

He shook his head. "This is your baby, Natasha. I don't know how many times you've told me you want to do this on your own, so do it."

She hugged him. "You are, without a doubt, the best person I have ever known."

"Just promise you'll be more careful." He drew away and gave her an intense look. "Try to watch yourself. Don't get pulled into anymore of these weird situations."

"I promise," Natasha said, smiling.

Striker rose, took her hand, pulled her up and into his arms. He gave her a quick hug followed by a kiss. "Now, go. I've got work to do and so do you." He turned her toward the door and lightly patted her bottom with the palm of his hand. She smiled at him as she walked away. He tried to return her smile, but had a hard time doing it.

Chapter 17

Natasha gave up on the postmarked envelope. There was no way she could trace anyone from Valdosta since, as far as she could detect, no owners were from that area or even had close relatives in that region. She picked up her list and glanced at the notes she had made before Myrtle fired her.

Okay, third place in Best in Show the prior year went to a dog owned by a local, Jerry Dawson, attorney at law. Curious if he had any other vocations or possible avocations, Natasha logged onto the Internet and keyed in the site for the Knox County Register of Deeds office to search for any property Dawson might own. Wait a minute, she thought, reading the data displayed. He held title to a residence in West Knox County — what attorney didn't? — but had purchased a large tract of land five years before outside the city proper. Wondering about his intent for the property, Natasha jotted down the address, deciding it wouldn't take her long to find it. But first she had to make a pit stop.

Natasha crept by Dugan's house, checking the driveway and behind the house, making sure no cars were about. The garage door was open this time and the enclosure stood vacant. She turned around at the end of the block, swung her Jeep into his empty driveway, lugged out a garbage bag filled with horse manure — she had begun saving the stuff when she mucked out the stalls at her parents' barn — and sprinted to the front porch. She jumped when the front door banged open.

"I been waiting on you," Dugan roared.

Natasha backed away.

"Damn it, where'd I put my gun? I'll teach you to come on a man's proper—"

Natasha didn't wait around to hear the rest. She picked up the garbage bag, slung it at Dugan, slammed the door, and ran like hell for her car. She figured she left about fifty feet of skid marks, but, hey, tires were more easily replaced than her body.

Natasha took her time driving to Dawson's property, trying to calm her thudding heart, allow the adrenaline to settle to a decent level, and stop shaking. Maybe it was time she gave up the manure-dumping visits.

She slowed down as she passed a long, graveled drive barricaded from entrance by an iron bar with a guard shack to one side. A large, rough-hewed sign mounted over the drive read "Jaybirds Inc." She speculated about the need for the bar and the guard. Noticing the shack was empty, she braked to a stop and studied the area. After a few moments, she drove further down the road and found a pull-off. She parked her car, locked up, and headed back the way she had come.

At the drive, Natasha skirted the bar and crept into the woods hugging the roadway, trying to stay out of sight. After a hundred feet or so, she encountered a tall, wooden fence blocking her way. She studied the upright boards, looking to either side, wondering if it fenced the entire property. The tall gateway was locked, so she walked to her right along the barrier to search for a way inside. She traveled a good half-mile before stopping. Her eyes roamed the wooden wall, marveling at its cost. Curious about what Dawson could be hiding within, she continued on, trying to find a peephole.

After another fifty yards, Natasha found a loose board in the fence. She wiggled it until it came free in her hands, almost sending her toppling. She placed the plank aside as quietly as she could. Hearing voices, she peeked into the space formerly occupied by the strip of wood and her eyes widened. She pivoted, placing her back against the wall. *Dang.* She turned back around, flattened herself against the fence, and tilted the left side of her face into the barren space. Several people were walking around, talking and engaging in various activities, wearing nothing but grins.

Jaybirds as in naked-as-a. So, old Jerry wasn't your typical badass lawyer. But then again, maybe he was. Natasha retrieved the wood plank and propped it into its previous berth as best she could. She retraced her steps, breaking into a run by the time she reached the road.

~~~

Back at Striker's, Natasha logged onto the Internet once more to search for Jaybirds, Inc. She smiled when she got a hit. Perusing their home page, she wondered about the declaration that this was a nudist resort offering an alternative lifestyle for those so inclined.

Alternative—did that mean "nudist", or something else? Her eyebrows shot up when she read that as an incentive to join the group, a free getaway weekend was offered to anyone interested in exploring that type of lifestyle. Thinking no way was she going to go get naked with people she didn't even know — well, with anyone but Striker — she grinned at the proclamation that clothes were accepted. She picked up the phone and dialed the number listed on the website.

Natasha was back, handing the earplugs to Gloria.

"Uh-oh," Gloria said, with a teasing glint in her eyes.

Natasha gave a solemn nod. "I don't know if you'll need those or not, but just in case."

Gloria watched Natasha walk toward Striker's office, considering the changes in her boss. Women used to flit in and out of his life more often than the moon changed phases, but that had come to an abrupt halt once Natasha caught his eye. Striker, usually a stoic, reserved, affable-enough businessman, now episodically morphed into a raving, ranting madman due to one constant factor: Natasha.

Used to controlling burly, testosterone-driven men with one hardened look, he couldn't seem to dominate a woman with maybe half his body mass; something Gloria suspected would never happen, much as Striker might want it to. She grinned. *Striker, you have finally met your match.*

Several minutes later, Gloria heard the now infamous "You did what?" She removed the earplugs and picked up the phone. She had just won five bucks.

"That man could have Chumley, Striker. His dog lost to him last year, which makes him a logical choice."

Striker shook his head with disbelief. "A nudist colony."

"I talked directly to Dawson — he answered the phone when I called — and told him we were thinking of doing something like that, but we were novices, you know. Weren't sure if that was for us or not but would like to see what they have to offer."

Striker rubbed his face.

"It's a free getaway weekend. And we don't have to walk around nude." She rolled her eyes. "Like I'd do something like that."

Striker gave her a look. "Yeah? Well, didn't I catch you skinny-dipping in Roger's pool last year with Roger, Pit, and Bigun?"

Natasha flushed with embarrassment. "Well, yeah, but we had the lights off and the agreement was they stayed that way until everybody was out of the pool and dressed. Besides, you're the one who turned on the lights," she added in an accusing tone.

Striker looked heavenward.

"Fine. You don't want to play my husband for a weekend, I'll get Roger to."

Striker stiffened, his mouth forming a thin line. Roger's love for Natasha was no secret to Striker. And if that weren't bad enough, Natasha had indicated before she and Striker began their relationship that it wouldn't be hard for her to reciprocate Roger's feelings. Striker found it irritating the nights Natasha spent at Roger's place, acting like she was having a sleepover with girlfriends. The only problem was that these girlfriends had the names Roger, Pit, and Bigun.

"When is this thing?" he growled.

"This weekend."

"I'm probably going to end up having to go to Nashville this weekend to kick a couple of my lazy investigators' asses."

"Oh, okay. That's fine, no big deal. I'll just go ask Roger." Natasha knew she had won, knew it was the name "Roger" that did it. It worked every time.

"Hold it," Striker said when she reached the door.

She turned back to him.

"Okay, I'll go."

Natasha grinned. "We'll have the best time."

"Uh-huh."

"Um, darlin', you wouldn't happen to have any wedding rings we can use?"

He looked heavenward again.

"Maybe you ought to keep those earplugs," Natasha told Gloria when she left.

Laughing, Gloria deposited them in her desk drawer.

On her way home, Natasha called her mom. When Stevie answered, she said, "Hey, Mom, Striker and I are going to a nudist colony for the weekend. You and Dad want to go?" She laughed at her mother's shocked response but stopped laughing several minutes later, when her dad called.

Chapter 18

During the drive to Jaybirds, Inc. early Saturday morning, Natasha studied the gold wedding band on her finger. She liked how it looked, how it felt. Striker had borrowed the ring from Gloria, who was a widow. He tried her husband's wedding band but his finger was too big.

"You'll just be one of those guys who doesn't wear a wedding ring, I guess," Natasha told him, adding, "Although don't get any ideas."

Striker braked to a stop next to the guard shack and told the man who stepped out to greet them that Mr. and Mrs. Jonce Striker were there for the weekend. They watched him trail one thick finger down a typewritten list on a clipboard and tap the paper when he reached their names. He gave Striker a curt nod, lifted the bar, and waved them in.

Striker drove slowly up the drive, through the now-open, tall wooden fence and onto the complex. Natasha tried not to gape at all the naked bodies wandering around, everyone acting friendly, smiling and waving at them as they passed.

Cozy-looking log cabins lay scattered around the resort, all attractively arranged around separate courts for tennis, volleyball, and basketball, with an Olympic-sized swimming pool, sauna, and picnic area beside a man-made lake. Striker parked in front of the largest building on the grounds, the one with the sign in front that read "Clubhouse."

A short, naked, wiry man with graying hair emerged to greet them. He extended his hand to Striker and introduced himself as Jerry Dawson—"Owner, manager, you name it," he said, grinning. Shaking hands with Natasha, Dawson's eyes slid up and down her body appreciatively. Striker resisted the urge to punch him. Natasha resisted the urge to kick him someplace she was trying not to look but knew it would hurt.

Jerry escorted them inside the building and got them seated in a comfortable-looking office. Just as her derriere hit the chair's cushion, Natasha remembered someone's naked ass had been there before her. Trying not to look repulsed, she vowed to herself as soon as they were in their cabin, these jeans were coming off. No telling what kind of germs occupied that seat with her.

Jerry gave them brochures, explaining about the complex, the fee for joining, and everything the community had to offer. He emphasized the word "free" often during his spiel. Afterwards, he told Natasha and Striker he would take them to their cabin, and when they were ready, to come back down to the Clubhouse and someone would give them a tour of the grounds.

Back outside, Natasha and Striker climbed into Striker's Porsche and Jerry stepped into a golf cart. Natasha watched him drive away, thinking how weird that looked, a naked man behind the wheel of a golf cart.

At the cabin, Dawson made a big production of unlocking the door, opening it, and waving his hand for them to precede him inside. Natasha strolled around, admiring the rustic design. Dawson's gaze followed her while he told Striker they were welcome to dress or undress; however they were most comfortable. He looked back at Striker and, with a glint in his eyes, added, "Most couples, by the end of their weekend, choose to undress."

He focused his attention on Natasha once more. Striker stepped in front of him, barring his view, and gave him a challenging look. Dawson got the message and left.

Natasha spent the next half-hour spraying Lysol on any surface she suspected a stranger's naked butt might have occupied.

They held hands during their guided tour. Natasha tried not to stare, thinking how much she envied anyone comfortable enough with their body to walk around nude in front of a group of people. There were all shapes and sizes of the human form on display and she guessed the age range from small children to men old enough to be her great-grandfather.

A volleyball bounced on the path in front of them, forcing them to stop. Natasha cringed at the sight of an overweight man running to fetch the ball, his penis and breasts merrily bouncing around. He came within a few feet of them, turned around, and bent over, offering a sight Natasha hoped she never saw again.

"There goes my appetite," she said, putting her hands over her face.

Striker grinned.

Later, in their cabin, in the bedroom, she told him, "I love your body, Jonce. I love watching your nude body, and I think you have the most beautiful physique of any man I've ever seen. But do me one favor, don't bend over in front of me. I might not look at you the same way after that."

With an amused look, Striker picked up the remote and turned on the TV to search for the Braves game.

Natasha didn't have the patience for baseball and quickly became bored. Exploring the room, she found a box in the closet labeled "Playthings." She hauled it to the bed and opened it.

"Dang."

"What?" Striker said, his eyes on the TV.

"Just a sec." Natasha picked up the can of Lysol and liberally sprayed inside the box before reaching in. She held up a strap-on dildo with one finger.

Striker glanced at her, then back to the TV.

She dangled it in front of him. "You want to know what it feels like?"

He slanted a bored look her way.

She threw the dildo down and began looking through the various sex toys and porn movies, finding what looked like a riding crop.

"What's this for?" she asked Striker, holding it up.

Suddenly he wasn't so bored anymore. "What else is in there?"

They played around on the bed, enjoying each other, until it grew dark outside. Then Natasha got up and began pulling on dark clothing.

Striker sat up, watching her. "What are you doing?" he said with irritation.

"I'm going to go snoop around a little, see if I can find where he's keeping Chumley."

Striker leaned his head back and stared at the ceiling.

"What?" she said.

"We've been all over these grounds. What makes you think the damn dog's here?"

Natasha gave him a stubborn look. "He may not be here, but I won't feel comfortable until I rule that out for myself."

"How many dogs do you think we've seen today?"

She shrugged her shoulders. "I don't know. Maybe half a dozen or so."

"Did you see a short, wrinkled, fat dog anywhere in that group?"

"Well, no. But we wouldn't, you know, because he's a show dog. They wouldn't want to throw him in with the mongrels."

"They probably did and he started humping every dog in the group, probably got the shit beat out of him by one of them."

"Striker."

He lunged off the bed. "I hate that dog."

Natasha watched him reach for his jeans. "What are you doing?"

"Gonna go make sure you don't do something stupid."

She frowned at this, but kept her mouth shut. After all, she needed his help. They'd talk about that comment later.

They turned off the lights in their cabin and stole outside, keeping to the shadows.

"I guess we start with the owner's house," Natasha whispered.

"You remember where it is?"

"Yeah, I think so."

"Lead the way."

They crept into the woods, staying just inside the tree line, trying to watch where they stepped and to be as quiet as they could. When Dawson's home came into view, they stopped. It was well lit, inside and out.

Natasha turned to Striker. "What do you think?"

"Don't know. Maybe they're having a party or meeting of some kind."

"Looks like something's up, for sure."

"Okay, keep to the shadows," Striker said in a low voice. "I'll lead, you follow. If you hear anything, freeze. Don't move until I give the signal to go forward."

Natasha nodded with a wide grin.

Striker took the time to look heavenward.

She gave him an irritated look, which he ignored. *Okay, another thing we're going to talk about.*

Natasha followed Striker to the outer perimeter of the yard. Both froze when a dog began barking, sharing the same thought: *Shit.* They stood still, waiting for the dog to either break from the shadows and chase after them, or lose interest. After a few minutes, Striker moved again, testing. Apparently the dog had gone away or was barking at something else.

They stole into the yard, keeping to the shadows of the large trees, checking each window facing their way to make sure no one was looking out before darting from cover to cover. When they reached the outer wall of the house, both leaned against it to catch their breath.

Striker turned to Natasha and began giving her weird hand signals.

She watched with fascination. "What's that mean?" she whispered, loud enough for a dog in the neighboring yard to start yapping away.

Striker put his hand over her mouth and leaned close to her ear. "Shhh." He withdrew his hand.

"Well, how do you ex—"

He clamped his hand over her mouth once more. Drawing close to her, he stared into her eyes, and said, his voice barely audible, "Shut up."

A hurt expression crossed her face.

He put the side of his head against hers. "I'm sorry I said that, but you're gonna get us caught, you keep talking out loud."

She brought her mouth to his ear and whispered, "I don't know what you're saying when you use your hands like that."

Now his lips were at her ear. "I'm going to boost you up. Take a quick peek in that window, then dart back down. If no one sees you, go back up, look again, longer if you think it's safe enough, and let me know what you see."

Natasha nodded.

Striker laced his fingers together and Natasha put her left foot into the cup he made with his hands. She pushed off with her right foot, bracing against the wall with her right arm, her left hand clutching his shoulder for balance. She popped her head up at the window, took a quick glance, and darted back down, the way Striker had told her to. She shook her head and repeated the process. She was staring into what appeared to be an office of some kind, devoid of people. Searching the floor for Chumley, she noticed a lot of movement in a room across the hall.

Natasha stepped down and spoke in Striker's ear. "It's an office. There's no one there. It looks like they're on the other side of the house, directly across from this room."

Striker nodded and began to lead the way around the domicile, staying in the shadows.

They squatted beneath the room where Natasha thought she had seen activity. The windows were closer to the ground, so Striker wouldn't have to boost her up this time. He put his hand on Natasha's arm and made another hand motion, which she recognized meant to stay down low. She nodded her understanding.

They both took quick peeks. The room was full of people. Naked people.

Striker glanced at a wide-eyed Natasha. He rose back up and stole another look, but the people in the room were too involved with what they were doing to notice anyone spying on them.

Natasha followed suit. There were a lot of nude bodies rolling around on the floor; some butts upended and pumping away, arms and legs everywhere. She clapped her hand over her mouth, knelt down, lost her balance, and fell over, right into the spill of light from the window.

Striker glanced warily at the window, reached out, and pulled her back toward him.

She opened her mouth, but he held up his finger, meaning *shhh.*

She leaned close to him, stared into his face. Her eyes asked him, *Did you see what I saw?*

He nodded.

They're having an orgy in there.

Another nod.

What should we do?

He shook his head. *Nothing, it's none of our business.*

Did you see the dog?

Another shake of his head.

All with the eyes.

Striker cocked his head, meaning *let's go,* and led the way back around the house. They peeked in each window, searching for the Pug, but no luck.

By the time they reached the woods, Natasha was practically dancing on air. Once they were in the shadows, far enough away from the house so as not to be seen or heard, she threw her arms around Striker and kissed him with a passion that surprised him.

"What?"

"Don't you realize what happened back there, Jonce?"

"Happened?"

"We talked to each other without saying a word. You knew what I was saying and I knew what you were saying."

The realization jolted him.

Natasha gave him a strange look. "I've read about this but never knew it existed. We're connected, Jonce. Don't you see? We were telepathic with each other, communicating without language, only with eyes and facial expressions."

He shrugged; he'd think about that later. "Come on."

"You think that's what they mean by alternative lifestyle?" Natasha whispered as they crept along.

"It's a definite alternative to my lifestyle."

At each cabin within the complex, they peered in windows and studied yards, searching for Chumley. Unable to find him, they gave up and returned to their cabin. By this time, Natasha was more interested in exploring what had happened between them. When they stepped inside, she was back in his arms.

"Love me, Jonce. Talk to me, as you're loving me, with your eyes. Tell me how you feel with your eyes, but don't say a word."

The next morning, they ate breakfast at a small country restaurant located inside the resort. Natasha watched the others, still curious about what "alternative lifestyle" meant. The brochure didn't reveal any formal explanation, and from what she could detect, these people were as normal as anyone else. Well, other than the fact that some of them liked to engage in orgies. And all of them liked to walk around naked most of the time, which probably made them more normal than she was. After all, who was the one sitting in this restaurant with a hangup about her body image?

Dawson wandered over to their table and told them that during the course of the day there would be various meetings and symposiums taking place, as well as get-togethers for certain activities, leaving them to decide how to occupy themselves. He kept flashing Natasha lecherous looks while talking to them. Striker resisted the urge to take the guy outside and teach him some manners. With Dawson's lower abdomen at eye level, Natasha kept her eyes on the food and nothing else.

Natasha and Striker strolled around, acting as if they were enjoying the scenery while searching for signs of Chumley. They walked to the man-made lake and watched several nudists canoeing, then rambled around the complex.

They entered the clubhouse, noticed a meeting was in progress in one of the rooms. *What the heck.* Natasha stopped at the entrance to pick up a flyer. The logo was two large, bold D's, with some kind of drawing inside each one. *Huh.*

A scattering of people sat in wooden pews near the front of the room. Natasha and Striker slid onto a long bench seat in the back to listen. Natasha kept her eyes on everything but the unclothed bodies while trying to pay attention to what was being discussed.

A man and a woman stood before the small group, giving testimonials, it sounded like. The woman was short and mousy and about as wide as she was tall; the man beside her was rangy and thin as a rail. Natasha focused on the woman's statements, which had something to do with what a terrible wife she had been.

The man interjected, "Nag, nag, nag," and rolled his eyes, drawing laughter from the other men in the room.

Natasha stole a glance at Striker and was glad to see he didn't think that was funny.

The woman gave her husband an indulgent smile and continued to describe what a horrible person she used to be: moody, rageful, unhappy, didn't show her husband any respect, didn't want to make love...

Yadda, yadda, yadda. Natasha tuned her out until she heard the woman claim that the DD Club had saved their marriage and made her into a new person. She picked up the flyer to study the strange drawings within the two D's. The first one looked like a wooden grain inside the letter, as if it were made of wood; the second one resembled a pink peach.

"The first time my husband disciplined me, I have to admit, I was resentful," the woman was saying.

Natasha stared at the logo. She turned to Striker and whispered, "What are they talking about?"

Striker leaned down close to her ear. "Domestic discipline."

She gave him a questioning look.

He raised his eyebrows, darted his eyes to the flyer and back to her, indicating, *think about it.*

Natasha's eyes widened when she read the description on the flyer. "Shit."

Several of the people in the room turned and looked at her.

The woman was now giving testament that she needed this sort of discipline in her life, she needed her husband to be in control, she needed him to punish her whenever she —

Natasha moved to stand and Striker pulled her back down. She glared at him. Was he listening to this crap?

The man began testifying how much better their marriage had become since his wife acknowledged him as ruler of their universe, allowed him to be the one in control, dictate how things should be, and accepted the fact that she was in need of discipline from time to time —

"Shit," Natasha said and received more stares.

Striker nudged her.

She might have kept her mouth shut until she witnessed the ceremony that came next. The woman presented her husband with a wooden hairbrush and he gave her an apron. This was greeted with much applause from the others.

Natasha stood.

Striker grabbed her arm but she shook him off with an angry look. He rubbed his face. *Ah, shit.*

Natasha held her hand in the air when the applause had died down. "Excuse me. Could I say something here?"

"Go ahead," said the man up front.

Natasha looked around at the audience. "What the hell is wrong with you people?"

This was met with stunned silence.

"This is like a *Twilight Zone* version of the *Stepford Wives*," she went on. "What the hell are you doing, letting some guy hit you?"

"I think you misunderstood the whole concept behind the DD Club," the testifying husband said.

"Yeah? DD, as in domestic discipline, as in you beating your wife when she doesn't do what you want her to?"

He frowned. "We don't beat our wives."

"You hit her with that hairbrush, don't you? Punish her physically. What else would you call it?"

"We call it domestic discipline," he answered in a haughty tone.

Others in the audience nodded in agreement.

"Well, I call it beating pure and simple. What comes after the hairbrush? A belt? A public flogging? What the hell do you think you're doing hitting your wife for whatever infraction you come up with? And what the hell are you women doing letting your husbands beat up on you like that? That's wrong. I mean, okay, I can understand a love spanking..."

Striker, warily watching the man up front, looked at Natasha when she said that. *Wait a minute.*

"...as a form of foreplay, but this goes way beyond that, if what I'm reading here is correct."

"What we do behind closed doors is our business, and you don't have the right to come in here and tell us what's right and what's not right," the man with the hairbrush said, waving it around, growing angry.

"Oh, yeah? Well, what you gonna do to stop me? Hit me with that hairbrush? Try to repress, suppress, oppress, and subjugate me like you do your wives? Who, by the way, let me tell you, I have no respect for if you let some man beat up on you."

The man stepped forward.

Natasha waved him over. "Come on, pervert. I guarantee you'll be the one getting swatted with that thing in your hand. You just try it."

The man stalked toward Natasha, his face bright red.

Striker stood and glared at him.

Seeing Striker's size, he backed off and addressed him. "You should do something about your wife. She needs to be controlled."

Striker put his hand on Natasha's forearm and drew her closer. "She has the right to say anything she damn well wants to and I don't have the right to stop her, nor do you. And you want to wave that hairbrush around at anyone, you better be waving it at me, not my wife."

"Yeah," Natasha agreed.

Everyone grew silent, waiting for what the man with the hairbrush would say. He tried giving Striker a challenging look but obviously felt intimidated, so he stepped back and looked away.

"Come on, Natasha, we're leaving," Striker said.

"You women do not have to take this kind of treatment," Natasha said, as Striker pulled her along. "This is not right. Do not let these men try to control you. It's not normal. It's not the way things are supposed to be."

Striker got her outside the door and slammed it closed behind them. "Why don't you shut up before you make this situation worse than it already is?"

That surprised her. "What?"

"We were outnumbered in that room, in case you didn't notice."

"Come on, Striker. There couldn't have been more than ten people in there. Besides, they're all naked. They're not going to do anything to us."

"Famous last words. But let me remind you, Natasha, dear; what people do in the privacy of their own homes is none of our business. If they choose to practice that, they have the right. And if you didn't agree with what they were saying, you should have just simply gotten up and walked out."

She drew back. "So you agree with them?"

He scowled at her. "Did I say that?"

"Well, I don't recall you getting up and walking out."

Striker huffed. "That's because I had to make sure you didn't decide it was time to beat up on somebody. After all, it's been a while —"

"Hey."

"Listen, I know that's a trigger point for you - a man hitting a woman. I understand. I feel the same way. But those women choose to live that lifestyle. For whatever reason. And you have to respect that."

"Why are you defending them?" she said with an angry glare.

"I'm not defending them, for Christ's sake. Just let it be, all right? I don't feel like tangling with a bunch of naked people."

Natasha grinned at that image.

Striker ignored that. "Come on, we're going to the cabin to pack our stuff and we're out of here. I've had enough of this place." He took her hand and tugged her along with him, expecting resistance. He was surprised when Natasha didn't object.

The entire time they packed their bags and loaded the car, Natasha remained silent. She kept giving Striker strange looks but she wouldn't say anything.

They were in the car, ready to leave, and she was staring at him again. Unable to stand it, he said, "What? Why do you keep looking at me like that?"

"I was just wondering if, deep down inside, you agree with what those men in there are doing to their wives."

"Damn it, Natasha. I don't believe in hitting a woman or child. You know that."

She continued to watch him.

He leaned toward her. "If I ever had the inclination to do something like that to you, believe me, my dear, I would have done it long before now."

"You did threaten me with violence once, you know."

Striker shook his head. "Here we go."

Their gazes locked.

"As I told you at the time, I only did it to get your attention, to try to get you to calm down. I will admit that there have been times during the somewhat short course of our life together when I've been sorely tempted, but I don't believe in that, and I will not do that. Ever. We clear on that?"

Natasha smiled at him. "I love you, Jonce. You know that, don't you? I love the hell out of you."

"Yeah, well, I do you, too, but I sure wish you'd learn to keep that mouth of yours shut sometimes."

She gave him a lecherous look. "Yeah, but not all the time."

He couldn't stop the grin.

"I guess we found out what 'alternative lifestyle' means," she said, as they sped away.

Back home, on the deck, in the nude, shrouded in darkness, Striker reclined in the lounge chair with Natasha in his lap, resting her head against his neck with her eyes closed. Glad to be home, Striker lightly stroked her velvety skin with his fingers while watching a cruiser maneuver downriver, tracking buoys with a bright light.

"I wish we could be this way forever," Natasha said in a soft tone.

"Me too," he said, his voice matching hers.

She held out her hand and studied the wedding band. "I liked being married to you."

He smiled. "It was fun."

She straightened and gave him a serious look.

"What?"

"Do you know how happy you make me, Jonce? How wonderful my life is with you?"

"If it's any small part of how happy you make me, yeah."

"I love you more than my life, you know that, don't you?"

"As I do you."

She settled back against him and they lapsed into a comfortable silence.

Natasha could feel Striker staring at her and tilted her head back to gaze at him. "What?"

"I was thinking about what you said in that meeting, your reference to love spankings."

She grinned.

He raised his eyebrows. "There something you want to tell me?"

She playfully slapped his chest.

Chapter 19

Perched on the chair in front of Striker's computer, Natasha frowned at the keyboard and muttered to herself. Cat sat on the desk, watching, with interest, the changing images on the monitor.

"What's going on?" Striker said from the doorway.

Natasha gave him a distracted smile and raised her face when he leaned his down for a kiss. "I've been going over these lists, cross-matching the two years and researching in-depth the owners of the dogs at the shows."

"I thought Roger was helping with that."

Natasha made a face. "He's occupied."

Striker gave her a knowing grin, which she ignored.

He studied the computer screen with her. "And?"

"Well, it's obvious to me that the ones whose dogs placed but got beat by Chumley would be the ones who would have the most to gain from his absence at the show this year."

"Makes sense."

"I'm having trouble locating the reserve winner's owner, a guy named Peterson."

"Reserve winner? What's that?"

"According to Myrtle, it's kind of like being a stand-in. If the winning dog gets disqualified for whatever reason, the reserve winner moves up and takes the points. So far I haven't been able to track this Peterson down. So tomorrow, I figured I'd check out the owner of last year's third-place winner in Chumley's group."

"Who is…?"

Natasha flipped her fingers at the screen. "Happy. Wasn't that the name of one of the Seven Dwarves?" She glanced up. "Can you imagine going around with the name Happy? Shoot, darlin', most of these dogs have better names than their owners."

Striker could sense her frustration. "How long you been doing this?"

She shrugged. "Since this morning. As of now, I have most of the owners' home and business addresses, vocations, avocations, Social Security Numbers, driver's license numbers, and criminal and credit histories. Not to mention how many times they pee a day."

Striker sat down on the corner of the desk, picked up one of Natasha's legs by the ankle, rested it on his thigh, and began untying her sneaker. Cat rose, padded over, and swatted at the moving laces.

Trying to ignore the effects Striker's hands had on her body, Natasha picked up her list and ran her finger down the page. "Okay, we got us a strip-club owner, attorney-nudist, and Happy, who works at a massage parlor. Are any of these people normal?"

Striker shrugged with a grin.

Natasha watched him drop her sneaker to the floor, lift her other leg, rest her foot on his thigh, and begin removing the shoe. Cat followed the dropped sneaker.

"Hey, sweetie, you ever been inside a massage parlor?"

Striker's eyes remained on her foot. "Not as a paying customer, no."

She thought about asking him in what way but knew he wouldn't tell her until he was ready. Striker was like that, guarded about his past and what he had done. Although she knew more than anyone else, she felt she didn't know much of anything at all, actually.

Now his rough hands were removing her anklets, sliding them slowly off her feet.

Natasha reveled in this, then forced her mind to focus on the rosters. "Don't most of those massage parlors front prostitution rings?"

"Yeah, I think a lot of them do." Striker gently placed her feet on the floor. He pulled the chair toward him and his hands traveled to the button on her shorts.

Natasha leaned forward, interrupting his efforts to pull the zipper down. "Hey, I know what. Why don't I go in there, apply for a position as a masseuse, get close to that Happy, feel her out about her show dog, find out if she knows anything about Chumley?"

Striker's eyes hardened.

"What?"

"Yeah, and do what if a guy comes in there and doesn't want you to massage his back but another area I better not ever catch you massaging on another man, if you get my drift."

Natasha grimaced. "Nasty."

"You better think that," he said, glaring at her.

Natasha stood and leaned into him, her shorts dropping around her ankles. She shivered when Striker's hands dipped into the waistband of her bikinis, cupped her buttocks. She drew her face close to his and gazed into his eyes.

"Baby, you have ruined me for any other man. How many times I got to tell you that?" She put her lips on his while his hands continued with the removal of her panties, and then raised her arms over her head so Striker could pull her tank up and off.

Natasha unbuttoned his shirt, her mouth busy with his. She unbuckled his belt, then unfastened and unzipped his jeans before drawing back. "Wait a minute."

"Forget it," he said, knowing what was coming.

"You could go in there, ask for Happy, let her give you a massage, start talking to her, see if you can find out anything."

Striker thought about it. "Okay, fine. I'll go, get naked, lie on the table, let that Happy give me a massage and whatever else she might feel the need to do."

Her eyes darkened. "You wouldn't."

He stared at her.

"That won't work anyway. You're too beautiful, too manly. She probably wouldn't be able to contain herself."

Striker grinned; he liked that she felt this way about him.

Natasha gave him a skeptical look. "Say you actually did that, went in there, and she wanted to give you more than a massage. What would you do?"

"What do you think I'd do?"

"Let me get one thing straight, Bucko. You go planting that big guy someplace other than my place, you ain't gonna be in the world long, I promise you that."

Striker laughed, pulling her closer. "Natasha, you are so bad. It's the same with me, darlin', don't you know that by now? You have ruined me for another woman. No one else but you will do, baby."

Natasha forgot all about Happy and the roster until the next morning. After Striker left for work, she returned to his office to straighten up the mess they made on his desk the evening before. She picked up the list, debating the best way to penetrate the massage parlor. She needed to send someone in, but whom? Striker was definitely out. Roger? No, he'd probably be so embarrassed he wouldn't even be able to talk. Her mind moved to her two bodyguard friends. Pit? Yeah, Pit was good. He looked like the type that would frequent massage parlors. But wait a minute. Bigun fit that stereotype even better than Pit. Plus Bigun was a little denser, easier to maneuver.

She picked up the phone and called Roger's house. Bigun answered. She knew he would. It was breakfast time.

"Hey, dude," she said.

"Dudette." Bigun sounded glad to hear from her.

"What's going on?"

"Nothing much. Pit and I got to go to Asheville this weekend, so Striker gave us the rest of the week off."

Perfect. "Hey, dude, I was wondering if I could hire you to do something for me."

"I don't know, dudette. Things get weird when you're involved."

"Come on, dude. You'll like this. All I need is for you to find out some information and get a massage in the process."

"Yeah? Hey, dudette, that sounds like fun."

"I'll pay for the massage, plus I'll pay for your time."

Bigun didn't respond to this.

"What?"

"Does Striker know? Striker won't get mad, will he? 'Cause he's a real bad-ass when he gets mad."

"No, dude, he won't get mad. I talked to him about it last night and he knows all about it. I asked him if he wanted to go, but he said no, so I thought I'd ask you."

"Oh, okay."

"All you have to do is go into this massage parlor, ask for Happy, let her give you a massage, and while she's doing that, query her about Chumley."

"Oh, the stinky dog."

"Yeah. Her dog lost to him last year, so I need someone who can find out if she knows anything about that letter or who's got Chumley now, and your name popped into my head."

"Well, why don't you just ask her?"

"If she took Chumley, why would she tell me? And if I ask her, being the one who's trying to find the dog, if she did take him or knows who did, they might do something to him. You know, to get him out of the way."

"Oh, dudette, that would be terrible. That nice Miss Myrtle would be awfully upset."

"That's true. So, what, dude, you willing to help me or not?"

Bigun thought some more. "Well, I don't have anything else to do. Okay, Nattie, I'll help."

"Great. I'm coming over. We'll plan our strategy when I get there."

Natasha had to wait for Bigun to finish eating breakfast before he called the massage parlor to make an appointment with Happy. He got one for eleven that morning.

Hearing this, Pit was a little put out Natasha hadn't asked him.

She hated to lie but didn't want to hurt his feelings. "Well, Bigun answered the phone. I would have asked you if you had answered."

"Oh, well, okay," Pit said.

"Where's Roger?" Natasha said, knowing he usually ate breakfast with the boys.

"Upstairs," Pit said.

Both men's eyes traveled in that direction.

"Misty?"

They nodded.

"She's still here?"

More nods.

"Man, I got to tell you, that woman's weird," Pit said.

Natasha leaned toward him, interested. "You think so?"

"Yeah, man. She slinks around here, watching everybody, never saying anything, only talking to Roger."

"She does?"

"Spends all day at the pool."

"Wait a minute. I thought she was supposed to be doing research."

"That's what we thought, dudette," Bigun said.

Natasha read their expressions. "Y'all don't like her."

Pit glanced in the direction of the doorway to make sure Roger or Misty wasn't lurking about. "No, man. She's just using Roger."

"Maybe I need to check her out," Natasha said.

Pit shook his head. "Hey, man, I talked to Striker about it, but he says it's Roger's business, to leave it alone."

"Yeah?" Well, what Striker didn't know wouldn't hurt him. Natasha made a mental note to look into one Misty Bellows's past.

The plan was for Bigun to go to the parlor at eleven and, while Happy was manipulating his muscles, talk about Brutus, the Weimaraner Natasha and Roger shared, to get her started on the subject of dogs.

"Then just steer the conversation toward her dog," Natasha said. "If she's anything like Myrtle, she'll brag about it being a show dog, so you say something like, 'I have a friend whose dog won a championship but he ended up missing.' Be sure and watch her face when you say this, see how she reacts, see what she says."

"Sure, dudette, no problem," Bigun said, making movements to leave.

"I'll drive you."

Bigun gave her a look.

"Don't worry. I'll wait outside."

He gave her another look.

"There's a laundromat right next door. I'll park there."

"Hey, man, since I don't have anything else to do, I think I'll tag along," Pit said.

After they were parked at the laundromat, Natasha dug her wallet out of her purse. "I forgot to ask, how much does it cost?"

Bigun glanced away. "Fifty."

Natasha handed over two twenties and a ten. "Okay, how long is this going to take?"

"Well, I got the hour massage, 'cause I figured that'd give her more of a chance to talk."

"Hour? What the heck can she massage for an hour?"

Both men were quiet.

"Okay, just go," Natasha said, irritated.

After Bigun disappeared inside the massage parlor, Pit and Natasha looked at one another. They had an hour to kill with nothing to do.

"Hey, there's a Wendy's down the street. You want to go get an early lunch?" she asked.

Pit's eyes brightened.

An hour later, Natasha was finishing up a Frosty when Bigun stepped out of the massage parlor. Pit climbed out of the Jeep and waited for his friend to get in the back seat. Bigun settled back, looking awfully relaxed.

Natasha stared at him in the rear-view mirror. "Well?"

"Well what, dudette?"

"What'd you find out?"

Bigun's face wore a guilty look.

"Don't tell me," Natasha said.

"We never got around to talking about dogs," Bigun said, with an embarrassed glance.

Natasha turned around to face him. "What the heck did you talk about?"

Bigun shrugged.

"You did get a massage, right?"

"Yeah."

"By Happy?"

A blush worked its way up Bigun's neck. "Yeah."

"And?"

He looked caught. "What?"

"Oh, man, you had *sex* with her," Natasha said, cringing inside.

Bigun's face turned brick red. "Well, it came with the price, if I wanted it."

"Damn it, Bigun, I didn't send you in there to get screwed, I sent you in there to find out some information."

"I'll pay you back. Next week, okay? I don't have enough right now to pay you back the full fifty."

"What the hell am I going to do now?"

After a moment's silence, Bigun said, "They accept walk-ins."

Natasha glared in the rear-view mirror.

Pit turned and looked at him. "Yeah?"

"Yeah, dude, and that Happy said she was free for a couple of hours."

"Hey, man, I'll try it if you want," Pit said.

Natasha had been expecting this. "You gonna go do the same stupid thing he did, get a blowjob or whatever —"

"Hey, I got more than a blowjob," Bigun said.

She ignored that, saying, for Bigun's benefit, "Go in there and forget all about doing what I'm paying you to do, by the way."

"Hey, man, I'll get what you want. Don't worry about it."

Natasha fished her wallet out of her purse. "You come out of there without any information, you better just keep on walking, Pit. I mean it."

"All right, already." He grabbed her money and climbed out of the jeep.

Bigun moved to the front seat, eyeing her Frosty. "Hey, dudette, I sure am hungry."

Natasha sighed, drove to Wendy's, and bought Bigun's lunch, just like she had Pit's.

An hour later, there came Pit, with the same damn look on his face.

Pit got into the jeep, glanced at Natasha, and looked away.

"Don't tell me," she moaned.

"Hey, man, that woman is *good*," Pit said.

"Yeah, dude, she's the best," Bigun agreed.

Natasha threw her hands in the air. "What am I doing here, funding prostitution?"

"Hey, man, I tried to talk about the dog, but she didn't want to talk about crap like that."

Natasha faced him. "Oh, yeah? And what the hell did she want to talk about, Pit?"

His face turned crimson.

"That's what I thought." Natasha opened her door and lunged out of the jeep.

"Hey, man, where are you going?" Pit said.

"To get the information you two idiots couldn't get, 'cause I, thank God, think with a different head than y'all do."

"Hey," both said.

A few minutes later, police cars began pulling up outside the massage parlor.

"Shit, man, you think Nattie shot somebody or something?" Pit said.

"Aw, dude, what are we gonna do?" Bigun said.

"I don't know, man, but we better wait. She'll kill us if she comes back and we're not here. You know how mad she gets."

The two men watched their first raid on a prostitution ring inside the City of Knoxville, gawking at Natasha being led outside along with other women.

Natasha looked their way and yelled, "You better not call Striker. You do and I'll —" Her words cut off when she was shoved inside a paddy wagon.

Pit picked up his cellphone.

Natasha was back in the holding cell, a different one this time with different women, most of whom, once again, were prostitutes. She hoped against hope that Pit and Bigun, those two dumb-asses, would bail her out. No way was she calling Striker, or her mother. Shoot, she'd never hear the end of this if Stevie found out she'd ended up in jail and God help her if her mom found out the reason why. She looked down at her form of attire, wondering why the cops took her for one of the hookers in there. Well, she was wearing a short skirt. But it was *denim*, for Pete's sake, something cool for such a hot day. And the halter-top, yeah, that might look like something a prostitute would wear, but it was lined, and besides, it was hot today. And hey, look at what was on her feet: flip-flops. No way did that look like a hooker doing business.

She studied the other women, noting their hard looks, raspy voices, and unhealthy hair. Glancing around, she called out, "Anybody in here named Happy?"

A woman broke apart from the others and approached Natasha. She had frizzy red hair, small brown eyes, and freckles everywhere. Her extremely obese body was stuffed into a strapless halter and spandex shorts, both of which bulged in too many places to count. Curious why Pit and Bigun had found her so, well, *great*, Natasha wondered if Happy maybe knew a secret to this sex thing she might divulge. Her thoughts were interrupted when Happy spoke in a rude tone.

"What the hell you want with me, bitch?"

Natasha frantically tried to think of a believable lie. "It's just, I have a friend who was telling me what a great masseuse you are. I came in to talk to you about that, thinking I might want to get into the business, and got caught up in this raid thing." Natasha paused. *Uh-oh.* Did that sound like she wanted to get into prostitution?

Happy gave her the once-over. "Yeah?"

"Yeah," Natasha said, feeling uncomfortable.

"Who's your friend?"

Natasha figured Pit was probably the better lover of the two Samoans, judging from the way he acted. "Pit."

Happy gave her a knowing glance. "Man, that dude is *hung.*"

Natasha didn't want to hear it.

Happy stepped back and ran her eyes up and down Natasha's body. "So, you're thinking about being a masseuse?"

"Yeah. I tried breeding and selling dogs — I have a Weimaraner — but there's not much money in that."

"Yeah? I got a dog myself."

"Really? What kind?"

"Little Shih-Tzu. A real beauty."

Natasha smiled. "Those are such cute dogs."

Happy's demeanor changed to that of a proud parent. "She's a show dog."

Natasha mentally kicked herself. *You doofus.* Look how easy this was, and she had to do it the hard way. She'd lost a hundred bucks today, plus having to pay Pit and Bigun for their time, not to mention the bail money. *Shoot.*

"I have a friend that has a show dog," Natasha said.

"Yeah?"

"Myrtle Galbreath. Has a little Pug named Chumley."

Happy glowered. "I hate that dog."

"I don't know. He's kind of sweet, even though he stinks to high heaven and humps everything in sight."

"Yeah, well, I'd like to know how in hell that little shrimp won a championship," Happy grumbled.

"Somebody apparently stole him."

Happy looked surprised. "Really? Well, hell, I might hate that dog but I feel bad for Myrtle. She's a real sweetie-pie."

Okay, cross Happy off the list. "Somebody even threatened to kill the dog," Natasha said, pretending to relay a big secret.

An angry expression settled on Happy's face. "Who in hell would ever kill a poor defenseless dog? I mean, yeah, I can understand a human being. We can defend ourselves, but not a sweet little doggie."

Yep, she was definitely off the list. Hearing her name called, Natasha waved bye to Happy and left.

The jailer led her into a room to retrieve her personal belongings. And who should be there, leaning against the wall, arms crossed, sending a wide scowl her way? *Damn it.* She was going to kill Bigun and Pit. She gave Striker an embarrassed grin.

Striker watched her the entire time, not saying anything, then led her outside to his SUV. Natasha thought he was probably so mad he couldn't talk. Striker held the door open for her and closed it with more force than necessary after she climbed inside. He settled into the driver's seat, turned, and looked at her.

"I told Pit and Bigun not to call you."

He didn't answer.

"If they hadn't been so stupid, acted like hormonal teenagers, none of this would have ever happened."

He remained silent.

"I guess you're wanting to know what happened," she finally said.

Striker raised his eyebrows.

Natasha told him, ignoring his laughter at what Pit and Bigun had done. "Dangit, Striker, I hadn't been in there five minutes when that parlor got raided. Now tell me what kind of luck I'm having with this friggin' case."

"Not much," he said, shaking his head.

She told Striker about her conversation with Happy.

He leaned back. "Okay, you lost a hundred bucks plus what you have to pay Pit and Bigun for their time, *and* got arrested for prostitution, when all you could have done was called the lady up and talked to her on the phone, saved yourself all kinds of trouble and me to boot. But no, you, Natasha, dear, have to do it the weird way, the not normal way. You have to con my guys, *my guys*, Natasha, into going into a massage parlor, a.k.a. 'house of prostitution', all for nothing."

She looked out the window. "Tell me about it."

Striker waited for her to bring her eyes to his. "What the hell is the matter with you?"

Natasha shrugged. "Well, you're always saying I'm wacky."

"Darlin', I think you've gone way beyond wacky," he said in an angry voice.

She decided to ignore that. Then registered what he had said to her. "Am I really going to be charged with prostitution?"

Striker keyed the ignition. "I talked to the ADA, explained who you are, that you were investigating a case, implying you worked for me. He understands you're not part of that group, so as far as I know, the charge won't be made."

"Thank goodness." Natasha glanced around. "Where's my jeep?"

"I had Pit and Bigun drop it off at the house." He leaned toward her with a frown. "You think if I take you home you can manage to keep that cute butt of yours out of trouble the rest of the day?"

The activities at the massage parlor had gotten Natasha in a randy mood. She scooted closer to Striker and smiled. "Hey, I have a great idea. Why don't we go home and play hooker and arresting policeman?"

His forehead furrowed.

"I'm serious." She slid her hand up his thigh. "You've got the handcuffs, the attitude, the big gun."

"Let's go," he said in a gruff voice.

"Yeah, boy."

Chapter 20

Natasha snuggled against Striker, waiting for the buzzing sound in her head to subside and the throbbing between her legs to stop. When her cellphone emitted a demanding chirp, she debated letting her voice mail pick up, but the thought that this might be about Chumley got her moving. With a groan, she stretched across Striker's lap and reached over the side of the bed for her skirt and phone.

Striker idly feathered his fingers down her spine, smiling when her body broke out in goose bumps.

"This better be good," Natasha said into the mouthpiece. She straightened up with a shocked expression on her face. "Grammy."

That got Striker's attention. *Grammy? Who the hell was Grammy?*

Natasha scrambled off Striker. "How am I? I'm fine. How are you?"

She listened, and then said, "You're fine. Good, good, you're fine. That's good."

"What am I doing?" She cast a guilty glance at Striker. "Uh, nothing, really, at the moment."

Striker raised his eyebrows.

"What was I doing? Oh, well, uh, exercising. Yeah, that's right. Exercising, you know. That's why I'm so, well, sweaty, and why I sound out of breath. That's what I was doing, exercising."

Striker frowned.

"I'm being 'echolalic'? What the heck? Okay, maybe I'm repeating back certain words you're saying to me, Grammy, but if I were actually being echolalic, I would be repeating word for word what you were saying, so I am not committing echolalia." She nodded for emphasis.

Striker grinned.

Natasha reached over, grabbed the sheet, and covered herself, acting modest.

What the hell? "Who is that?"

She shook her head and made a shushing motion with her hand. "Who's here? No one, Grammy. That was the TV."

Striker scowled.

"A man? No, it wasn't a man." Natasha sent Striker an apologetic look.

"Mom told you I had a boyfriend? Why the heck would she tell you that?"

Striker stiffened.

"I have a man friend, Grammy. He's no boy, believe me." She glanced at Striker, pointed at the phone, and made a face.

"Yes, he is. He's beautiful, in fact, if you want to know the truth of the matter."

Striker's expression relaxed.

"That's none of your business." She mouthed, "Can you believe this?" to Striker.

He shrugged.

"No, that's none of your business, either. That's no one's business but mine and Striker's." She covered the mouthpiece and said, "Shoot."

"What?" he whispered.

She shook her head.

"No, Grammy. *Striker*, not Lighter. For Pete's sake, quit being difficult."

"No, I don't want to talk about him. He's none of your business. Why'd you call anyway?"

She concentrated on the phone, her expression growing alarmed. "You're coming here? When?" Her mouth formed the words, "Oh, no."

"What are you coming here for?"

"A family conference? Why the heck do we need to have a family conference?"

"We'll discuss it when you get here? Well, thanks, but no thanks. I want to know now."

"No, I'm not being obstinate and I'm not being echolalic. Would you please get off that subject?"

She sighed, listening, and said, "I suppose you'll be staying with me."

Her posture told Striker the answer was yes.

"Well, Grammy, that may be a problem."

"Why? Well, I'm working on a case right now. I won't be home much. I won't be able to spend any time with you. Besides, why don't you stay with Mom? She's your daughter, you know. You two should spend time together."

She held the cellphone in the air, much like she did when she was on the phone with her mom and had said something to elicit an angry reaction.

After the noise from the other end of the line died down, Natasha brought the phone back to her ear. "Okay, already. I'll see you tomorrow." She hurled her cell at the chaise on the other side of the room. "Dangit."

"What?"

She turned to him. "You know who that was?"

"Grammy?"

"Yeah." She lunged off the bed.

"I take it she's your grandmother."

Natasha nodded. "She's coming in for a family conference. That can mean only one thing: Mom's called in the BK."

Striker grinned. "BK? As in Grammy?"

"Yeah. Mom can't talk me out of being a bodyguard, so she's called in the mistress of manipulation, the master at shaming, the butt-kicker of all time."

"Grammy."

"Yes."

"How come you never told me about her?"

Natasha gave him a *well, duh* look.

"What?"

"I told you about her."

"No, you didn't."

"I said I have a grandmother that lives in Atlanta. That's her. That's Grammy. And now she's coming here." She was beginning to sound panicked.

Striker didn't see what the problem was. "What's her name?"

"B.S. Elliott."

His face changed. "The author?"

"The one and only."

"The one who writes those books —"

"Yeah, that's the one. You know what B.S. stands for? Bullshit, pure and simple."

"They're best-sellers, aren't they?"

"Yeah, well, go figure."

"I'd like to meet her."

Natasha looked alarmed. "You can't meet her."

"Why not?"

"She hates men. You know about the books, so surely you know how she feels about men."

"I didn't read the series. I just heard about it."

"You know what it's based on? Her theory that men are the weaker sex and are doomed to become obsolete."

"Come on, I thought it was science fiction."

"A fictional story, but her theory. She really thinks that."

"Is she a lesbian?"

Natasha gave him a look.

"What?"

"That is so sexist."

"Okay, I apologize."

"And no, she isn't a lesbian. Shoot, she's had so many lovers in her lifetime, it's a wonder she doesn't walk around like John Wayne."

Striker chuckled at that image.

"I'm serious. She uses men for sexual purposes. Other than that, forget it. She says men aren't worth our time."

"What?"

"That's why Mom won't let her stay with them, 'cause she can't keep her opinions to herself, has to take jabs at my dad all the time. Has to lecture my mom about being a weakling and marrying one of those things."

Striker's amusement sobered at Natasha's look. "You're serious?"

"As a heart attack. She's a man-eater, Striker. She'll chew you up and spit you out, and I'm not kidding. I haven't introduced one man to her yet who hasn't gone running for the hills with his hands protecting his genitals when she got through with him."

"Oh, come on. She can't be that bad."

"Yeah? Did you hear about her getting arrested last month?"

"No, I didn't hear about that. Why didn't you tell me B.S. Elliott was your grandmother?"

"She called the President an illiterate redneck who's so stupid he thinks that smirk he wears on his face passes for amiability."

"Well, everyone's entitled to their opinion."

"But to say it to his face? Then slap a sign on his back as he's walking away with an arrow pointing down, saying, 'Insert here'?"

Striker lost it.

"You think it's funny now. Wait till you meet her."

"I thought you didn't want me to meet her."

"She knows about you now. She'll make sure she meets you, and God help you, Striker." Natasha searched around, found her panties, and pulled them on.

Striker's brow furrowed. "What are you doing?"

"I've got to go home. She's coming in tomorrow."

"So?"

"So? She's like a drill sergeant. She sees one item out of place or one speck of dust, I'll never hear the end of it."

"Come on, baby. Stay awhile."

Striker's heated look caused her body to tingle. She stopped dressing and stared at him.

"Come on, darlin'. I'm not through yet."

Natasha looked at him longingly as she walked toward the bed. She reached down, picked up her skirt, and pulled it on.

He sat up, surprised. "Damn, Natasha, it's not like you're going to get sent off to prison or anything, she finds your house dusty. What's wrong with you?"

She pulled her top over her head. "Yeah? Tell me that after you meet her." She grabbed her flip-flops and cellphone and dashed out the door.

After a couple of hours, Striker called Natasha's house. She sounded breathless when she answered.

"You finished yet?" he asked.

"I wish. I just now got through with the bathrooms. Shoot, darlin', I'm spending way too much time at your house. This place is a mess."

"So? Hey, I've got a great idea. Let her stay there and you stay here. That way you won't have to deal with her."

"Yeah, right." Natasha hung up the phone.

After another hour, Striker hit the redial button. "You coming back over here tonight?" he asked when she answered.

"Heck, no. I've got too much work to do."

"Come on, Natasha, that's a one-bedroom cottage. What the hell's taking so long?"

She disconnected without replying. He fetched his car keys and left.

Striker stepped out of his SUV and took a moment to admire Natasha's cottage, designed and built by her father, Jacob, a building contractor. Striker, who fancied himself a carpenter in a previous life, liked the rustic design, which blended well with the pastoral area surrounding the small house.

A large wooden porch wrapped around the cottage with artisan cane rockers strewn about, inviting visitors to sit and enjoy the view. A mulched flowerbed filled with blooming plants circled the porch, broken only by a sidewalk leading up to the front steps. Inside, the downstairs was open throughout; the living area, kitchen, and dining alcove flowing together in cozy warmth, filled with overstuffed furniture and houseplants.

Her grandmother's high antique iron bed, along with heavy wooden beams on the slanted ceiling, dominated Natasha's bedroom, which took up most of the loft. A half-bath nestled in the space beneath the stairs, and a more spacious bathroom adjoined Natasha's bedroom. Although it was small, the dimensions were perfect, with no unused space, yet allowing enough room for Natasha's comfort.

Striker could hear the vacuum cleaner when he walked up the steps to the front porch. The wooden door was open but the glass door was closed. He yanked hard, knowing how flimsy the lock was, and walked on in.

Natasha screamed when she saw a tall, powerfully built silhouette framed in her doorway.

"It's me," Striker yelled over the loud cleaning machine.

She stomped her foot down and the vacuum fell silent. "You scared me to death."

Striker stormed over to her. "How many times have I told you that lock on your glass door isn't going to stop someone from coming in?"

She shrugged.

"Damn it, Natasha, I could have been a rapist or a murderer standing there."

"Yeah, but you weren't. Why'd you come anyway? In case it hasn't hit you by now, I don't have time to entertain you. I've got company coming."

"Okay, first things first. Promise me that from now on, you'll keep the wooden door closed, at least until you get a better lock for the glass door."

"Come on, Striker. How many times have we had this conversation?"

"I'll tell Stevie," he said in a warning tone.

She frowned at him. "You'd do that? You'd tell my mom on me, like some little kid?"

"If it'll make you be safe, sure."

"Okay, already. I'll start closing the wooden door." She stepped back and gave him a suspicious look. "Why'd you come anyway?"

"I figured I'd help you clean."

"You mean, here?"

Striker held out his hands. "Hey, you've seen me clean my place. You know I can do it."

Natasha couldn't suppress her smile.

"Tell me what you need me to do."

"I love the heck out of you, you know that?"

Natasha, too busy playing with Striker and having way too much fun to even think about it, forgot to set the alarm, and they overslept the next morning. Someone banging on her front door got them untangled and standing, eyes darting around, searching for clothes.

"I'm coming," Natasha yelled out her bedroom door. She glanced at the clock. "Thank goodness. I thought it was Grammy, but she isn't supposed to be here until noon and it's only eight now. It must be Mom. I'll be right back." She snatched Striker's shirt off the floor and hurried out.

Striker watched her walk away as he reached for his pants. Hearing voices downstairs, he debated whether to join them or stay in the bedroom and wait for Stevie to leave. Although Natasha's mom knew they slept together, she wouldn't be happy about that fact until a wedding ring rested on her daughter's finger—if then. When the voices grew louder, he decided maybe he better find out what was going on.

An older woman stood in the living area lecturing Natasha about dressing herself properly before answering the door. Natasha had buttoned Striker's shirt so that it hung crookedly on her body, exposing one bare shoulder. The shirtsleeves hid her hands and the tail fell almost to the backs of her knees. Her hair was tousled and she kept rubbing at her eyes like a small child.

Striker grinned, thinking how cute she looked as he walked down the stairs. The woman stopped talking when she noticed him. Natasha followed the woman's gaze and her eyes widened with alarm.

"Grammy, I'd like you to meet my — Jonce Striker. Jonce, my grandmother, B.S. Elliott," Natasha mumbled.

Natasha's grandmother glared at Striker. Although he had heard of her, he had never looked at one of her book jackets long enough to study a photo. She was tall and slender, like Natasha and her mother. Her cotton-white hair was cut in a short, masculine style. She wore a man's white, long-sleeved shirt tucked into dark jeans, with hiking boots on her feet.

"So, you're Stroker," she said.

Natasha rolled her eyes.

Striker held out his hand. "Jonce Striker."

B.S. gave him a firm, quick shake. She withdrew her hand as though she had touched something vile.

Striker put his arm around Natasha in a possessive way.

B.S.'s eyes narrowed. She turned to her granddaughter. "Well, Nat, I'll say one thing for you. You always pick the good-looking ones."

Striker's jaw muscles clenched.

"Grammy," Natasha said, in a warning tone.

B.S. turned back to Striker. "I hear you're a rich man."

Striker kissed Natasha's temple. "I didn't consider myself rich until I met your granddaughter."

B.S. made a face as if to say, *hmmm*. She made it a point to stare at his naked chest. "I also hear you're having sex with my granddaughter."

"Grammy," Natasha said.

"That's between Natasha and me and no one else," Striker said in an affable voice.

"Does he know who I am?" B.S. asked her granddaughter, continuing to stare Striker down.

Natasha sighed. "Yes, Grammy, he knows."

"Well?" B.S. said.

Striker resisted the urge to smile. "Are you talking to me?"

B.S. cocked her head and waited for his reply.

"I haven't read your books, if that's what you're asking."

B.S. gave him a smug look. "Oh, an illiterate."

"No. I just don't happen to read science fiction."

B.S. bristled. "The books are not science fiction."

"Really? I must have read the wrong article then."

"And what do you think about my theory?"

"You mean about men and our eventual obsoletism?"

"Is there any other?" B.S. said in a haughty tone.

"Actually, I think that's pure bullshit, B.S."

They glared at one another.

"I understand you're the reason my granddaughter got into this idiotic career she's trying to cut out for herself," B.S. said.

"The very one," Striker agreed.

Natasha shot him a look of surprise. So did B.S.

"Listen, Ms. Elliott, I don't hide the fact that I don't want Natasha to be in the bodyguard business. I think it's too dangerous, and I'm afraid for her. But it's her choice, whatever she decides to pursue. And I don't have the right, you don't have the right, no one has the right to tell her what she should be doing with her life. It's her decision, and I may not like it, but I respect the hell out of it."

Natasha smiled.

B.S. glowered. Ignoring Striker, she turned to Natasha. "An imbecile could be a bodyguard. What kind of an IQ does one need possess to babysit another person, Nat? Is that what you went to college for, what you wasted an education on?"

"Looks it," Natasha said.

B.S. drew herself up, darting angry glances between Striker and Natasha. "I don't particularly care to have a discussion with you dressed like that," she said to Natasha, waving her arm at Striker's shirt. She turned and gave Striker a hostile stare. "And I'd like to talk with my granddaughter in private, if you don't mind."

"I need to leave anyway," he said.

Natasha looked from her grandmother to her lover and back. "Okay," she said defiantly, shrugging out of the shirt.

B.S. watched in astonishment, Striker in amusement.

Natasha handed the shirt to Striker. She kissed him with passion, murmured, "Thanks for everything, darlin'," and sashayed up the stairs toward her bedroom.

Striker turned back to B.S. and stopped smiling when he saw the look she was sending him. He strode toward the door, pulling on his shirt. "It was a real treat, Ms. Elliott," he said over his shoulder, ignoring the exasperated huff she cast his way.

Chapter 21

After a lot of whining and pleading, Natasha persuaded her mom to take her grandmother to Gatlinburg for the day. Natasha escaped to her office and was back to her list for the prior two years' participants. Okay, here was a judge from the first year Chumley won Best in Show, a Mr. Harold Wright, occupation: banker. She recognized the name of the bank, one of the largest in Tennessee. She'd pay a visit to Mr. Wright, check him out, see if he could remember anything about the —

Her office door opened to reveal a large, masculine frame filling the doorway, blocking out most of the light. Natasha smiled, recognizing that form, and goose bumps broke out over her body.

Striker stepped into the room and closed the door, removing his sunglasses.

Natasha decided to ignore his angry expression; she needed something from him. She rushed over to him, flung herself into his arms, and kissed him long and hard.

"I have missed you so much. You wouldn't believe," she whispered against his lips. Pressing as tightly against him as she could, she smiled at his body's response.

Striker gently pushed her away.

"What?"

"What's going on?" he said, his voice low, his eyes shooting daggers.

"Going on? Nothing. I was just going over the list —"

"That's not what I'm talking about, and you know it."

She gave him a trapped look.

"It's been two days now and I haven't seen you, haven't heard from you. What is this? Your grandmother comes to pay a visit and all of a sudden I'm *persona non grata* with you?"

"Oh, sweetie, it's not like that at all. It's just I've been busy with her. She's staying at my house, she's always hanging around, watching everything I do, listening to everything I —"

"What? Grammy comes to visit and you turn into a ten-year-old?"

"Well, no, not exactly."

"You can't say, 'Excuse me, I'd like some privacy' or 'I'll be back later, I'm going to see Striker'?"

"You've met her. You try saying something like that to her."

"Just say it, Natasha, then do it. What's wrong with that?"

She looked away, mulling over his comments. After a few moments, she brought her eyes back to his.

"You're right. I'm an adult; I'm entitled. What the hell is the matter with me?" She stood on tiptoes and wrapped her arms around his neck. "Can we now proceed to other, more important things?" she said with a teasing smile.

His reply was physical.

They were in the chair behind Natasha's desk, their clothing shoved up and down and every which way, when the office door opened. They froze, staring into one another's eyes.

"Didn't you lock the door?" Natasha mouthed.

Striker shook his head. "I thought you did."

Natasha rose up from Striker's body to peek over her high-backed executive chair, thankful it was lodged against her desk and not in danger of toppling over. Her grandmother stood on the other side of her desk with arms crossed. Natasha glanced down at Striker, relieved for his sake that her body hid most of his nakedness.

Natasha gave her grandmother a guilty look. "Um, I'm a little bit occupied right now, Grammy. I'd appreciate it ever so much if you'd… well, leave."

B.S. leaned over the desk and tilted her head sideways, trying to see what was going on in the chair. Her eyes widened at the sight of one furry forearm and thigh.

"Hello, Ms. Elliott," Striker said between gritted teeth.

Raising her eyebrows, B.S. turned her eyes to Natasha. Natasha tried giving her a defiant look but couldn't quite manage it.

B.S. backed off a step, pivoted, and walked away, saying over her shoulder, "Well, Nat, I'm glad you figured out the one thing men are good for."

After the door closed behind her, Natasha looked at Striker. "You see?"

He shook his head with frustration.

After Striker left, Natasha hurried into the bathroom to do a quick cleanup and straighten her clothes. When she stepped into her office, B.S. was sitting in the chair across from her desk. Natasha cleared her throat while darting uneasy glances toward her grandmother.

B.S. reciprocated with a bored look. "You really should try locking the door, Nat. You'd be surprised how easy a task that is."

Natasha ignored her, settling in behind her desk.

B.S. watched Natasha pick up a computerized list and pretend to study it. She leaned back, fishing in her pocket for a cigarillo. She pulled one out, followed by a butane lighter, and lit up, all the while studying her granddaughter.

Unable to resist any longer, Natasha glanced at her.

"Judging by the look on your face, I'd say that Streaker knows what he's doing."

"*Striker*, Grammy. How many times do I have to tell you?"

B.S. ignored that.

"And while we're on the subject, Grammy, he's my life mate, okay? I love him more than I've ever loved anyone. I like the fact that he's a man and I like the things we do with each other. So don't start on me about the male species and the role they should play in a woman's life."

B.S.'s eyebrows lifted.

"I like the role Striker plays in my life just fine." Natasha nodded for emphasis.

"Well, sweetheart, from what I just witnessed, it looks to me like he fits the role he should play in your life just fine."

"No, Grammy, it's more than sex with us. He's also my friend, my mentor, my companion, my confidante, my soul mate, as well as my life mate. I not only love him, I respect the hell out of him."

B.S. looked bored. "You're young. You'll get over it."

Natasha bristled. "I thought you were going to Gatlinburg with Mom today."

Her grandmother's eyes roamed the room. "We decided today wasn't a good day for a trip."

"In other words, you had a fight."

B.S. chose not to respond.

Natasha pushed up out of her chair. "I need to leave. I've got to go talk to this banker about a dog show he judged."

B.S. looked interested. "You're investigating?"

Natasha nodded.

"I'll go with you."

At the bank, Natasha paused before entering the revolving glass door and gave her grandmother a wary look. "You *are* gonna behave?"

With an indignant glare, B.S. pushed past her into the building.

They stood in the lobby, studying the ornate fixtures, colorful flower arrangements, and marble floor, counters, and pillars. A gray-haired security guard ambled over and asked if he could help them.

Natasha handed him her business card. "I'd like to speak with Mr. Wright, please."

The guard led them to a sitting area arranged outside a group of offices and motioned for them to wait. He approached a stocky, middle-aged woman perched behind a simple wooden desk and spoke to her in a low voice, waving his hand in the general direction of Natasha and B.S.

The woman stared at them, then at the card the security guard handed her. After examining it for a moment, she said something to him and he disappeared. Glancing at the office door behind her desk, she rose and joined Natasha and her grandmother.

"Ms. Chamberlain?" she said, her eyes darting between the two women.

Natasha stood. "Yes?"

"May I ask what business you have with Mr. Wright?" Her nasal voice signified serious sinus problems.

"I'm investigating the disappearance of a dog at one of the shows Mr. Wright judged in the past. I'd like to speak with him for a moment about that particular show, see if there's any information he can share with me that would help in my endeavor to find the dog."

The woman's expression grew piqued. "Mr. Wright is an extremely busy man. Unless you're here to discuss banking matters, you'll need to call ahead and make an appointment."

Natasha resisted the urge to suggest that the woman go blow her dang nose. "How about I make one now?"

B.S. stood, drawing attention. "You'll have to excuse my granddaughter's lack of manners," she said in her most charming voice. "I'm B.S. Elliott."

The woman's demeanor changed from irritated to gushy. "The author?"

"Yes, that's me," B.S. said humbly.

Natasha glanced at her grandmother, knowing it was an arduous endeavor for her to act demure.

"Oh, my gosh," the woman said, her voice raised, her face flushed. "Just wait until Mr. Wright hears you're here to see him. His wife loves your books. Well, so do I. We talk about them all the time."

Natasha grew irritated. "Actually, she's just along for the ride. I'm the one who needs to speak with Mr. Wright."

A loud bang issued from the lobby of the bank, startling the three women.

"What in the world?" B.S. said.

Natasha grasped her grandmother's arm. "Get down, Grammy. That was a gun."

The woman who had been gushing over B.S. bent over, duck-walked into an office, and closed the door behind her as quietly as she could.

Natasha and B.S. watched in horror as two men with ski masks covering their faces strode into the lobby of the bank. Each held a gun in the air, with smoke wisping from the barrel of one of the firearms. The helpful security guard lay facedown on the floor in front of the revolving door. Natasha couldn't tell if he had been shot or was knocked unconscious. She quickly prayed it was the latter.

"Don't panic, just do what they say," Natasha whispered.

The men waved their weapons around in a crazed way, yelling at everyone to lie face down on the floor.

"You've got to stop them, Nat, before they shoot someone," B.S. said.

Natasha gave her a look of amazement. "You expect me to stop two armed men?"

"Of course, I do, sweetheart. After all, you're a bodyguard, aren't you?"

"That's two against one, Grammy. I don't think that would be a very fair fight."

"I know that, but from the stories you've been telling me, I doubt you would have much of a problem overcoming those two fools."

"Two crazy fools, Grammy. For Pete's sake, look at them," Natasha said, pointing at the two men.

Both men glanced toward the only other people standing in the bank. After waving his gun in their direction, the lead robber headed toward the tellers' stations. The other hurried over to Natasha and her grandmother, brandishing his firearm and yelling at them to get on the fucking floor or he'd shoot their brains out.

"Oh, really, can't you come up with something better than that?" B.S. said in a bored voice. "You sound like someone straight out of a B-movie. I wouldn't even put that in one of my books."

The man stopped in front of them. His mud-colored eyes glared behind the ski mask. Natasha moved to stand in front of her grandmother.

"Get down!" he yelled.

"Okay, Nat, you've been bragging about all these self-defense classes you've taken, along with your bodyguard training, about how well you can handle yourself. Here's your chance," her grandmother said, peeking around Natasha and pointing at the man in the ski mask.

Natasha looked at her. "Are you *serious*?"

"You seem to think you have the ability to protect another person. Well, sweetheart, I'm hiring you to guard my body. Take him out."

"You're crazy," Natasha said.

"Get on the fuckin' floor, lady," the man yelled, pointing the gun at Natasha's face.

Natasha tracked the other bandit, moving toward the open vault behind the tellers' stations. She turned to the one in front of her. "Do you mind? I'm talking to my grandmother and I don't appreciate your interrupting me."

He drew closer. "Get on the fucking floor."

Natasha's booted foot made contact with his groin. He didn't even see it coming. His eyes bulged and his hands, including the one holding the gun, converged at his genitals as he sank to his knees.

Natasha kicked the gun out of his hand. "Pull the friggin' trigger now, why don't you?"

B.S. watched the weapon clatter to the floor. She walked over and picked it up, holding it by the trigger guard.

The man doubled over, making gagging noises. Natasha checked the whereabouts of his partner; he'd disappeared into the vault. She circled around the gunman, as if studying an interesting specimen, before kicking him in the right kidney area. She waited for him to straighten up and quickly placed another kick to his nose. She watched him, now flat on his back, screaming as the blood from his crushed septum spurted onto his face.

The other man hurried out of the vault and approached at a half-run with his gun pointed in front of him. He stopped when B.S. aimed the firearm at him.

"I do believe what we have here is a standoff," Natasha said.

"Tshe brothe my thuthkin nothe," the robber on the floor wailed, struggling to sit up, holding his crotch with one hand and his leaking nose with the other.

"Shut up, you big weenie," Natasha said, "or I'll kick you again."

B.S. gave Natasha a proud look. "Well done, sweetheart."

"Thanks, Grammy," Natasha said, keeping her eyes on the armed man.

"Put the fucking gun down!" he yelled.

B.S. gave him a cocky look. "Why don't you make me?" she said, spurred by her granddaughter's actions.

Natasha reached behind and pulled her Glock .40 from beneath her blazer. "Okay, now, you got two against one," she said mildly.

The man's eyes widened when he saw what she held in her hand.

"So why don't you put your fucking gun down?" Natasha said sweetly.

"Why don't you make me?" he mimicked.

"Don't take your eyes off him, Grammy." Natasha glanced around. Bodies remained splayed on the floor, although people had their heads up, watching the scenario playing out between Natasha, B.S., and the gunmen. All the office doors were closed but she could see faces peeking through the beveled glass strips beside the doors.

"Did anybody in here hit the alarm button or call 911?" Natasha called out.

No one responded.

Natasha clipped her cellphone off her belt.

The armed man waved his gun at her. "You open that phone or move one step, you're dead."

Natasha hesitated.

B.S. stepped closer to the gunman. "You pull that *trigger*, you're dead."

Natasha dropped her cell into her jacket pocket. "Okay, what's it going to take to call an end to this standoff we got going here?"

No one answered.

"I mean, the way I see it, you shoot me, she's gonna shoot you. Or if you shoot her, I'm gonna shoot you. So either way, you're gonna get shot. You can't shoot both of us at the same time."

The man on the floor pointed at Natasha. "Thoot her."

Natasha scowled at him. "How about I shoot you just 'cause I feel like it?"

He closed his mouth and gave her a sullen look. The armed man's eyes shifting back and forth, along with the firearm, made Natasha nervous.

"Okay," she said. "How about we all put the guns down and you just leave?"

The robber gave her a crazed smile. "How about I leave with my gun?"

"You thant leathe me theere," the man on the floor whined.

"Yeah, what kind of a partner in crime are you, you leave your injured buddy on the floor, bleeding to death?" Natasha said.

"Yeath," the injured man said.

B.S. shook her head with disbelief. They watched the gunman think about this.

Natasha glanced at the robber on the floor. "I don't think he likes you so much."

"Hey!" the standing man said.

"You donth helth me, I'm thelling Momth on thu," the injured man said.

Natasha nodded. "Oh, you're brothers. Surely you're not going to leave your brother behind, injured as he is? What will your mother say? Dang, guy, have some principles, do something decent for once."

B.S. looked as if she couldn't believe this.

"Besides, you leave, who's to say I won't just go ahead and shoot the man? I mean, y'all have ruined my day, ruined the day for every person in here, I would think. I can't let you walk out and someone not pay for it, you know."

Sirens undulated in the distance, drawing closer. Natasha glanced toward the windows. "Whoever summoned the cops, I would like to thank you," she shouted. She turned to the gunman. "Okay, the cops are coming. Unless you want to be some SWAT guy's target in the next few minutes, I'd suggest you put your gun down and sit on the floor until they get here. What say?"

The man began backing up.

Natasha trailed him with her Glock. "Uh-uh."

He stopped moving, giving her an innocent look. "What?"

"You're thinking you'll grab a hostage, pick up someone off the floor, take them with you. Can't let you do that, guy. It's not going to happen."

The man looked disappointed.

"He was gonna do it," Natasha said to the man on the floor. "He was gonna leave without you. Just go, not try to help you at all. I think that's terrible."

"If I hadth my gun, I'dth thoot you righth now," the injured robber said in an angry voice.

"You tell him," Natasha said.

B.S. sighed.

"Put the gun down, go sit by your brother, and wait for your destiny like a good little boy," Natasha said to the gunman.

He backed away, shaking his head.

"Don't make me have to shoot you," Natasha said, hoping she wouldn't have to back down, knowing she couldn't pull the trigger.

The police crashed through the door, crowding into one another, frantically looking around the bank lobby. The armed robber turned his head in their direction and Natasha took the opportunity to snatch his gun out of his hand.

"Shit," he mumbled.

She engaged the safety and tucked it into the waistband at the back of her jeans. "Back here," she yelled.

Natasha was allowed to interview Mr. Wright while she waited for the police to take her statement. Although he seemed a little miffed with her, he was more than anxious to answer any questions she put to him, and he seemed greatly relieved when she told him she was through. Everyone *ooh*ed and *ahh*ed over B.S. but stayed as far away from Natasha as they could while giving her strange looks. Natasha couldn't figure out what that was about.

She was relieved to learn from the EMTs that the security guard had been knocked unconscious, suffering a slight concussion, which wasn't considered life threatening.

Striker arrived when they were winding things up.

"What took you so long?" Natasha said.

"I just now heard." He pulled her against him and kissed her hard and fierce. He ran his hands over her arms and back while his eyes inspected her body.

Natasha smiled at the concern on his face. "Everything's fine."

Striker's brow crinkled.

"What?"

"Why the hell didn't you call me? If I hadn't been in the car, listening to the news, I wouldn't have known anything about it."

Natasha shrugged. "I didn't want to worry you. Besides, everything was under control. How'd you know I was here anyway?"

"I saw your notes this morning, and when I heard there was a commotion going on down here, I figured that could only mean you."

"Hey."

Joining them, B.S. smiled at Striker. "Have you heard what a hero our Nattie is?"

Striker gave Natasha a look. "No."

Natasha glanced away.

"She stopped those gunmen from robbing the bank and saved everyone's lives," B.S. said with a proud look.

Natasha watched Striker's face while B.S. told him what had happened, including Natasha taking the gun away from the robber. She winced as his expression flowed from puzzled to worried to outright angry. She looked away when his dark eyes flashed toward her, knowing he was furious at how she had handled the situation.

After B.S. finished, she told Natasha she was going to go home, pack her bags, and take off.

"But I thought you were planning on staying awhile. I mean, we haven't even had the family conference yet."

B.S. gave her an indulgent smile. "I found out what I wanted to, so there's no reason to stay."

"Which was?" Natasha asked when she didn't elaborate.

"I think you've found your niche, sweetheart. You were born to be a bodyguard. I'm proud of you."

Striker walked away, shaking his head. "Damnation."

"Thanks, Grammy." Natasha kissed her, ignoring Striker's ire. "But what about my fee?"

B.S. looked confused.

"You hired me to guard your body and I did what you wanted me to."

B.S. glanced toward the bank of windows in front of the building, anxious to get to any reporters that might be hovering about outside. She didn't want to miss this chance to get her name in print, which in turn would help sell books.

Striker stood to the side, eyes hard, his lips in a thin line.

B.S. rummaged in her purse for her checkbook. "Certainly, sweetheart. How much do you charge?"

Natasha watched her grandmother gaze with longing out the window at a local TV news van parked across the street. "Apologize to Striker."

A shocked expression crossed B.S.'s face. "What?"

"You've been very rude to him. In your eyes, he may be only a man, but he's much more than that to me."

B.S. gave her granddaughter a cool look, then turned to Striker. "I apologize if I've been rude to you in any way, Mr., uh, Striker."

Striker gave her a faint smile.

B.S. kissed her granddaughter on the cheek and whispered in her ear, "I hope for your sake, sweetheart, he's everything you think he is." She began to make her way through the bank, signing autographs as she went.

Natasha looked at Striker. "In case you didn't notice, I did it the right way, the honest way, the way you keep telling me to do it, and look what happened."

Striker groaned.

Chapter 22

"Hey, girl, I like what you got going on with your hair," Natasha said.

Gloria smiled her thanks. After straightening her hair for years, she had decided to go natural and wore it short and curly, emphasizing her large brown eyes and high cheekbones.

"You think I could get my hair to do that?" Natasha said, fingering the fine strands.

"I hate to tell you this, girlfriend, but you're the wrong color."

Natasha grinned. "Yeah, I was afraid of that. Hey, you still got those earplugs I gave you?"

Gloria reached into her desk drawer and held them in the air.

"You better keep 'em handy, just in case," Natasha said before stepping into Striker's office.

Striker sat behind his desk, staring out the window, contemplating something that occupied his mind a lot lately—how to talk Natasha into marrying him. He didn't hear the door open or her footsteps and was surprised when she plopped into his lap, seeming to materialize from his very thoughts.

He smiled down at her. "Well, hey."

"Hey, back." She kissed him hello. "I brought us some lunch. Hope you didn't have plans."

"Nope."

"You hungry for deli?"

He gave her a lewd grin. "How about I have you instead?"

They shared a leisurely lunch, feeding each other between tender kisses and heated murmurings. Natasha was slowly returning to the real world when a glance at Striker's antique clock cleared her mind.

"Oh, shoot. I've got to get going."

Striker leaned forward. "I'm glad I got to see you," he said, his mouth on hers.

She smiled against his lips. "Yeah, boy."

While they were picking up their discards from lunch, Natasha said, "I finally found out more about the owner of the reserve winner from last year, that guy named Peterson. You know of a Ned Peterson, lives up on Norris Lake?"

Striker thought for a moment. "No, don't think so."

"He owns a bar right outside North Knoxville. A place called Hells Bells."

"What?"

"Hells Bells. I thought I'd head over there and —"

"You what?"

"I thought I'd see if anyone in there has seen Chumley or knows anything about the let —"

"Huh-uh, no way," Striker said, giving her a stern look. "You are not going in there."

Natasha frowned. "Why are you telling me no?"

"That's a biker bar, Natasha. Strictly a biker bar. You have any idea what sort of people hang out in there?"

"Bikers, I guess."

"Right. The one percent kind."

"One percent?"

"The legitimate criminal bikers, the one percent of the biking population that do get in trouble with the law."

"You mean like the Hell's Angels?"

"The original Hell's Angels. The criminal biking population."

"How can you tell they're one percenters?"

"They wear a patch or have a tattoo. I'm not kidding, they're the worst kind of bikers, dangerous as hell."

"Yeah?"

"You're not going."

Natasha glared at him. "You don't tell me what to do."

"It's too dangerous and I don't want you going in there."

"Hey, if I want to go in there, I'll go in there. You do *not* tell me what to do, Striker."

The vertical furrow between her eyebrows told Striker he was starting to tread dangerous ground. "Okay, why don't we do it this way? I'll send someone in there, an investigator who works for me, a man who will blend in with them, see what he can find out."

Natasha smiled. "Hey, I've got an even better idea. Why don't you go with me? I'll be your woman, we'll pretend we're bikers. That should be fun."

Striker wanted to look heavenward, but she had talked to him about that, so he forced himself to keep his eyes focused on her. "Forget it."

"But Striker, you're so big and intimidating and can look like a real badass when you want to, so you'd fit right in."

"Hell, no. You're not going in there."

Natasha put hands on hips. "Hey, this is my case, and if I feel the need to go there, I will go there."

Striker forced his voice to a reasonable level. "Listen to me, baby. Hear what I'm saying. They don't accept outsiders in there. You go in, you're gonna get in a lot of trouble. Now, come on, use your head here. Let me send someone in, someone who won't get made the minute they step through the door."

Natasha busied herself repacking her backpack.

Striker took her silence to mean acquiescence. "I'll even bill you for his time, if that will make you feel better." He watched her sling her backpack over her shoulder. "Don't get mad at me because I love you and want to protect you."

Natasha gave a reluctant shrug. "I know."

Striker pulled Natasha close and kissed her. Her response wasn't as passionate as it normally was, but he thought she was pouting, that she'd get over it.

Natasha waved at a grinning Gloria when she left. She stood waiting at the elevator, thinking this thing through. The one person she knew who would be more than willing to accompany her and not give himself away was standing inside when the doors opened.

"Pit." Natasha dropped her backpack and waited for him to step off the elevator. She put her arms around him.

Pit hugged back. "Hey, Nattie. How's it going, man?"

"Great. Hey, listen, you still got that Harley?"

"Yeah," he said, as if it were a question.

"You still keep it at Roger's?"

"Yep."

"You working on a case today?"

He shook his head.

"You think I could hire you to work on something with me?"

Pit thought about it. "I don't know. What's Striker say?"

"He told me he'd let me have someone and bill me for their time. But if you don't tell him, I'll pay you under the table. Striker doesn't have to know anything about it."

Pit grinned.

In the elevator, on the way down, Natasha told Pit why she needed him.

"That's a biker bar."

"Yeah, I know. Striker told me."

Pit looked as if he were thinking about saying no.

"Hey, you still owe me for that Happy thing, you know," Natasha reminded him.

Pit's expression grew suspicious. "Striker's okay with you going in there?"

"Well, he said he'd give me someone who would blend in, and I figured he had to be talking about you." She stepped back and eyed Pit, with his gargantuan stature, shaved head, and black goatee. He was dressed in his normal attire—black T-shirt under a leather vest, jeans, Western boots, and diamond stud earrings. "It had to be you."

Pit shrugged, agreeing.

"What about me? You think I'd blend in?"

Pit studied her low-riding jeans, cowboy boots, and cropped tank showing about an inch of abdomen under a jeans jacket. "Yeah, you could pass for a biker's woman, I guess."

"So I'll be your woman, okay? We'll be together. That will work, won't it?"

Pit shrugged. "Should."

At Roger's estate, Pit headed directly for the garage.

"Is Roger home?" Natasha asked, thinking she'd go in and say hi.

"Yeah, man, but I wouldn't go in there if I was you," Pit said, waiting for the garage door to roll up.

"Why not?"

"That weird woman's here, man, that grad student."

"Oh."

He gave her a look.

"*Oh.*"

Pit uncovered the bike, stood back, and gazed at it with pride.

"Oh, man, what a beauty," Natasha said, admiring the chrome, running her hand over the leather upholstery.

Beaming, Pit picked up two helmets and handed one to her.

Natasha strapped it on and waited for Pit to straddle the motorcycle. "Damn, I feel bad," she said with a wicked grin, climbing on behind him.

Pit laughed.

On the way to the bar, Natasha wondered why Striker didn't own one of these things. She liked the freedom the bike offered, the air hitting her face, the nice vibration going between her legs. She wondered if that was the reason so many guys liked motorcycles.

At the bar, Pit braked in the gravel lot, slinging small rocks and dirt in their wake. After Natasha stepped off, he put the kickstand down, leaned the bike over, and dismounted. Natasha handed her helmet to him. Tilting her head toward the ground, she shook out her hair.

They stared at the boxy wooden building. The bar appeared rundown, decrepit, as if it had been neglected for years. The windows were grimy, the once-white planks peeling to reveal wood bleached dull gray by the sun.

Natasha glanced at Pit. "You don't happen to have one of those one percent patches or a tattoo, do you?"

"Hell, no," he said, sounding offended.

"It's just, we might be accepted more if you had one of those things. You don't, by any chance, know where we could get one, do you?"

"Damn, Nattie, if I wore one of those when I actually *wasn't* a one percenter, I'd be a dead man walking, going in there. They don't take kindly to that."

"Okay, here's how we'll play it. We're together, trying to help out a friend who's lost her dog, and someone told her they saw it hanging around the bar."

Pit nodded.

"You packing?"

His hand fluttered toward his back. "Always."

Natasha reached around to make sure her Glock was tucked securely into the waistband at the back of her jeans, covered by her jacket. "Let's go."

They stood inside the doorway long enough to allow their eyes to adjust to the dimly lit room. The pungent, malodorous blend of beer, cigarette smoke, and sweat hung heavy in the air. Natasha resisted the urge to wave her hand in front of her nose, thinking that somebody needed to air this place out. The buzz of conversation going on when they opened the door ceased as everyone stared at the two intruders.

Natasha and Pit stepped into the room and crossed over to the bar, trying to act like bikers who belonged. The bartender took his time drying shot glasses while studying them. After a few moments, he ambled over and said, "What can I get for you?" around the toothpick tucked into the corner of his mouth.

Pit ordered a bottled beer. Natasha almost ordered water with lemon, but thought maybe that would look WASPish, so she ordered a beer, too.

Natasha glanced around at all the unkempt, hairy men in the place, each casting suspicious looks their way. The women gave them sullen glares behind bored eyes.

"How's it going?" Natasha said.

Pit grabbed her arm.

She turned to him. "What?"

"A biker's woman don't say nothing, not unless he gives her permission to," he said in a low voice.

"Oops."

Pit leaned down, put his hand on the back of her neck. He brought his face close to hers and whispered between gritted teeth, "Pretend I'm giving you hell for speaking. Act like you're sorry."

"I'm sorry," she yelled.

Pit released her.

"Damn, what century are they from?" she asked, *sotto voce.*

Pit ignored her.

They drank their beer and waited for conversation in the room to begin again.

Natasha leaned against Pit, uncomfortable with all the stares and continued silence. "You think they've made us?"

"We'll know it the minute they do."

A young woman with platinum blond hair showing an inch of black roots framing her heart-shaped face sidled over to them. She perched on the stool the other side of Pit.

"Hey, man."

Pit nodded but kept quiet.

The woman tilted her head in Natasha's direction. "That your old lady?"

Pit gave another curt nod.

Natasha studied the woman's long, tangled hair and slender build. She had a pretty face until she opened her mouth, revealing blackened teeth.

A stockily built man who looked to be in his late thirties wandered over to stand next to Natasha. His sandy-colored beard, mustache, and hair were long and uncombed. A conglomeration of tattoos covered his forearms and hands. Natasha couldn't make out the design on his large silver belt buckle for his bulging stomach. His black jeans, T-shirt, and boots had seen cleaner days, and a musty odor drifted off him. She surreptitiously edged away, closer to Pit.

"You here for a reason?" he asked Pit.

"Just passing through, man."

"That your hog out there?"

"Yeah, man. I've had that baby since I was a kid."

The man smiled, and he and Pit began talking motorcycles and the like. Growing bored, Natasha stepped back to allow the biker room to get closer to Pit while she half-listened to their conversation. She noticed the young woman watching her.

"That your man?" Natasha said.

"No, man, I'm just a sheep. I don't belong to nobody."

Natasha was curious what "sheep" meant but didn't dare ask. She stepped closer to the young woman. "I'm helping a friend try to locate her lost dog. I was wondering if you might have seen it." She fished in her pocket and pulled out a picture of Chumley.

The woman studied the photograph, twirling her hair between her fingers. "I don't know — "

"Did I tell you you could talk to her?" the man roared, startling Natasha.

The woman flinched.

The biker backhanded her, knocking her off the stool.

"Hey," Natasha said.

The woman cringed on the floor, holding her hand to her face. She gave the biker a look, as if maybe she liked this sort of treatment.

The man hauled her up and pushed her toward a small, wooden stage. "Get up there and do a strip."

A young male biker fed money into a jukebox and the room thrummed to a heavy bass. The woman slumped to the stage area, moving to the music with a detached apathy while she removed her clothes. Most of the men in the room watched her with listless expressions. The women ignored her.

Natasha glared at the biker. "What the hell do you think you're doing?"

"Nat," Pit growled, giving her a warning look.

The man turned to Pit. "Control your woman."

"Hey, nobody controls me but me," Natasha said.

Pit grabbed Natasha by the arm and dragged her with him toward the door. "I'll take care of this," he said over his shoulder.

"Let me go," Natasha yelled. She tried to squirm out of his hold but Pit only tightened his grip. Realizing he was too strong for her, Natasha stopped trying to pull away, knowing she was going to have one hell of a bruise where his hand clutched her arm.

Pit shoved the door open and hauled her over to the bike, Natasha cursing all the way.

"What the hell are you trying to do, man, get us killed?" he yelled, releasing her, glancing back at the bar.

Natasha pointed at the building. "You saw what he did to her. You gonna stand by while he beats up on someone, makes her strip? Huh?"

Pit yanked the helmets off the cycle and pushed one into Natasha's hands. "Hey, that's their world in there. That's what they do. She chooses to be there, to take that, ain't nothing I can do to change that situation, and I ain't even gonna attempt to, or I'll be hauled out of there feet first."

The male biker stepped outside the door and crossed his arms. "Don't look to me like you're taking care of anything," he shouted at Pit.

"Don't worry about it, man," Pit said, strapping on his helmet. "Once I get her home, she'll learn."

"Shit, man, that bitch ain't gonna learn nothing, not with a mouth like that," the biker said.

Natasha threw down the helmet and headed off.

"Aw, hell," Pit whined, and went after her.

"What'd you call me?" she said when she drew close to the biker.

"I called you a bitch, *bitch*."

"That's what I thought you said." She kicked his feet out from under him.

The man sprawled on his back in the gravel, wheezing.

"Shit," Pit said, sounding afraid.

Natasha leaned over the man, reached behind, and pulled her gun. Holding it against his head, she glanced up at the window. Several angry bikers were watching them.

"Go get the bike, Pit," she said.

Pit didn't waste any time breaking into a run.

She cocked the Glock and pressed the muzzle against the biker's temple. "Man, you need a bath. What woman in her right mind would have anything to do with the likes of you, I wonder?"

The biker grunted in response.

Natasha pulled out the picture and flashed it in his face. "I came here to ask one simple question and you have to go and ruin it all, make a fun day not so much fun anymore, you dick."

The biker looked like he might want to kill her.

"You seen this dog around?" she asked, as Pit pulled up behind her on the bike.

He glanced at the picture, then back to her, but remained mute.

"I like to shoot people, it don't bother me none. So, you want to give me a good day, make my day better, don't answer me, you asshole. I'll just shoot you in the head, coat myself in your blood and gore, and go home happy."

His eyes changed. Now he looked as if he thought Natasha just might be crazy.

"You seen him or not?" she shouted.

"No, I ain't seen nothing that ugly around here," he said in a raspy voice.

"Except maybe yourself when you look in the mirror." Natasha straightened, pointed the gun at the window, and watched the people move back. She brought it back to the biker with a grin. "Anybody thinks they're crazy enough to follow us, come on. I like a good gun fight." She climbed on the motorcycle behind Pit, yelling like a banshee and shooting the gun in the air as Pit exited the parking lot.

Pit drove as fast as he could to Roger's house without saying a word. Natasha grinned the whole way there.

As soon as the bike was parked, Pit gave Natasha a dark look. "Man, you are one crazy fucker," he said, heading toward the house.

"Well he shouldn't have hit that woman," Natasha yelled after his departing back.

Pit ignored her.

"Hey, Pit, you're not going to tell Striker, are you?"

Chapter 23

In her mind, Natasha genuflected against the fierce scowl Striker gave her when she stepped through his kitchen doorway. "I have had the worst afternoon ever," she said, trying for sympathy.

He approached her, eyes flaring. "Yeah? Well, I got news for you, Natasha, dear, it's about to get a whole hell of a lot worse."

And it did.

Pit had told Striker everything, including Natasha's lie about how Striker wanted him to help her.

"Well, actually, it wasn't a lie so much as I dodged the question and was maybe a little ambiguous about certain things," Natasha said.

Striker was incensed she had gone to the bar, even though he hadn't wanted her to, even though she had agreed not to.

"I never actually agreed," she said. "I just shut up about it."

He couldn't believe she had kicked that biker, had held a gun to his head.

"He hit that woman, Striker, then made her do a strip. What the hell did you expect me to do?"

Natasha watched Striker pace and yell, and grew defensive. Why couldn't he comprehend her reasoning? Why was he so mad? He would have done the same, after all.

"And what's with this acting like a nut, waving your damn, friggin' gun around, shooting the fuckin' thing, yelling like a mad woman? What the hell is with that?"

She shrugged. "I kind of got caught up in the heat of the moment."

Striker's eyes bugged. "What the hell is the matter with you?"

Natasha didn't know how to answer that.

"It's this case. Because of that perverted, idiotic dog, you're going around lying, beating up on people, manipulating people, shooting at people —"

"Hey, I didn't shoot at anybody."

"Okay, how about waving your gun around at people. What the hell is the difference anyway?" he roared.

She chose not to answer.

Striker stopped pacing and studied her. Natasha tried to give him a defiant look but failed miserably.

He drew closer and lowered his voice. "I want you to think about this, Natasha, and think about it long and hard. This case is affecting your integrity, it's affecting our relationship, it's affecting everything about you and me, and I want you off."

"What?"

He gave her an intense look. "Think about it. What's more important here—our relationship or this case? Because I cannot stand by and watch you get into any more of these crazy situations that are right on the verge of you getting seriously hurt. You got that? I refuse to do that anymore."

Before she could respond, Striker left the room. A few minutes later, banging sounds drifted down the stairs. She knew he was, metaphorically, beating up on her once more.

Natasha sat down, wondering if he was serious. Of course he was. This was what he had wanted all along. Okay, she had to admit, she had lied, she had manipulated, she had kicked the guy — but hey, he deserved it — she had gotten a little bit carried away with the gun. Well, maybe more than a little bit. Okay, so maybe this case had made her act a little bit too extreme. Maybe.

Did he really mean that—the dog or them? The answer was simple. She would choose Striker over anything. *But wait a minute.* What right did he have to make her choose? Would it be that easy for him to give up something he had committed himself to, for her? But she would never put him to that test, she thought, somewhat haughtily. Then again, he was concerned for her safety, and she did seem jinxed with this case for some reason.

Natasha didn't know what to do. She could call Myrtle, she supposed, tell her she was backing off the case, and refer her to someone else. But then she was giving in to Striker and his wants, and what about *her* wants? Okay, she wanted him more than anything. However, if she caved in here, if she let Striker have his way on this…well, what would be next? Why couldn't he understand that this was her job, this was what she had chosen to do, even though she was growing tired of this particular case? It seemed to be nothing but a dead-end, and a jinxed one at that.

Cat jumped onto her lap and settled down with a contented purr. Natasha stroked the pet, considering her options. This was what she'd do. She'd leave Striker a note. She didn't want to face him; she was too emotional right now, too vulnerable, and she might cave in. Plus she knew how he reacted to her tears and that wasn't fair to him. So she'd tell him in the note how much she loved him, how much he meant to her, but that she had an obligation to remain with the case. She would promise to be more careful, not so impulsive, to listen to him more and accept his guidance. Maybe that would appease him. But he wasn't being fair, asking her to choose. He had to understand that.

Natasha put Cat on the floor, found paper and a pen, and wrote a long note to Striker. She declared her love, offered her compromise, and ended by asking him to call her if that was agreeable, implying if it were not and she did not hear from him, that would be that.

She placed the note on the counter by the refrigerator, gave Cat a goodbye kiss, gathered up her backpack and keys, and left by the back door.

Natasha drove to Roger's mansion to confront Pit, knowing that if she went home, she would have to endure a visit from her mother and listen to her say, "I knew this was going to happen," before continuing on to the infamous cow-and-free-milk lecture, the same one she had heard too many times to count.

Pit was where she knew he would be, in Roger's kitchen, eating, with Bigun right alongside him. She slammed into the room, glaring at Pit. "I hope you're happy."

"Huh?"

Bigun said, "Hey, dudette, what's wrong?"

"You big old tattletale," Natasha shouted, ignoring Bigun. "Bet you couldn't wait to get in here and call Striker and tell on me, you jerk."

"Hey," Pit said.

"And now, thanks to you, I got Striker giving me ultimatums, you squealer."

"Hey."

"You make me sick." Natasha plopped down in a chair and sent Pit an angry look.

"Listen, man, you're getting carried away with this case," Pit said. "You got to be reined in, or you're gonna get yourself in a whole hell of a lot of trouble, you keep going at it the way you are. And we all know the only one can rein you in is Striker."

"Says you."

"And besides, who the hell do you think you are, coming in here yelling at me, acting mad? I'm the one who should be mad at you. You lied to me."

Bigun's eyes traveled back and forth between the two of them, giving them a confused look. "Dude, dudette, what happened?"

"You could have gotten my ass killed out there today," Pit continued, ignoring his friend. "Knocking that biker down, all those other bikers in there. It's a wonder they didn't all start shooting. It's a wonder we both aren't dead."

"Yeah, and you just had to go and tell Striker, didn't you?"

"Hell, yeah, I told Striker." Pit pointed a finger at her. "You're out of control, Nattie."

"Says you." Natasha leaned toward him and said, her voice low, "Thanks to you, Pit, Striker is probably finished with me. The love of my life will no longer be such, and if that's the case, I will be the most miserable wench on earth. So let me assure you, Pit, dear, it will be my intention to make sure you're just as miserable as I am." She lunged to her feet and stalked out of the room.

"Hey, you're the one put you there," Pit called after her.

Natasha pretended she didn't hear him.

Later that evening, Roger noticed a strip of light shining beneath Natasha's bedroom door at the end of the hall. He told Misty he'd be back in a minute and walked in that direction, curious about his best friend being there. He gently pushed the door open. Natasha sat in the rocker in front of the window, her knees drawn up to her chest, staring out, looking lost.

"Hey, Nattie," he said.

Natasha glanced at him and he saw the tears glistening. Roger stepped into the room and closed the door. He didn't see Misty watching with a frown on her face.

Roger sat on the window seat in front of Natasha. "You okay?"

Natasha didn't answer; she was too busy trying to keep from bursting into wailing sobs.

"What happened?" Roger said.

She told him, in between the crying bouts.

"Oh, Nattie, I'm sorry. He'll call; you know he will. Striker loves you too much to end it like this."

Natasha gave him a forlorn look. "I don't know, Roger. He's pretty upset with me."

Roger didn't know what to say. He reached over and patted her on the shoulder. "I'm here if you need me. You know that." He left to join Misty.

Late that night, looking for sympathy, Natasha called B.S. at her home in Atlanta. She grew irritated when her grandmother sided with Striker and went on to remind Natasha she had a real problem controlling her mouth as well as her temper. When B.S. asked her to repeat the bar story, in greater detail, Natasha grew suspicious.

"Why do you want to hear about the bar fight?" she asked in a piqued voice.

B.S. told her she was thinking about using it in one of her books.

"Oh, for the love of Myrtle," Natasha said and hung up.

Chapter 24

Natasha tried to keep her mind off Striker and her constant angst about his not calling by focusing on the investigation into Chumley's disappearance. The next morning, she paid a visit to Ned Peterson's home, located on wooded acreage fronting Norris Lake, a popular body of water thirty minutes outside of Knoxville. She hid behind a large oak and smoked cigarettes while studying the log-cabin-style house, its weathered logs and dark-green, aluminum roof blending with the forest surrounding it. A sliver of blue water shimmered about a hundred feet from Peterson's front porch. She took the time to appreciate the view, thinking that this had to be one of the prettiest lakes in Tennessee.

A chopper sat in the driveway alongside a white monster SUV. She glanced about, listening for signs of life. It seemed preternaturally quiet here. She wondered about that and decided everyone must still be in bed.

She crept closer to the house, searching for Chumley. Staying low to the ground, moving a few feet, stopping and listening before continuing on. She reached the back of the house and peeked inside. Staring into the kitchen area, she admired the bright color scheme, combining yellows with blues. A small dog waddled into the kitchen, and her heart lightened, thinking it was Chumley. The mutt looked toward the window and she almost sagged with disappointment. The dog perked its ears and began yipping in a high voice.

"Shoot." She got the hell out of there.

Sitting on her bed at Roger's mansion that evening, smoking more cigarettes, Natasha again pored over the names from the previous year's show, checking out the locals, trying to find a way to rule each one in or out. Okay, Jerry Dawson, the attorney/nudist, was still a suspect, but so far, zilch. The same went for Ned Peterson, the bar owner. That Happy chick was definitely ruled out. Fourth in Best in Show last year was a woman named Sondra Blain who lived in Knoxville and worked for the county clerk's office in the marriage license department.

It would be easy enough to pay a visit to the bureau, show the woman a picture of Chumley, and find out if she knew where the dog could be. No, wait; if the woman had Chumley, of course, she wasn't about to reveal anything to her. Natasha thought about it and soon hit upon an idea.

The next morning, she went downstairs early, hoping to find Roger in the kitchen. Instead, Bigun was there with his head stuck in the refrigerator.

He looked around when he heard movement in the doorway and smiled her way. "Dudette."

Uh-oh.

"Hey, Nattie, you feel like making pancakes?"

Natasha was going to tell him she didn't have time but remembered there was some information she wanted from him. "Sure, dude," she said with a smile.

They sat together at the table, Natasha watching Bigun wolf down a stack of pancakes covered in butter and syrup, picturing his arteries slowly clogging. She listened to his mangled compliments and said, "There's something I've been wanting to ask you, dude."

Bigun smiled around his food and nodded for her to continue.

"I've been wondering why y'all thought that Happy was so good. I mean, is there something she does that maybe other women don't know about?"

Bigun's brow crinkled.

Natasha sighed. "Hey, I made your breakfast, you know. Plus you haven't paid me the fifty back yet, and if you'll just tell me what the heck was so great about her, I'll forego that."

Bigun considered this while chewing. Natasha rolled her eyes. He finally swallowed. "Okay, dudette, I'll tell you."

She smiled.

"But I won't owe you the fifty anymore, right?"

"Right."

Bigun forked more pancakes into his mouth.

Come on, Natasha thought.

He shrugged. "I don't know, dudette. I guess she's so good 'cause she did everything. I didn't have to do a thing."

"I can't believe I paid you fifty dollars to tell me nothing."

"It's true, dudette."

Natasha eyed him with suspicion.

"Honest."

She leaned toward him. "Tell me, step by step, what she did, Bigun, or I'm gonna throw your pancakes down the garbage disposal."

Bigun checked his plate to see how much was left. He gave Natasha a resigned look. "Okay, first, she gave me a body massage."

"I hope so, for fifty bucks."

"Then she washed me, you know, down there." A flush crept up his face.

"Well, that's probably more for her benefit than yours."

"Well, yeah, but it felt good, real good."

"Okay, what'd she do next?"

"Well, you know, I just laid there while she, you know." Bigun looked away.

Natasha leaned toward him. "Performed oral sex?"

He looked relieved. "Yeah, dudette, while she did that."

"Is that all she did?"

Bigun's gaze wouldn't meet hers.

Natasha grew frustrated. "What'd she do, dude? Go 'round the world? Stick a corncob up your butt? Set a ferret loose in there? What'd she do?"

Their eyes locked.

"What?"

Bigun sighed. "Okay, she went 'round the world, but I didn't have to do anything. That's what was so great about it. I just laid there and let her, you know, get me ready and do all the work."

Natasha drew back. "Are you *serious*? That's what it takes to make you guys happy? Just let you lie there while we service you? Is that what you want?"

"Sure, dudette, didn't you know that?"

No, she didn't know that. Was Striker like that? No way. He was too physical when they made love, too kinetic, too involved to want to just lie there, too — *Don't think about it,* she told herself. Besides, what was the point of wondering about it anyway? He hadn't called and they weren't together anymore. Tears sprang to her eyes.

Bigun crammed the rest of his pancakes into his mouth, trying not to look at Natasha. "Hey, dudette, it's late, I've got to get going," he said over his shoulder, hurrying away.

Roger wandered in just as Bigun left. He sent a sleepy smile in Natasha's direction, shuffled to the cupboard, pulled out a box of cereal, and tucked it beneath his arm. Moving to another cupboard, he took down a bowl, pulled open a drawer, removed a spoon, and placed it in the bowl. He scuffed to the refrigerator for the milk and retired to the table.

Natasha kept her back to Roger, wiping her eyes. After she had herself under control, she turned to her friend and gave him as bright a smile as she could manage.

Roger returned her smile, shaking cereal into his bowl. "Hey, Nattie, what's going on?"

Natasha watched him pour milk over the dry food. "Roger, I was wondering if I could ask you something."

"Sure, Nattie, anything," Roger said, scooping cereal into his spoon and raising it toward his mouth.

"Would you marry me?"

Roger's eyes widened. He dropped his spoon into the cereal and glanced upward.

So Misty was around. Natasha watched Roger fidget and gulp while his face reddened.

"I don't mean literally," she said, feeling a little disappointed he wasn't jumping at the chance, as he once might have.

He looked relieved. "Oh, okay."

"The lady whose dog came in fourth place at the cluster last year works downtown at the marriage license bureau. So, what I was thinking, why don't you go down there with me, act like you're my fiancé, and on the pretense of inquiring about a marriage license, I'll try to work the conversation around to Chumley and see what happens."

Roger stared at his uneaten cereal.

"I'm not asking you to actually buy a marriage license, for Pete's sake," Natasha said.

Roger looked relieved. "Sure, Nattie, I'll marry you."

Neither one noticed that Bigun had just stepped into the kitchen. Hearing this, he quickly backed out of sight and began to eavesdrop.

Natasha hugged her friend. "Thank you, Roger. You're the best."

"When do you want to go to the marriage license place?"

Bigun clamped a hand over his mouth, fearful he would make some sort of sound and give himself away.

"How about this afternoon? Myrtle and I are paying another visit to the animal shelters this morning to look for Chumley, but we should be finished by noon. So, say, one o'clock?"

"Sounds good to me."

Natasha leaned forward and kissed him on the cheek. "I really love you, Roger."

"I love you too, Nattie." He straightened up with a worried look. "Wait a minute. What's Striker going to say?"

Natasha's face fell into the hurt expression she'd been wearing so much lately.

"Oh, Nattie."

"He's made it clear he doesn't want anything more to do with me, so what can he say? It's none of his business anymore." She rose from her chair, tears in her eyes. "I need to get going, Roger. I'll be back around noon or so."

"I'll be here."

Bigun breathed a sigh of relief when Natasha left through the kitchen door. If she had chosen the front door, she would have caught him slinking down the hall, trying to get away. He hurried upstairs, thinking he'd go back to the kitchen and get his cellphone later. For now, he needed to find Pit.

Everyone in the office had complained about Striker's foul mood, so Scott sent him to Atlanta the day before on the pretense of overseeing a case, but really to get him out of the way. Gloria sat at her desk, feeling a little antsy, knowing Striker was headed back into town, hoping he was in a much better frame of mind than when he left. Pit and Bigun appeared before her, interrupting her thoughts.

"Hey, fellas. What's going on?" she asked, noticing their glum expressions.

"Where's Striker?" Bigun said.

"Driving back from Atlanta."

"Hey, man, have you heard anything about Nattie and Roger getting married?" Pit asked her.

Gloria stiffened, a shocked expression on her face. "You're kidding."

The two bodyguards gave her solemn nods.

"Bigun overheard her and Roger talking this morning," Pit said. "They're going to the marriage license place today at one, gonna buy a license, get married."

Gloria looked upset. "But Nattie doesn't belong with Roger. She belongs with Striker."

"Yeah, man, that's what I said," Pit agreed.

"Is that why he was so mad? Is that what's got him so upset? I thought he only had a spat with Nattie. I didn't think it was this serious."

"That's what we thought," Pit said, feeling guilty, knowing he was the one responsible for the quarrel.

Bigun shook his head. "No, dude. Nattie asked Roger to marry her this morning, so Striker couldn't have known anything about it."

Gloria's voice rose with alarm. "Nattie asked *Roger*?"

Scott had been sitting in his office with the door open, watching the conversation at Gloria's desk. Curious about the look on her face, he joined them.

"What's going on?"

"Did you know Nattie and Roger were getting married?" Gloria said.

"What? Nattie doesn't belong with Roger. She belongs with Striker."

"Yeah," three other voices agreed, all nodding.

"Does Striker know?"

"No, dude," Bigun said. "I heard Roger ask Nattie what Striker would say if he found out, and she said it didn't matter, he didn't want her anymore, that it wasn't any of his business."

They stood around, considering that.

"Then why the hell's he so upset, if he doesn't want her?" Scott said. "I thought it was the other way around, the way he was acting."

The others shrugged in response.

Scott read their expressions when they focused their attention on him. "Hey, I'm not going to tell him."

"Well, somebody should," Gloria said. "What if this is all a misunderstanding on their part and Nattie marries Roger and puts an end to them forever? Y'all know she needs to be with Striker. They love each other. And if she marries Roger, Striker will never forgive her, you know that. So you can't just sit back and let her do this. She should marry Striker."

Scott thought this thing through. Maybe he'd better let Striker know, in case Gloria was right. If it had been a misunderstanding and he didn't tell Striker what was about to transpire and Natasha married Roger, then Striker found out about it later — or what's worse, found out he knew and didn't tell him — well, he didn't want to think about it. "Where is he?"

"He's on his way in from Atlanta. He should be here by noon," Gloria said.

"They're getting the license at one, dude," Bigun said.

Scott reached over, picked up Gloria's phone, and dialed Striker's cellphone.

Striker answered on the second ring, sounding in a worse mood than when he left.

"Striker, it's me," Scott said, glancing at the others. "Listen, there's something I need to tell you."

"Wait, wait." Gloria put her hand on Scott's arm and pulled the phone away.

"What?"

"Tell him to pull over. Don't tell him while he's driving; he might have an accident. You know how he gets when it comes to Nattie. He's not his normal self."

Striker yelled into the phone, but they ignored him.

"Yeah, you're right." Scott brought the phone up to his ear. "Striker, you need to pull over and call me back after you're stopped."

Striker sounded panicked. "What? What the hell happened? It isn't Natasha, is it? She's all right, isn't she?"

Scott hung up the phone. They stood looking at one another, waiting for it to ring.

It took only seconds. Scott snatched up the receiver before the receptionist even thought about it. It was Striker, wanting to know what the hell was going on.

"Are you pulled over?" Scott said.

"Yeah, I'm off to the shoulder. What the hell are you doing, scaring the shit out of me like that?"

"I didn't mean to, but we all know how upset you can get when it comes to Nattie."

"Where is she? What's happened? Is she all right?"

"Yeah, yeah, she's fine. We just now found out something and figured you might need to know. Of course, you might not care at this point, if what Nattie told Roger is true, but still, we thought it best you —"

"Will you shut the fuck up and tell me?"

Gloria and the bodyguards gave one another uneasy looks, hearing this.

Glad this was being done over the phone and that he wasn't facing Striker, Scott said, "Okay, I'll tell you. Did you — I mean, we — well, Bigun overheard a conversation between Nattie and Roger, and it — well, it seems they're planning to get married."

"They what?"

"They're going to get the license today."

"They're what?"

Scott didn't know what else to say. "That's what Bigun heard them talking about."

"Let me talk to Bigun," Striker said.

Scott held the phone out to the huge bodyguard. Bigun backed away, shaking his head.

Scott gritted his teeth and hissed, "Here, talk to him."

With trepidation, Bigun gingerly took the receiver and put it to his ear. "Hey, dude, what's happening?"

"Tell me the conversation, word for word," Striker said, his voice low, his speech pressured.

And Bigun did, as best he could remember. Of course, he made it sound worse, especially the part where Natasha and Roger said they loved one another. Without saying a word, Striker disconnected.

Bigun stared at the phone. "He hung up."

Pit said, "Hey, man, I don't think I want to hang around here, not with Striker coming in mad like that."

"Yeah, dude, he sounded pretty upset," Bigun said.

Gloria stood. "I'm not feeling so well. I think I'll take a sick day."

"You bunch of cowards," Scott called after them. He hurried to his office, trying to come up with an appointment that would take him out of the office for the rest of the day.

Returning home shortly after noon, Natasha entered the kitchen through the back door. Pit and Bigun sat at the table, preparing sandwiches.

"Hey, guys. I forgot to charge my cellphone last night and the battery's dead. Did anybody call for me this morning?"

Both men glowered at her while shaking their heads.

Natasha forced a smile on her face to hide the defeat she felt. "Okay. You seen Roger?"

They didn't answer, continuing to glare.

"What? What'd I do?"

"It's not what you did, dudette. It's what you're *gonna* do," Bigun said.

"Hey, man, you need to think this thing out," Pit said.

Natasha didn't know what they were talking about, but she was in a rush and didn't want to take the time to get into anything with them. "Sure, I'll think about it," she said, and left.

Pit and Bigun returned to their sandwiches, debating what they should do next. When Pit's cellphone bleeped, both jumped.

Pit glanced at the display. "Oh, man," he whined, before answering.

"Where are you and what are you doing?" Striker said.

"We're at Roger's, man, eating lunch."

"Where's Natasha?"

"She and Roger just left."

"Why the hell didn't you stop them?" Striker yelled at the top of his lungs.

"Hey, man, if Nattie wants to marry Roger, I can't stop her. You know that."

"All right, listen. I've been calling her all morning but she's not answering —"

"That's 'cause her cell's dead."

Relieved she wasn't ignoring him on purpose, Striker said, "Oh, okay. Listen, I'm still half an hour outside of Knoxville. You and Bigun get down there, try to talk some sense into her. Tell her to wait for me; I'm coming. I want to talk to her first."

"Well, I'll try, man, but I got to tell you, this is Nattie we're dealing with, and you know how stubborn she gets. Besides, she's still mad at me for telling on her the other night. She'll probably do it just to spite me."

"I don't care what you have to do. I don't care if you have to blow the friggin' building up. You get your butts down there and keep her from getting that license or I'll be all over you and it will *not* be pretty," Striker raved into the phone.

"But she's back on the cigs, man. You know how she gets when she's doing smokes. She's not gonna —"

"Are you still sitting in that fucking kitchen?"

Pit surged to his feet. "We're gone."

"Why'd you have to tell on her, dude? Why'd you have to start this mess?" Bigun said, looking forlornly at his unfinished sandwich.

Natasha held Roger's hand as they walked toward the Marriage License Department in the City-County Building, hoping the lone woman standing behind the counter with her back to them was Sondra Blain. If not, she guessed they'd have to hang around until Sondra showed up. When they reached the counter, the woman turned toward them. Natasha glanced at her nametag, relieved to see this was, indeed, Sondra Blain. Just as Natasha opened her mouth to speak, Sondra snatched up a ringing telephone.

"What?" Sondra blared into the phone. Natasha and Roger exchanged uneasy glances. Sondra listened for a few minutes, her face growing hard. "Are you kidding me?" she asked with disbelief. "You choose to tell me this on the worst day of my life, the day your father informs me he's leaving me, the day your brother gets suspended from school for fighting. And why the hell do you think it'll be any better living with your dad, who is one sick bastard, let me tell you?" Apparently she didn't like the answer, because she slammed the phone down without responding. She seemed to notice Roger and Natasha standing before her, trying to act as if they hadn't heard a word.

"What?" she said.

Natasha forced a smile on her face, which withered under the woman's belligerent stare. She backed up a step, wondering if she had offended her somehow. Roger squeezed her hand reassuringly.

"Um, we're here to inquire about a marriage license," Natasha said.

"Biggest mistake of your life," Sondra huffed. While she robotically barked out the procedure for obtaining the license and the proper form that was required, Natasha glanced around, trying not to look at the woman, thinking maybe they should come back at a better time. Her gaze landed on the framed picture of a dog on the desk behind the counter. She nodded at it.

"What a beautiful dog," Natasha said.

Sondra ignored her as she searched for the form they needed to complete.

"I'll bet you show that dog, as pretty as he is."

Sondra raised her head with a scowl. "It's a she."

"Oh." Shoot, if she only knew my life's just as miserable as hers is, I bet she'd be nicer, Natasha thought.

Sondra pulled out the form. "Okay, here's what —"

"Do you show that dog?" Natasha said.

Sondra glared at her.

Natasha decided that as angry as this woman was, maybe the honest approach would be best. "Actually, I'm looking for a champion show dog. He's turned up missing, and I was thinking, if you show her, maybe you've seen him around." She fished in her purse for the picture of Chumley.

Sondra's face began to redden and she stepped back with a baleful look in her eyes. "Are you saying I took a *dog*?"

Roger put his hand on Natasha's arm and drew her closer.

Natasha thought her accusation had been subtle, so Sondra's response must signal possible guilt. "No, of course not. I was just wondering if you knew this dog, if you've seen him around." She held the picture out for Sondra to see.

Sondra's eyes darted to the photograph. "All I got going on in my life, you think I have time to steal an ugly mutt like that." She leaned closer to the picture and her eyes narrowed with recognition. "I'd like to know how in the world that ugly, squat creature took the prize away from my beautiful, elegant Sophie," she said, her voice rising in pitch, a finger jabbing at the air.

We got motive, Natasha thought. She decided to push some more buttons, see what developed. "Listen, lady, if you know where this dog is, you need to tell me. That's a federal offense, you know, kidnapping a dog." She didn't know if it was or not, but it sounded good.

Sondra lurched toward the counter, but seemed to catch herself. She stood rigid, her fists clenched, her mouth pinched into a thin, hard line, her face crimson.

"Nattie," Roger said in a warning tone, watching the clerk's bulging eyes.

"Just tell me where he is and I'll go get him. I won't report you to the police," Natasha said appeasingly.

Natasha and Roger were shocked to see such a short, stocky woman move as quickly as Sondra did. She lunged over the counter and grabbed Natasha just as she turned to flee. Sondra's weight propelled Natasha forward, onto her hands and knees. She landed on Natasha's back, flattening her out. She grabbed Natasha's hair and slammed her face into the floor.

Roger tugged at Sondra in an effort to pry her off Natasha. Sondra, in the spirit of the battle now, endorphins charging right and left, backhanded him, catching him square in the stomach. Roger flew back, hit a wall, and slumped down.

Striker drove like a madman, running red lights and weaving in and out of traffic. Ignoring the "No Parking" sign, he braked to a stop in front of the City-County Building and shot out of his SUV. He didn't notice Pit and Bigun passing by, searching for a parking space. He ran into the building and, hearing all the commotion, raced toward the source, knowing that could only be Natasha in one of her crazy situations.

A portly woman straddled Natasha, her hands in Natasha's hair, slinging her head into the carpet. Striker went a little crazy when she saw this. He ran like a lunatic, pushing people right and left.

"Get off her!" he roared at the woman.

She ignored him, ramming Natasha's head into the floor one more time.

Natasha was beginning to see stars. "Help," she said in a muffled voice.

Striker put his hands over the woman's hands and held them. "You don't get off her, I'll make you," he yelled in her face.

The woman gave him a sinister look. "Yeah? Why don't you just try?"

Pit and Bigun lumbered over to them. In one smooth motion, they yanked the woman off Natasha. After handing her off to a security guard standing nearby, watching all this with a shocked expression on his face, they picked Roger up off the floor.

Groaning with relief, Natasha turned over, wincing with pain. "My back. My head."

Striker held three fingers in front of her face. "How many fingers do you see?"

She tried to focus but couldn't. "What fingers?"

"That's it. You're going to the hospital." Striker plucked her off the floor and carried her outside to his vehicle.

"Who are you?" Natasha asked him once, which frightened him. He didn't know she wasn't serious, that this was her way of getting back at him for not calling.

Forced to remain in the waiting room while the emergency room technicians sent Natasha upstairs for a CAT scan of her head, x-ray of her back, and whatever else they deemed necessary, Striker paced back and forth, nearly out of his mind with worry. He ignored Pit, Bigun, and Roger, thinking how much he hated that damn dog. This was it. This time, Natasha was off the case, even if it meant he had to hog-tie her.

When they finally allowed Striker to see Natasha, he found her on a bed in an examining room. Her face was pale and sweat was beading on her forehead, already showing the first hints of bruising.

Striker put his hand in hers, leaned down, and gave her a chaste kiss. "How are you feeling?"

Natasha responded with a weak smile. "I'm a little bit nauseous, but the doctor said that's going to pass."

Striker pulled over an examining stool, sat down on it, and gently touched her face. "What's the doctor told you?"

"I don't know. They're waiting for the radiologist's report."

Striker nodded.

Natasha glanced past him at the door. "How's Roger?"

"He's okay. Got the wind knocked out of him, but he's fine now."

Tears shimmered in Natasha's eyes. "I thought I'd never see you again."

Unable to contain the question, Striker said, "Why'd you do it, Natasha? Why'd you leave me like that?"

She gave him a surprised look. "Didn't you read my note?"

"What note?"

"The one I left on the counter by the refrigerator."

He frowned. "I didn't see a note."

"I wrote it right before I left," she said, wondering what had happened to the note.

Striker was curious about the same thing. Giving up on that, he leaned forward and stroked her hair, thinking how much he loved this woman. "Tell me what the note said."

By the time Natasha finished, Striker was rubbing his face and mentally kicking himself for being so utterly stupid. He knew he had hurt her, but it had been unintentional.

She brushed away tears. "I'm sorry. I should have just told you but I couldn't. I wanted you to decide this on your own, without having to witness any emotionality from me."

"I thought you were through with me," Striker said, trying to conceal the anguish in his voice. "I thought we were over."

"I could never be over you, Jonce," she whispered.

He gave her a lingering kiss. *Wait a minute.* He drew back with a scowl. "Well, then, what's all this shit about you marrying Roger?"

She hesitated.

"Well?"

The doctor entered the room, directing their attention to him and granting Natasha a reprieve.

Chapter 25

Striker had been instructed to wake Natasha every two hours and ask her who she was, where she was, what day was it— enough to ascertain that her brain hadn't swelled. Each time he woke her, she gave him the right answers, to his great relief. He held her while she slept, constantly thanking God for placing her in his life, and stayed awake most of the night, worried about her. Toward dawn, he began to wonder about the note she had left and what could have happened to it.

They slept through the morning, no longer having to wake every couple of hours to make sure Natasha's brain was functioning normally. Striker rose at noon, curious about the note, and headed downstairs to the kitchen.

Natasha joined him, dressed in one of his T-shirts and nothing else, looking tousled and cute. She asked him what the heck he was doing with the refrigerator pulled out.

"I was wondering what happened to the note."

"Did you find it?"

"No. Where exactly did you put it?"

"Over here, on the counter, right by the refrigerator."

Striker considered that. "Then what'd you do?"

Natasha thought back. "I got my backpack and keys and left."

"By the front or back door?"

"This one."

Striker found a piece of paper, put it on the counter by the refrigerator, opened and closed the back door. The breeze this created lifted the paper into the air and sent it skittering over the floor and underneath the breakfast bar.

He got down on all fours and felt beneath the bar. His hand touched paper, and he pulled the blank one free. He fished around again and found the note. He stared at it for a moment before looking at Natasha.

"You mind if I read it?"

"I want you to."

Striker sat down on the tall stool by the cooking island while Natasha busied herself making coffee. He seemed to take a long

time reading the note. Finally, unable to stand it, she darted a
glance at him and saw he was watching her. She turned to face
him.

"What would you have done?"

"I would have gone and gotten you."

"I hoped so."

"I really love you, Natasha. You know that, don't you?"

She answered by smiling at him. But *uh-oh*, Striker's eyes were
flashing now.

"So what's this with you and Roger getting married?"

Natasha sighed and told him the plan.

He gave her a look. "Damn, Natasha."

She shrugged. "I know."

Striker shook his head. "This case is so fucking out of
control."

She crossed over to him. "I suppose you still want me to
quit."

"Yes."

"Does the ultimatum still stand?"

"No. It was stupid of me to even think that."

She nodded.

"Natasha," Striker reached out and pulled her against him.
He gently touched the bruises on her forehead before resting his
lips there for a brief moment. "This case is jinxed for you. How
many times have you gotten hurt? What will it take for you to
understand this is one job you need to back away from?"

"Can I ask you something?"

"Sure."

"How many cases have you backed away from?"

She had him there.

"If it were you, would you quit, just give it up?"

"I don't know. I know I'd want to quit, get rid of it, pass the
curse on to someone else." He gave her a concerned look. "I'm
worried for you. How many times now have you ended up in the
hospital? That woman yesterday could have killed you if she had
hit you the right way."

"But darlin', hasn't it occurred to you that I'm the one who
gets myself into these situations? It's not the dog or the fact that the
case is jinxed, it's me."

Striker shrugged. He didn't want to consider that.

"You were right about me, you know," she said.

He waited for her to tell him what she meant.

"I was way out of control. I see that now." She gave a small sigh. "I'm sure you've noticed I have a tendency to get caught up in a situation and lose all sense of rationale. That's one reason I need you so much, Jonce. You keep me grounded."

Striker put his hand on the back of her neck, pulled her to him, and kissed her.

"Why does this have to be so hard for us?" Natasha said, tears gathering.

"I just want you safe, baby. That's all I want."

Later that afternoon, Natasha reclined on a lounge beside the pool, nursing her wounds. Striker had gone to the office at her insistence. His hovering over her and worrying about her got on her nerves. There was tension between them now; with a little resentment on her part and a moderate amount of guilt on his. But she thought that probably wouldn't last long; at least, she hoped not.

Her cellphone rang, startling her. She answered, thinking it was Striker calling to check on her.

"Opened your mouth to the wrong person, I hear," her mom said.

"Mom. Who told you?"

"First, tell me how you are," Stevie said.

Natasha spent the next ten minutes assuring her mother she was fine, rolling her eyes while Stevie dispensed medical advice. When her phone beeped, she said, "Mom, someone's calling in, hold on a minute." She clicked over.

"Hey," she said, expecting Striker.

A man said, "I got your dog. It's gonna cost you if you want him back."

Natasha sat up. That voice sounded vaguely familiar. "Who is this?"

"Ain't none of your business. You want him or not?"

"Of course I want him."

"Bring ten thousand dollars in small bills in a black garbage bag to Northwest Middle School in North Knoxville. You familiar with it?"

"I've jogged the track there a few times."

"Where the track goes next to the woods, you'll see a dogwood tree with a red ribbon dangling off a limb. Put the garbage bag behind the tree, then leave."

"Not without Chumley."

"I'll be watching you. If you do what I tell you, he'll be in your jeep when you get back to it."

"How do I know you actually have him? I mean, I'm not leaving ten thousand dollars for anyone until I have proof."

"The mutt has a problem with table legs," he said.

"Well, I'd say a lot of dogs do."

"He can't stop farting."

"Again, I'd say a lot of dogs —"

"Okay. He's got a tag on his collar."

"Give me the number."

He read it off. Natasha had memorized it and knew it was correct.

"When do you want to do this?" she asked.

"This afternoon at five."

Shoot. The place would be packed with kids playing in the fields, and joggers and walkers would be using the track. She glanced at her watch. It was coming up on three o'clock.

"That doesn't give me much time."

"You got enough time. The banks don't close till four."

"Okay, I'll be there." Natasha hung up, forgetting all about her mother, still holding. That voice worried her. Where had she heard it? Who could it be? She debated getting the money from Myrtle. That would be the safe thing to do, but how could she ensure Chumley would be returned unharmed? And why in hell had the kidnapper waited so long to call? Wait a minute. How did he know she drove a jeep? It had to be someone she had come in contact with, or who had been watching her, or trailing her.

Omigosh. Barry Dugan.

Natasha hurried into the house and changed into jeans, a sleeveless tee, and sneakers. She left after arming herself.

Natasha parked on the street behind Dugan's house. She cut through yards, approaching from the rear. She huddled behind the leaning structure in the back yard to watch for any signs of life. Glancing at her watch, she noted it was now four o'clock. He would probably leave in fifteen minutes to half an hour. Staying low to the ground, she darted from tree to bush, advancing toward his residence.

When she reached the side of his house, she flattened herself against it and sidled along the length. A woman in the house next door glanced out a window and her mouth formed a shocked "O". Natasha put one finger to her lips and shook her head. She slipped around the corner and onto the porch, praying that the woman wasn't a friend of Dugan's who would call to warn him. She crawled beneath the windows to the front door. Standing beside it, against the wooden planks, she reached into the pocket of her jeans and waited.

Fifteen minutes later, the screen door banged open and Dugan stepped out, Chumley in hand. Natasha sprayed his eyes with pepper mace.

"Shit," he yelled, dropping the Pug. Natasha barely managed to catch Chumley before he hit the concrete flooring.

Dugan pawed at his streaming eyes, making mewling sounds.

"I'll get water if you'll calm down," Natasha said.

Dugan sank to his knees. "Give it to me. Hurry."

Natasha sprinted to the small flowerbed in front of the house. She turned on the water faucet, dragged the water hose onto the porch, and handed it to Dugan. While Dugan flushed his eyes, she checked the Pug for injuries, smiling at his happy response to her. Finding the little dog unharmed, she placed kisses over Chumley's wrinkled face. She put him on the porch behind her and told him to stay. He lay down with a grunt.

Natasha pulled her gun. After making sure the safety was engaged, she placed it against the side of Dugan's head. He stopped whimpering and froze, slicing his reddened eyes toward her.

"The pain you're feeling is at best one-tenth the pain poor Ben went through when you blinded him," she said, startled to find herself almost angry enough to pull the trigger.

"Hey, I didn't hurt that horse. Whoever told you that's shittin' you."

"Yeah, right. But we'll discuss that at a later time. For now, why'd you take the dog?"

Dugan dribbled more water over his eyes. "Thought I could make some money breeding the thing, but damn, who can stand putting up with the way he smells? Plus, the little fucker doesn't know what to do with a bitch. He'd rather hump a table leg."

Natasha tried not to smile. "That why it took so long to demand money?"

"Hey, champion dogs with good enough breed points can bring in big money, but he wouldn't cooperate. I was cutting you a deal."

Natasha shook her head. "You doofus. You didn't have the papers to prove he was a champion, or even registered, for that matter."

"I could, though. I got friends who know how to do those things."

"Sure you do. How'd you get my cellphone number?"

Dugan squeezed his eyes shut and opened them wide several times. "I called the dog's owner, told her I needed to talk to you about the dog."

"And Myrtle bought that?" Natasha asked with disbelief.

"It didn't take much to get her to give it up," he said.

With a shake of her head, Natasha pulled out her cellphone and dialed 911. She reported Dugan, the kidnapping, and his attempted demand for ransom. Dugan made movements to stand, but she pressed the gun tighter against his temple. He settled down with a disgruntled look, mumbling something about what he'd like to do to her with his rifle.

She cocked the gun. "Okay, before the cops get here, let's get some things straight. First off, I don't understand why you abuse animals, nor do I want to understand. If it's 'cause your mama punched you when you were little or your daddy took his belt to you, get over it. Stop the cycle. Secondly, you aren't gonna get any money; you don't have the brains for it, so don't try this again. And I see any more animals in your yard or hear about you having any in your house, I'm coming back here and we're gonna have us a serious conversation." She nudged him with the gun barrel. "You hear what I'm saying?"

"You damn bitch," he snarled.

"I can be that. And I see you following me in traffic anymore, I'm gonna come after you with my own rifle. Understand?"

"Well, quit dumping shit on my porch and maybe I'll leave you alone. You started this shit."

Natasha thought about it. "Okay. How about I'll leave you alone if you promise me, on your death, that you won't own any animals, harm any animals, and/or try to kidnap any animals. If you do that and stay true to your word, you'll never see me again. But if not, I'll be back, and I won't be as passive as I was before." She nudged him with the gun. "Well?"

"Okay."

"No, make the promise."

"Okay, damn it, I promise," he said, glancing up at the street at the police car turning into his driveway.

Natasha returned Chumley to Myrtle, smiling at their happy reunion.

"Oh, my dear Natasha, I can't thank you enough," Myrtle said, with tears in her eyes.

Natasha told her about Dugan's thwarted demand for ransom.

Myrtle hugged Chumley closer. "Well, dear, Chumley certainly looks fine. He hasn't lost any weight that I can tell."

Natasha shook her head at this, thinking it probably wouldn't have hurt Chumley any if he had.

"And he's acting like his old self, so I don't think he's suffered any kind of trauma," Myrtle continued.

"Thank goodness," Natasha said, thinking of Ben.

"Do you think this Mr. Dugan is the one who sent the letter?"

With a sigh, Natasha told Myrtle about her past history with Dugan.

Myrtle's expression relayed disappointment. "Natasha, dear, I'm afraid I have some bad news for you."

Uh-oh.

"It seems you haven't had any luck at all finding who sent that terrible letter, and, well, dear, you seem to keep getting yourself injured and into situations I wouldn't consider normal at all."

Natasha couldn't disagree with her statement, which depressed her.

"I don't think there's a need for any further investigation. No one has actually hurt Chumley or even tried to. Well, except this Mr. Dugan, and that's your fault, dear."

Natasha almost protested at this but found she couldn't. Myrtle was speaking the truth.

"Maybe the letter was just a threat and nothing else. So, it's probably best not to worry any further with the issue, wouldn't you think?"

Well, that solved Natasha's problem with Striker. "Unless a threat develops, you're probably right."

"I'm sorry this case has been so difficult for you, dear."

"Oh, well." Natasha's mind turned to Roger's case and the problems she had run into with that one. She was beginning to wonder if she shouldn't find another vocation.

"Send me your most recent hours and I'll mail you a check."

After kissing Chumley goodbye, Natasha left, humiliated at being fired. Shoot. This was only her second case. She hadn't even solved the damn thing and she'd been fired twice now. Was she good for anything?

As she headed home, feeling discouraged, Natasha's cellphone rang. She picked it up and muttered a depressed, "Hello."

"Nat, sweetie, it's Grammy," B.S. said.

"Oh, hey, Grammy. What's going on?"

"I just talked to your mother and she tells me you were attacked yesterday and nearly knocked unconscious. Are you all right, sweetheart? I've been so worried."

Ah, how sweet. "I'm fine, Grammy. I have a little bit of a headache, but that should go away soon."

"I'm so relieved, sweetheart. Listen, as long as I've got you, maybe you can help me out."

"Uh, sure. What do you need?"

"Describe for me what you felt when that woman attacked you and then after the attack. Both mentally and physically."

"What?"

"This will fit in perfectly with a manuscript I'm working on at the moment, and what better person to relay the attackee's feelings than one who has suffered through virtually the same thing?"

"Heavens to Mergatroid," Natasha said.

When Natasha told Striker what happened, he didn't know what to think. He was furious that she had faced Dugan alone but relieved to hear she was once more off the case. The fact that she felt so distressed over her ineffectual attempts to solve it and at being fired twice tamped his angry response to the Dugan situation. So he found himself comforting her instead of giving her hell for acting like a nut and taking on a man like Dugan by herself. He decided he'd save that conversation for later, when she wasn't feeling so bad. But, of course, he never got around to it.

Chapter 26

Natasha decided to contest the charges the police officer levied against her when she tripped him to keep him from taking Chumley. The day of her court appearance, she stood in Striker's bedroom wearing a black lacy thong and nothing else.

"What should I wear?" she asked in the direction of the open bathroom door.

Striker stuck his head around the doorjamb. Even with shaving cream covering the lower half of his face, he couldn't hide his lewd admiration of her body.

"Wear that and I guarantee the judge will let you off."

She gave him a frustrated look.

He shrugged. "I don't know. Wear something professional. Well, maybe something casual would be better. Hell, Natasha, I've seen people show up in bathrobes. I don't think it really matters." His head disappeared into the bathroom.

Natasha thought about it. *Okay, professional.* She'd look sophisticated, like she knew what she was doing. But wait—that might send the signal she was doing very well for herself financially, even though she wasn't. She didn't want anyone to think that, especially not the judge, particularly when a fine could be involved. Okay, the casual look. Khakis and a sweater? Jeans and a T-shirt? She rifled through her clothes in Striker's walk-in closet, wondering how in the world so much had accumulated there in so little time. She startled when his hands caressed her bare buttocks.

Striker nuzzled the side of her neck. "What time's your case?"

"I'm supposed to be there by nine."

His hands moved up to cup her breasts.

She leaned back against him and sighed. There was no better bra in the world than Striker's large, warm hands. His lips were against the nape of her neck now, and she felt a part of his anatomy inching toward a part of hers.

"I don't have time," she murmured. "I've got to find something for court."

"I know." His hand slipped inside the thong.

"I should have thought about this last night," she said, her voice barely a whisper, her lips seeking his.

When she came to herself, lying next to Striker on the floor of the closet, both doing some heavy breathing, a thought nudged her mind that there was something she needed to do that morning. She sat up. Striker reached out and stroked her back.

"Oh, shoot." She was due in court in less than an hour and she still didn't know what she was going to wear. She made a wild dash for the bathroom. Returning a few moments later with a warm washcloth, she dropped it over Striker's lower abdomen.

"Damn, baby, you have got to quit enticing me with that beautiful body of yours," Striker said in a lazy drawl, watching her don her panties, thinking how much he liked the sexy underwear she wore, not to mention the way she looked in them.

Natasha took the time to roll her eyes at him while stepping into a denim skirt. She pulled a pink cotton sweater over her head and slid her feet into sandals.

Striker stood, nodding.

"What?"

He eyed her legs. "That ought to do it."

She gave him an irritated look, running her fingers through her hair. "What is the matter with you?"

Striker leaned down, kissed her lips. "You."

Natasha darted past him, heading for the bathroom to apply lipstick. After giving him a quick smooch, she was gone.

Striker slid in beside Natasha, sitting on a bench near the back of the courtroom.

She looked surprised to see him.

"I thought I'd come offer support," he said.

She smiled.

"They haven't called your case yet?"

She shook her head.

He glanced around. "Where's Tommy?"

Natasha was silent.

Striker turned and stared at her. "You didn't call him."

Her eyes drifted away. "No."

Striker stiffened.

She returned her gaze to his. "I can't afford an attorney, Striker. You know that."

"I told you I'd pay." His voice was louder than it should have been and several people glanced their way.

Natasha lowered her voice to a whisper. "I know, but it's not right, you paying for my legal defense. Besides, this is General Sessions Court. It's not like some federal big-time court, so I figured I'd represent myself."

Striker shook his head.

She leaned toward him with a confident look. "Hey, I can do it."

"You can get yourself in a whole hell of a lot of trouble, you know that."

"Listen, I'll tell the judge my version of what happened, that stupid-upid officer will tell his version, and the judge will decide in my favor." She settled back with a smile.

"Yeah, right. Using legal terminology like stupid-upid ought to do it."

Natasha frowned.

"You better let me call Tommy."

She gave him a stubborn look.

Now Striker frowned.

Natasha's case was called, saving further argument. She flashed white teeth at her love, rose, and walked toward the front of the courtroom.

Striker moved to the first row.

Natasha and the police officer stood before the judge studying them over the rim of his bifocals. His pallid complexion, bald head, and hooded eyes reminded Natasha of a squat, albino frog dressed in a black, billowing robe. She glanced at the nameplate, which read Judge Weiser. That frog-beer commercial came to mind, and she resisted the urge to ask him if his first name was Bud.

"Does defense have counsel?" Judge Weiser asked Natasha.

"No, Your Honor. I'm self-employed and unable to afford a lawyer, so I'm here representing myself." She gave him a bright smile.

The judge ignored that, shuffling through papers. "You have been charged with assault of a police officer."

"Yes, sir."

"And you plead?"

"Not guilty, Your Honor. I don't see how tripping and falling into this man would constitute assaulting him."

"A simple guilty or not guilty will do, and thank you very much," Judge Weiser said in a singsong voice.

Natasha felt eyes on her and turned. The policeman was glowering at her, so she glared back.

Judge Weiser peered at the officer, then at Natasha. "All right. Let's hear what Officer Comer has to say. Then we'll hear your side of things, Ms. Chamberlain."

Natasha stopped scowling at the policeman and addressed the judge, sounding like a child complaining about a sibling. "Why does he get to go first?"

Judge Weiser gave her an *oh-please* look, which she ignored. He huffed into his microphone and spoke in a patient tone. "Because, Ms. Chamberlain, he made the charge against you. After he's told us his version regarding what happened, you can tell us your version."

"Oh, well, okay, that's fine," she said, her tone insinuating the opposite.

Natasha listened to the officer tell the judge that on such and such a day, at such and such a time, he had been trying to take one certain dog into custody due to a violation of the leash law —

"That's an outright lie, Your Honor."

Comer gave her an indignant glare. "It is not."

"Ms. Chamberlain," the judge intoned.

Natasha turned to him.

"As I've already stated, we'll hear what the officer has to say about what happened on the day in question, then you'll get your turn."

"Yes, sir."

"Now —" the jurist began.

She pointed at the policeman. "But tell him to quit lying, Your Honor."

Judge Weiser scowled. Natasha grew quiet.

"Go ahead," Judge Weiser told the officer.

Who then proceeded to tell how he had simply been approaching the dog that had been in violation of the leash law —

"Liar," Natasha said.

"Ms. Chamberlain, please." Judge Weiser gave her a flustered look.

Natasha resisted the urge to roll her eyes.

"Proceed," he said to the officer.

The officer went on to explain that when the defendant, Ms. Chamberlain, had attacked him, to keep him from —

"Your Honor, I object."

The judge threw his hands into the air in frustration.

"I did not attack him, sir. I was trying to move out of his way. Well, kind of, in a way. And I tripped and fell against him and we both went down. Actually, sir, you could say he attacked me, if you wanted, the way he yanked me up, not to mention how he dragged me over to the police car and threw me in the back."

"That's a lie and you know it," Comer shouted.

Natasha turned to face him. "You're just mad 'cause that humane officer cussed you out."

"Am not."

"You're mad 'cause you told the humane officer a lie, told him Chumley hadn't been on a leash, and when he investigated, he found out differently."

"That's a lie."

"I don't lie. You're the liar."

"No, you are."

"Quiet," the judge screamed, banging his gavel.

Striker only shook his head.

Natasha and Comer stopped glaring at one another and turned back to face a furious Judge Weiser.

"I will ask you once, and only once, to refrain from hurling insults at each other," Judge Weiser warned. "Do not address one another. Address me. Do not look at each other. Look at me. Do not point at one another. Do not point at all in my court. Am I clear?"

He should have been a drill sergeant with that voice, Natasha thought. "Yes, Your Honor," she replied meekly.

The whole courtroom was quiet now, with everyone watching and waiting to see what was going to happen next.

"All right," Judge Weiser breathed. "According to Officer Comer, as he was attempting to take the violating dog into custody —"

"Which he had no right doing to start with." Natasha gave an emphatic nod.

Judge Weiser leaned over his podium, his small eyes piercing hers.

"Sorry, Your Honor," she said in a small voice.

"As he was attempting to take the violating dog into custody, he was assaulted by Ms. Chamberlain." Judge Weiser glanced at the officer. "Am I right on the facts as they now stand?"

"Hell, no," Natasha said.

Judge Weiser banged his gavel. "There will be no profanity spoken in my Court."

"I'm sorry, Your Honor," Natasha said. "But I cannot tolerate liars, and he's done nothing but lie —"

Comer jabbed his finger at her. "If anyone in this courtroom's a shittin' liar, it's you."

"Hey. You don't call me a shittin' liar, not if you want to live."

"Shut up. Shut up. Shut up. Damn it," the judge shouted, emphasizing each word with his gavel.

Everyone stared at Judge Weiser, red-faced with rage.

He pointed his gavel at Natasha. "What did I tell you?"

"He said the cuss word. I didn't."

Comer gave the judge a beseeching look. "Yes, she did."

"You said it first."

"Yeah, but you've said two cuss words now to my one."

"You're not only a liar, you're a profane liar."

"Shut up, you fuckin' cunt," Officer Comer yelled, leaning close to her face.

Natasha drew back, offended.

Striker half-rose and then forced himself to remain seated, resisting the urge to pound that shithead's face into the floor.

Glowering, the judge slammed his gavel down once more. "You, sir, are in contempt of court."

Comer's face turned bright red. "I'm sorry, Your Honor."

Natasha, for once, was quiet.

Judge Weiser turned to her. "And what say you, Ms. Chamberlain?"

"Your Honor, I'd like to begin by saying I'm a bodyguard by profession."

"Not surprising," the judge scoffed.

Natasha ignored that. "And I had been hired to guard Chumley, the dog in question. That particular day, I had taken Chumley for his daily walk and he had…well, defecated in a woman's yard. And she wanted me to clean up the mess, but I didn't have anything to clean it up with. So I was going to go back to Chumley's owner's house to get something, and first thing I know, she's chasing me down the street —"

"Ms. Chamberlain, stick to the facts, please. Did you or did you not attack the officer?"

Natasha drew herself up. "No, sir, I did not attack him by any means. I simply objected to his taking Chumley into custody. I didn't know police officers could legally do that. I thought that had to be done by a humane officer, who, in fact, when he came upon the scene, determined that Chumley had not violated the leash law, I might add."

She waited to see what the jurist thought about that. Apparently not much, judging by the look on his face.

Natasha cleared her throat. "As I said, I had objected and was moving toward Chumley to protect him. I'm his bodyguard, but I think I told you that already."

The judge's eyes wandered toward the ceiling. So did Striker's.

"And I kind of tripped, Your Honor, and fell into Officer Comer. And next thing I know, he's yanking me up and throwing me in the back of his police car and charging me with assault." Now she sounded upset. "He took me to jail, Your Honor, had me thrown in this prison cell. I'd never been in jail before."

Striker found it ironic that she neglected to tell the judge about her hip-hop danceathon.

Natasha swiped at her eyes. "And I could have been raped or beaten up. You know what goes on in those places."

The judge frowned.

"It was horrible," she said, her voice cracking. "I was scared out of my mind, all because I tripped and landed against him. And if that wasn't bad enough, when I got out, the woman who owns the dog fired me."

Striker and Judge Weiser scowled at the officer.

"And that's all I have to say, sir." Natasha cast her eyes downward, looking helpless to everyone except for the policeman, whose clinched fists indicated he just might like to do some heavy pounding in her direction.

Judge Weiser thought for a moment. "Did anyone think to bring witnesses?"

Natasha mentally slapped her forehead. *D'oh.* Why hadn't she thought of that? "Your Honor, if I could have a continuance, I'm sure I could have several witnesses here who were present that day and saw the whole thing."

Judge Weiser looked at the crimson-faced officer, who shook his head.

"What we have here, I do believe, is a he-said, she-said situation." Heaving a sigh, Judge Weiser rubbed his jaw while he studied the two before him. "Okay, here's what I'm going to do. I dismiss the case against Ms. Chamberlain. Although she has failed to produce witnesses on her behalf, it appears that Officer Comer has not presented anyone to corroborate the alleged assault. And since there was no violation of the leash law, as determined by the Humane Officer, Ms. Chamberlain's objection to taking the dog into custody was a valid one. But I'm fining the both of you a hundred dollars each for using obscenities in my courtroom."

Natasha held up her hand. "Your Honor, if I might point something out to you, I have a slight objection here."

"Shit," Striker mumbled.

"You yourself said a curse word, sir, and he used the worst obscenity in the world, in my book, whereas I only used the one, sir — well, maybe two, but the second time, I was repeating his curse word. But I think he should receive a heavier fine because he used the C word. Or at least be made to apologize."

The judge's eyes bulged, making him look even more frog-like.

"Never mind, sir," she said, hurriedly. "I withdraw my objection."

"You two better hope to hell you never have a case in my courtroom again." Judge Weiser threw down his gavel and stomped off the bench.

Striker stepped between Natasha and the officer, who were back to glaring at one another.

"I think you owe the young lady an apology," Striker said, appearing ominous, towering over the rookie policeman.

"I'm sorry, okay?" Comer glanced at Natasha, then away. "Shit, I'm gonna be the laughingstock of the whole force now," he added, lumbering off.

"As well you should be." Natasha got out before Striker clamped his hand over her mouth.

"You never learn, do you?" he said.

"What? What'd I do?"

Chapter 27

Natasha lounged in a recliner on Striker's pool deck, a pocket calculator in her hands. Okay, Myrtle's latest check should last her maybe another month if she lived frugally. She didn't have to worry about paying rent on the cottage her dad had built for her, thank the good Lord and her dad. She was rarely there, which meant her electric bill should be minimal. Laying aside money for her office rental, cellphone, computer payment, electric bill, and the bare essentials, she could last at least another month before she needed to begin worrying about finding a new client. However, if something came along in the meantime, that would be even better. If not, she was having way too much fun to complain.

Tossing the calculator to the side, Natasha settled back and turned her face to the sun. This is the life, she thought while doing a checklist in her mind. Physically, she felt great. Emotionally, she'd never been better. And sexually… oh, *wow*. That was one area that never disappointed with Striker in the picture. She smiled, thinking about him. She figured from the way he was treating her that he was still trying to make it up to her for insisting that she back off the Chumley deal, even though it had been a real relief to her to let go of that jinxed case. And, boy, did she like how hard he was trying.

Natasha picked up her glass and sipped iced tea. She breathed in the sweet scent of mown grass, reminding herself to retrieve the clippings from Striker's lawn mower bag for the horses. Her gaze wandered from the silver-tinted river to the large, irregularly shaped pool and onto Striker's house.

She really loved his place. The style was contemporary, with brick and copper facades, angled so that the south and west sides faced the winding river. Windows and glass doors predominated throughout in order to encapsulate the view of the river or the wooded area surrounding the north and east sides. Spacious and filled with light, all of the rooms sported white oak floors with large, stone fireplaces in the great room, kitchen, Striker's office, and his bedroom. Brightly colored Native American crafts and artwork were displayed abundantly throughout the rooms. And Natasha, thankful that Striker gave her free rein and encouraged her to decorate if she felt so inclined, had added her own feminine touch here and there.

She sighed, laid her head back, and closed her eyes, thinking she could stay here forever and never grow tired of it. Her mind turned to the one concern that dominated her thoughts—her need, not to mention her lust, for Striker. She loved this man more than anyone or anything, and she was terrified that she would allow herself to become dependent on him. It would be so easy to let him care for her as he wanted, hang out here during the day waiting for him to come home at night. And oh, Lord, the *nights*...

The phone rang, interrupting her thoughts. Natasha snatched it up, hoping it was her love calling to say he was taking the afternoon off.

"Natasha, dear, it's me," Myrtle said.

Natasha's face fell. "Hello, Myrtle, dear. What's going on?"

"Well, dear, there's something I need to discuss with you."

"Okay."

"I'm afraid last time we talked, I might have told you a little white lie."

"You did?"

"Yes, dear, when I said there was no need for any further investigation. Actually, Natasha, my intentions were to hire another person since you seemed so jinxed with this case."

What? Natasha sat up.

"And I did hire someone. A man. But dear, it just hasn't worked out."

Uh-oh.

"So I'd like to rehire you to guard Chumley at the cluster a week from today."

Natasha sighed inwardly. *Well, shoot.* If she said yes, that would probably cause another upheaval in her relationship with Striker, just when things couldn't be more perfect.

"Are you there, dear?"

"Uh, yes, Myrtle, I'm here. And actually, to be honest, I'd rather you stayed with the other investigator. Like you said, I'm jinxed with this case for some reason, so I'd rather stay out of it."

Myrtle was silent in response. Natasha waited her out.

"Well, dear, I was hoping I wouldn't have to go into this with you, but you did sign a contract stating you would guard Chumley at the show."

Now Natasha was quiet.

"And I've discussed this with my attorney and he says everything is legal and binding and that you should perform the duties you contracted to do. If you don't, you're in violation of the contract."

"But you fired me. That should have made the contract null and void."

"Well, dear, actually, I fired you from any further investigation. I don't think we discussed the cluster."

"Striker's going to kill me."

"That nice- looking young man you're seeing?"

"Yes. He thought, like we did, that I was jinxed and wanted me to step away from the case."

"But this isn't Striker's decision, dear."

"Well, no. But he does have a point. I mean, after all, how many times now have I ended up in the hospital?"

"Maybe so. And I hope I'm not interfering in your business, dear, but you're making a drastic mistake if you're letting some man dictate to you what you should be doing with your career."

Natasha sat up straighter. "What?"

"It's obvious you love the man, but really, if you're going to allow him to tell you what to do this early in the relationship, I hate to think what's in store for you down the road."

"It's not like that at all."

"Maybe not from your perspective, dear."

"Look, Myrtle, let's leave Striker out of this. I was glad you fired me. Okay? I'm tired of getting hurt. It's a dead-end case, anyway. Like you said, there probably is no threat in actuality, so I see no need for me to —"

"If you don't guard Chumley at the show, I'm suing you," Myrtle said in a hard voice.

Natasha stared at the phone. *What happened to the "dears"?* "You wouldn't."

"Yes, I would, and I also intend to ask that I be reimbursed all the funds I've paid you to date."

Natasha's mouth dropped open. Oh, no. She had already spent most of that. How in the world would she ever come up with the money to —

"And I have the right. I have the contract to prove everything. I have an attorney ready —"

"Okay, I'll subcontract it out to Pit or Bigun. You know them, Myrtle. They're capable. They can handle it, probably better than I've been able to."

"I'm afraid I can't agree to that. I insist that you be the one to guard Chumley."

"Why the heck does it have to be *me*?"

"Well, apparently you're the only one Chumley feels comfortable around. He's had such a hard time with this other man. And as I'm sure you're aware by now, Chumley is very picky about the people he chooses to like."

Natasha chewed her bottom lip.

"I need an answer now, dear," Myrtle said.

Oh, so, we're back to dear again, huh? "I can't think about it?"

"No, I'm afraid there's not enough time. But if you say no, let me remind you, you'll be receiving a subpoena within the next day or two to appear in court and explain to the judge why you are refusing to abide by the contract."

Visions of Judge Weiser danced in Natasha's head. "All right, already. I'll be there."

"Oh, dear, thank you so much," Myrtle said, cheerily. "Why don't you come over this afternoon and we'll talk specifics?"

After disconnecting, Natasha stared at the phone, wondering how in the hell she was going to explain this to Striker.

Chapter 28

Striker stared out his office window, weighing things out in his mind, more than a little baffled at the depth of his feelings for Natasha. Women used to be nothing more than a pleasant distraction for him, a means to an end, but all that had come to an abrupt halt with this relationship. He wondered how in the world Natasha could make him feel like an awkward teenager with one look or a horny adolescent with another. If he wasn't thinking about her, he was thinking of things he wanted to do for her, or with her, or *to* her.

He loved Natasha deeply and knew in his heart he would never feel this passionate or intense about anyone else. And that was just fine with him. But he was sick to death of Natasha going to her house or over to Roger's place. Not a week passed that she didn't do that. She never stayed with him continuously. He wanted her with him; he didn't want to share her anymore. He knew how selfish this thought was, but she was his world now. There was no one else, and he needed to know if she felt the same toward him. He *had* to know.

Okay, he'd propose marriage to her. She loved him; she told him enough, showed him enough. So maybe it was time, maybe she was ready. Maybe — please, God — she would say yes.

His thoughts turned to the engagement ring he'd happened upon less than a week ago. Displayed in the window of an exclusive jewelry store, the ring had caught his attention, and he entered the shop, curious about the price. He liked the band's antique style, which appeared to be interwoven vines turned silver with age. A white diamond glistened brightly in the center of the band, like a delicate flower nestled within the vines, not too large, not too small. It was just perfect, Striker thought, knowing Natasha's dislike for big gems and gaudy jewelry. He purchased the ring on the spur of the moment, rationalizing he would keep it for later. He'd been carrying it in a velvet envelope in his pocket ever since. That ring bothered him, lying there, covered up. He would at times take it out and study it, envisioning it on his beloved's finger.

Okay, he had the ring. What about the proposal? Natasha was a romantic; she'd proved that enough by the things she did for him. So he couldn't just say, kind of as an aside, *Hey, what do you think about us getting married?* That would go over like a ton of bricks. The proposal had to be in a romantic place, at a romantic time. He considered this, images playing in his mind. Taking her to dinner, asking her there. No, that was too public. What if she said no? Okay, he would make intense love with her the way they did sometimes — well, a lot — that always got her crying and talking about how beautiful it was, how much she loved him, loved loving him. And afterwards, still joined with her, he'd ask her. No, that was a bad idea. She would probably say yes in the heat of the moment and later think he had exploited their lovemaking to get her to agree, that he'd caught her in a vulnerable mood.

He decided to ask Gloria what she thought and rose from his chair, then paused. What if she told Natasha he had sought her advice on how to propose? Knowing what a stupid idea that was, he sat back down and continued to ponder.

Okay, she loved the boat, loved to go cruising. Loved to make love on the boat. He'd suggest a boat ride. Maybe go to Calhoun's. Their food was great. Natasha liked to eat there on the deck overlooking the water. Have a fine meal, order some wine, and head back home on the cruiser. Find a cove and pull into it. Take her down into the galley, where he'd have a bottle of champagne on ice. He straightened in his chair, getting into this. *Yeah, that was good.* Have the ring resting in the bottom of her glass, pop the cork, kiss her, and ask her if she would pour while he wiped his hands or something. She'd pick up her glass, see the ring sparkling at the bottom and... He grinned. Perfect. He snatched up the phone.

"Hey, sweetie, what's going on?" Natasha said, sounding happy to hear his voice.

"Nothing much, gorgeous. Just thinking about you."

"So what's up?"

"How about we take the cruiser and go upriver tonight, stop off at Calhoun's, have some dinner, then go back home? What do you think?"

"Oh, gosh, didn't I tell you?"

"Tell me what?"

"I invited Roger and the boys over for dinner. I thought I told you. I'm sorry, darlin'."

Striker clamped his mouth shut to keep from cursing out loud. Tonight was supposed to be extremely romantic, special; an evening they would remember for the rest of their lives. Well, depending on what she said. Either way, one *he* would remember for the rest of his life, he was sure.

"We can go tomorrow night, if you want."

He didn't think he could wait another day. "We'll see."

"They'll be here around seven. You think you can make it by then?"

Striker was silent in response.

"Why don't I just have them over to my house?" Natasha asked, thinking he was irritated with this.

"No, it's fine. It's okay. I'll be home by six." Striker disconnected and began to plan another strategy. Okay, he'd go home, have dinner with Natasha and the boys, try to hurry them out as quickly as possible, ask her to go for a midnight cruise with him, find a cove and...

Natasha was in the kitchen preparing dinner when Striker arrived home. Cat was sprawled on the floor in front of the refrigerator, lazily watching her movements. Natasha gave Striker a warm hug and promising kiss, then returned to the salad. Cat yawned in Striker's direction, lifted a leg, and began cleaning his genitals.

Striker calculated in his mind. Okay, they'd get here at seven, eat, talk, and do the cleanup. Maybe they'd be gone by ten. Surely he could wait four hours. But he didn't think so; he was too anxious now, too worried about what her answer would be. He began to pace, darting glances at his love, frustrated because this was the night he had chosen and he wanted her all to himself. If she said no, could he handle it? What would he do? He'd have to leave, of course. Find an excuse to go away until he could deal with it. He stopped moving, staring at her.

Natasha gave him a questioning look. Striker flashed teeth at her and resumed pacing. Cat sat up to watch the scenario being played out between the two of them.

Natasha surreptitiously observed Striker pacing and rubbing his face and stealing glances at her, wondering what in the heck was going on. She could tell something had him agitated.

"Bad day?" she said, hoping an incident at work had put him in this state of mind. Surely he couldn't have found out about Chumley this fast.

"No, everything went smoothly." Striker gave her that look again.

Natasha stopped chopping vegetables. "Why don't you go watch the news or something? You're making me nervous pacing around like that. Here, let me fix you a quick snack, something that will tide you over until they get here."

"I'm not hungry," Striker said, sounding irritated.

With a shrug, she turned away, beginning to worry that he'd found out about Myrtle's call.

Striker glanced at the clock. Six-fifteen. Forty-five minutes until they got here, then another three hours at least before they left, then he'd take Natasha by the hand, go down to the boat...

Striker stopped pacing and his eyes traveled Natasha's body with an unquenched hunger. She was dressed in black this evening, wearing a long-sleeved, off-the-shoulder blouse over an ankle-length skirt made out of some kind of wrinkly material with a chained silver belt resting above her hips. Her feet were bare. Her hair had been pulled into some complicated style at the back of her head, directing attention to those incredible eyes and exquisite lips. God, she was so beautiful. His stomach knotted, and he wondered, as always, why he felt so incredibly inept in her presence. And how had he come to the point where a woman half his size could practically bring him to his knees with fear? He shook his head and his gaze moved to the view outside. She loved being out on the deck, watching the water.

Striker stepped up behind Natasha and touched her shoulder. She turned, her expression one he couldn't quite comprehend.

"I need to talk to you," he said in a low voice.

Natasha looked surprised. He didn't know it, but she was working herself into a panic, thinking he knew, and she didn't have the chance to explain first.

Striker trailed his hand down her arm and caught her hand in his. "Let's go outside on the deck."

"I was going to tell you."

"Tell me?"

"Honest, I was. But I wanted to wait until the time was right, and I knew tonight wouldn't be a good time, what with Roger, Pit, and Bigun coming for dinner."

Striker dropped her hand, wondering what in the heck she had done now.

"Okay, I admit it. I asked them over simply so I wouldn't have to tell you, so I could put off telling you, because I knew it'd make you mad. And yes, I lied today when I acted like I thought I had told you they were coming over. But Striker, I wanted to tell you in the right way, and I've been puzzling this out in my mind, how to say it without you getting mad at me and wanting to break up with me. And now it's too late; you found out without me explaining it. And you want to break up with me, don't you? You're afraid to tell me, you're afraid of my reaction, you're afraid I might start throwing things. That's why you want to go outside, so I can have a temper tantrum out there, without damaging anything, right? That's why you've been pacing and watching me. You've been trying to work it out in your mind the best way to —"

Striker put one hand over her mouth. "For Pete's sake, that doesn't even come close." He mentally sighed; there went his plans for this evening. "Okay, what is it you didn't want me to find out about?"

Natasha drew back. He didn't know. Damn it, did she ever step into that one. "Why don't we discuss what you wanted to talk to me about first, then we'll get to my news?"

He crossed his arms and waited. She stepped away from him and put her hands behind her back. He scowled, her posture reminding him of a child dealing with an irate parent.

Natasha gave him a beseeching look. "Really, Striker, I don't want to get into this now. Roger and the boys are coming and they'll be here in—" she glanced at the clock "—thirty minutes or so. And… well, this is going to be a major discussion we'll be having, and really, there's not enough time. And you don't want them to walk in on us having a disagreement, do you? Or us mad at each other? Or me crying? Or, in all probability, you kicking my butt out the door?"

Striker forgot all about the ring. "What the hell did you do, Natasha?"

Natasha looked away from him. "It has to do with Chumley."

He shook his head. "Don't tell me."

She nodded. "Myrtle called and reminded me that in the contract I signed with her, I agreed to guard him at the dog show." She rushed on, seeing the flare in his eyes. "Striker, I told her no, but she kept insisting I couldn't back out, that I had contracted for that. She said she talked to her attorney and they were going to sue me if I didn't uphold my end of the agreement."

Striker walked away from her. *Jesus.*

"I told her I'd get someone else to go. I was thinking Pit or Bigun. But for some unfathomable reason to me, she's insisting I guard him. She says I'm the only one that dang dog feels comfortable with, if you can believe that."

Striker glanced at her and began pacing.

"I would have offered to give her all her money back, everything, but I don't have it." Natasha hesitated for a moment before saying in a soft voice, "And then she said something that kind of made me feel bad about myself."

Striker ceased moving, his attention on her.

"She said I was letting you dictate to me, letting you tell me what to do with my career."

He waved his arms around. "How the hell do I come into this?"

Natasha shrugged. "I might have let it slip you were upset about me getting hurt and wanted me to step away from the case." She gave him her own dark look, lifting her chin in a defiant manner. "Which is true."

Striker stifled a groan. *Ah, shit.*

Tears glistened in Natasha's eyes. "I love you more than anything, but I can't let you decide what you think is right for me. Or whether or not I should take a job. It's my choice, not yours. So, even though I love you and I'll probably lose you, I have to abide by my agreement, my word. After all, what am I if my word is not good?"

Striker gave her an annoyed look. "For Christ's sake, quit sounding like a movie."

Natasha wiped at her eyes. "I'll get my purse and go. And later, when you're not here — you can let me know when will be a good time — I'll get the rest of my things." She walked past him, toward the door.

"So you just walk out?" he asked with disbelief.

"Isn't that what you want me to do? I mean, you made it pretty clear before, you couldn't tolerate my involvement with this case."

Striker gazed at her, processing what she had said to him. When she moved restlessly, he held up his hands. "Give me a second."

Okay, there it was in a nutshell, the one thing that would continue to come between them: her choice of a career and his determination to get her away from the dangerous field she had chosen. He was stunned by what she had revealed to him. Was he that domineering with her, that demanding? He didn't like to think he was. But he had pressured her pretty strongly about this frigging case the whole time she had been on it. And why had she been so anxious about telling him she had decided to abide by the contract and guard that perverted little mutt? Because she was afraid of his reaction? That stopped him.

"Just come outside with me," Striker said, his voice low, his eyes intense, reaching for her hand. He led her outside to the deck, stopping when they reached the railing. Neither noticed that Cat had followed them to the glass door and was watching them.

Feeling bad for upsetting her, Striker reached out and gently brushed her tears away. "Will you quit that? Please?"

Natasha drew herself up and tried to appear composed. Striker patted his pocket as he sank onto one knee. A shocked expression crossed Natasha's face.

He kissed her hand and looked into her eyes. "Natasha."

"Yes?"

"There's something I want to ask you, and I know I should wait until Roger and the boys leave, but damn it, I can't. I have to know. The suspense is killing me. So I want to do it now and get it over with, I guess, in case it's bad and —"

Natasha leaned down to stop his rambling with her mouth on his. She kissed him sweetly, straightened up, and smiled.

"Just say it, Jonce."

He swallowed before beginning. "Natasha Chamberlain, I love you more than I'll ever love anyone. I've chosen you as my life mate and I've committed myself to you. And I'd like to ask you to go the traditional route with me, become my wife, share your life with me, have a family with me, grow old with me, love me the way you do, for the rest of my life."

Tears were running down her cheeks, but she was beaming at him.

"And I know you're not ready for marriage or babies or any of that. So, we can make this engagement as long as you want, years if that's what it takes —"

"Yes."

Striker looked startled.

"I said *yes.*"

"Oh, yeah." Striker reached into his pocket, found the ring, drew it out, and kissed it. He slid it on her finger, putting his lips to it as it rested there.

Natasha knelt with him, exclaiming over the ring, kissing it, kissing him, throwing her arms around him, telling him how much she loved him, thanking him for loving her the way he did.

They forgot all about their guests. When the doorbell rang promptly at seven, they were upstairs, in bed, enjoying one another, thanking each other, busy consummating the engagement, Natasha wearing nothing but the ring. Both were oblivious to the fire alarm going off in the kitchen from the burned pots or Cat screaming his head off at the irritating noise or the doorbell ringing.

Hearing the alarm's shrill blare, Roger, Pit, and Bigun entered the house and ran into the kitchen, yelling at the top of their lungs. They turned off the stove, used a broom to whisk the smoke away from the fire alarm, and opened the door to air out the room. Seeing the trail of discarded clothing, hearing the noises from upstairs, knowing what was going on, the three men gave each other disgusted looks and left. So did Cat.

Chapter 29

Natasha's mom, now a bona fide health nut, ran four to five days a week, occasionally managing to shame Natasha into joining her. Since the cluster was five days away and Natasha didn't have anything better to do, she couldn't weasel out of it when Stevie called, wanting to jog along the river in Sequoyah Hills.

Natasha drove by Myrtle's to pick up Chumley, telling her she was taking him for a walk in the park, thinking that was a good excuse not to run since all the Pug could do was waddle. But Stevie, knowing her daughter, came prepared with a baby carrier from Natasha's infancy. Chumley fit perfectly, to Natasha's great disappointment.

Running in place, Stevie admired Natasha's engagement ring, expressed her happiness over the upcoming wedding. When she started talking about possible dates, Natasha took off.

By the time Stevie caught up with her daughter, she had decided to drop the wedding talk, not push things just yet. Jogging along, Chumley's little head peeping out of the baby sling on Natasha's chest, Stevie said, "Oh, did I tell you I've signed up at the gym to take belly dancing lessons?"

Natasha stopped dead.

Stevie ran on a few feet before missing her daughter's presence. She turned back to her. "What?"

"Belly dancing lessons? You? At your age?"

Stevie rolled her head back and sighed.

"You're twenty years older than I am."

"So?"

"So act your age, Mom. You should be joining gardening clubs, quilting circles, book discussion groups..." Natasha drew back at the look in Stevie's eyes. Ever since her mom had entered this crappy perimenopause stage, Natasha never knew whom she was dealing with anymore, what with Stevie's personalities ranging from June Cleaver to the Terminator.

"I am only forty-five. I am not quite ready for the old folks home, thank you very much. When I'm sixty-five or seventy-five, I might think about joining one of those sedate groups, but until then, what I choose to do with my time is none of your business. Especially if you're going to question every damn thing I take on."

Natasha's eyes widened at the D word coming out of her mom's mouth. She placed her hands over Chumley's ears.

"Sure, Mom, whatever you want is fine with me. I didn't mean anything."

Stevie eyed her with suspicion.

"Really. Hey, you'd make a great belly dancer, Mom, you've got the perfect stomach for it."

"What about my stomach? Are you saying my stomach's fat? It's too flabby?"

"Uh, no, it's great. Maybe a little round, but that's the way belly dancers' tummies are, aren't they? Round?"

Stevie stared down at her stomach, bulging in her jogging shorts.

"Come on, Mom, you've had a baby, you're entitled. Besides, women look better, healthier, with meat on their bones, not like all those models and actresses who look like they've just been released from a concentration camp. Regardless of what the fashion magazines or Hollywood try to push down our throats."

Stevie gave Natasha a look she knew all too well, the one that meant a storm was brewing and heading her way. She glanced around for help.

"Omigosh."

"What?" Stevie's gaze followed Natasha's to a couple sitting on a blanket beside the water, enjoying a picnic. "Whoa. Look at those babies."

"You know who that is?" Natasha said, eyes flaring.

"Nope. But I've been thinking about a breast enlargement. What do you think?"

"Ah, geez, Mom, you don't need a breast enlargement. How old are you anyway? Fifteen?"

Stevie put her hands on hips, another danger signal.

"Anyway, Mom, that's Misty," Natasha said hurriedly, pointing.

"Who?"

"Misty Bellows, Roger's girlfriend."

"Sounds like a stripper's name."

Natasha nodded. "That's what I thought." She continued to watch the couple. "I knew she was up to something."

"Who?"

"Misty, Mom. Pay attention." At her mother's irritated look, she rushed on. "She's weird. She's supposed to be doing research on Roger but never seems to do anything but hang out at the pool and screw him."

"Watch your mouth, young lady."

"This from a woman who's decided it's okay to become a mid-life cusser."

"I keep the cussing to a minimum, unlike some people I know," Stevie said, glaring.

"Mom, we're getting off subject. Pit and Bigun think she's up to something, and so do I, but we can't get Striker to run a check on her. He says it's none of our business, to leave it alone."

"Well, he's right. If she doesn't have a genuine interest in Roger, she'll show her colors sooner or later."

"Yeah, but the thing is, I think Roger's falling in love with her. If she isn't on the up-and-up, I'd rather he found out sooner than later. That way, he won't be so hurt."

"Why don't you investigate her?"

"I tried to but couldn't find out much. She's telling the truth; she *is* a grad student working on her dissertation. She hasn't committed any criminal offenses, hasn't been arrested. Hell, I couldn't even find a traffic violation."

"And you think *I* cuss too much?"

"Mom, stay with me here. Look at the man she's with. That has to be her lover, which means she's running around on Roger. I knew it."

Steve studied the couple. "He's too old, Nattie. That's probably her father."

"Fathers and daughters don't have picnics alone."

"You and your father do."

"No, we don't."

"When we go trail riding, when we stop and eat lunch, that's a picnic."

"That's a *trail-riding* lunch, Mom. That's different. Besides, you and Striker are usually with us. What do you want to bet it's one of her professors and she's carrying on this torrid affair with him?"

"Here we go."

"What?"

"You always make mountains out of molehills, Nattie. It's an innocent picnic lunch between two people. Stop twisting your panties in a bind."

Natasha pulled her mother behind a large poplar. "Okay, I'm going to sneak up on them, behind that tree, and listen to what they say. If you see them looking in my direction, distract them."

"How?"

"I don't know. Yell and wave your arms like you're trying to get someone's attention." Natasha plucked Chumley out of the carrier and pushed him into Stevie's hands.

"They'll see you coming."

"Nah, I'm stealthy, I'll be quiet. Their backs are to me, so the only way they'll see me is if they turn around. That's where you come into the picture."

Stevie gave her a look.

"What?"

"This is what you call investigating?"

Ignoring that, Natasha took off.

Stevie made sure Chumley's leash was securely attached before placing him on the ground. She leaned against the tree, her eyes darting between the picnicking couple and her daughter weaving in and out of foliage, working her way toward them.

Natasha rested against the maple tree behind the couple, quietly trying to catch her breath. *Dang,* she needed to get more running time in, no doubt about it, or she wouldn't be in shape when soccer season started. She squinted her eyes in her mother's direction and saw Stevie stretching out, with one leg against the poplar, glancing in their direction every few seconds. Natasha pointed around the maple, as if to say, *What are they doing?*

Stevie made a gabbing motion with her hand.

Natasha stood still, held her breath and listened, wishing the branches weren't so low to the ground, hindering her view. When the wind kicked up, one of the smaller limbs smacked her across the face.

"Shit," she muttered, falling to her knees, cupping her left eye. She clasped her hand over her mouth.

Stevie began yelling and waving at no one.

Tears were running down Natasha's left cheek. She opened that eye and everything looked blurry. *Damn it.* While she waited for the pain to subside, she tried once more to hear what the couple was saying, but the tree acted as a buffer, filtering their voices so that all Natasha could pick up on were a few murmurs.

She studied the maple, which branched out at least twenty feet. What if she climbed one of the lower limbs high enough so she was over them? Surely she would be able to hear something. She motioned her intent to her mother. Stevie vehemently shook her head. Natasha put her foot on the lower branch.

Misty and her escort were several feet away, so Natasha didn't worry about them hearing her scurry up. Besides, Stevie was making noises again. Natasha quietly scooted on her belly along a limb horizontal to the couple, only five feet or so above them. She stopped when she was directly overhead. She still couldn't hear what they were saying, so she hung her head off the branch, knocking a few leaves loose.

Misty looked up and shrieked.

Startled, Natasha fell out of the tree and landed on her back in the middle of their food. She stared at the sky, trying to catch her breath, wishing she could disappear into thin air.

Misty stood, giving Natasha a furious look. "You."

"Hey, Misty," Natasha squeaked.

"What the hell are you doing here?"

Uh-oh.

"You were *spying* on me."

Stevie joined them, clutching Chumley to her chest. "Did you get it?" she asked Natasha.

Natasha didn't know what to say.

Stevie gave Misty an apologetic smile. "I was playing Frisbee with Chumley and threw it too high and it got stuck in the tree. And Nattie here was kind enough to offer to climb up and get it for me. You're probably thinking, a Frisbee? Why does she care about a Frisbee? But it's the only one Chumley will play with. Isn't that right, Nattie?"

Natasha tried to smile, but she was still trying to catch her breath and couldn't manage it.

Stevie extended one hand. "I'm Stevie Chamberlain and this is —"

"I already know who that is," Misty said with a sneer in Natasha's direction. "I'm Misty Bellows and this is my father, Frank."

Natasha squeezed her eyes shut. *Shoot.*

After introductions were made, Stevie and Frank helped Natasha to her feet. Natasha smiled her thanks at Frank and received a stiff one in return.

"I'm really sorry about this, Misty," she wheezed, stepping off their blanket. Her back felt all gooey and wet. She looked over her shoulder, trying to see what was back there. It was something dark and black. *Yick.* She swiped her butt, brought her hand around, and took a good look. The aroma was enticing. "Gee, I ruined your chocolate cake. I'm really sorry about that." She put her fingers in her mouth.

Stevie gasped with horror.

"Well, Mom, I guess we better get going," Natasha said. "Sorry I couldn't get that Frisbee for you." She gave Misty and her father a small wave and got the hell out of Dodge, limping all the way.

"You need to find another career, Nat," Stevie said on the way to the car.

Natasha pretended she didn't hear her.

Natasha talked Stevie into returning Chumley to Myrtle, so she could drive directly to Striker's for medical attention. She hobbled into the kitchen to put something cold on her face. A welt had begun to form, traveling from her left temple, across her eye and the bridge of her nose, ending at her right cheek. She held a bag of frozen peas to her face, wondering if she had broken her tailbone when she landed. Something back there felt sprung, for sure. She needed to clean the mess off her jeep seat, but the act of bending over sent the muscles in her back into agonizing spasms. She jumped when her cellphone rang.

"Hello," she groaned into the phone.

"Well, I've just received some very disturbing news," B.S. said.

"Oh, hey, Grammy. What's wrong? Did your manuscript get rejected?"

"My manuscripts don't get rejected," B.S. huffed.

"Did one of your books get slammed at Amazon again? Maybe you should do what Anne Rice did when — "

"I understand you're engaged," B.S. said in a steely voice.

"Oh. Yes, I am, and I couldn't be happier."

"Natasha, really, I thought I taught you better than that."

"Than what?"

"How old are you?"

"Almost twenty-six. And what the heck does that have to do with anything?"

"You're way too young to even think about committing yourself to a relationship, that's what. Try to look to the future, sweetheart. Where will you be ten years from now? An overweight housewife with a pack of babies nipping at your heels. Is that what you want out of life?"

"Grammy, whoever said I'm going to be a housewife? I like being a bodyguard and I intend to remain one as long as I'm able."

"And the reason for the marriage?"

"I love Striker, more than I'll ever love anyone. He's the only person I can ever conceive of spending the rest of my life with. That good enough for you?"

"Really, sweetheart, if you think you love the man, that's acceptable. But don't throw your life away by letting him put a ring on your finger and babies in your belly. Honestly, have you not studied anthropology? Are you not aware it is not the nature of the beast, shall we say, for humans to remain monogamous?"

"Well, I intend to be an anomaly in that regard," Natasha said. "Now, if you don't mind, I need to go. I fell out of a tree and my back is killing me."

"Stephanie told me about your little caper in the park. Before you go, sweetie, tell me how it felt as you were falling and then when you landed. For future reference."

"Oh, for cripes' sake," Natasha said.

Behind her, Striker said, "Natasha."

She startled and dropped her phone into the sink. When she turned around, Striker and Roger loomed in the doorway.

"You scared the crap out of me. Hey, Roger," she added, smiling his way.

This was met with stern frowns.

"What? What'd I do?" she said, feigning innocence.

"Did you get the Frisbee?" Striker asked.

Yikes.

"Funny thing about Chumley chasing a disappearing Frisbee," Striker said to Roger. "Chumley's too fat to run after one and his mouth's too small to hold it. We know 'cause we tried once. Isn't that right?" His eyes flashed at Natasha.

Roger's face reddened with anger. "So Misty was right. She *was* spying on her."

"Well, spying may be a little too extreme," Natasha said.

Both men looked as if they weren't buying that.

She sighed. "Roger, I didn't follow her there, if she's telling you that. Mom and I were running in Sequoyah Hills, you know, by the river? And I saw Misty having a picnic with a man. I mean, a couple on a blanket by the river having a picnic. What does that imply?"

"You and your dad have picnics all the time," Striker said, eyebrows raised.

"Well, yeah, but only when we go trail riding."

"So you couldn't go over and introduce your mom to Misty? You had to sneak around, climb a tree, spy on them, like some little kid, right?"

Natasha shrugged. She was out of excuses.

Striker looked at Roger. "She's all yours. I'll take what's left when you get done with her."

Natasha had never seen Roger so angry. At first, he stuttered around, seeming unable to formulate words. When he finally found his voice, he didn't let up for several minutes, in essence, telling Natasha to stay out of his "effing business." Roger rarely cursed and had never said the F word in front of her. Upset that her sweet, even-tempered best friend would use profanity toward her, she burst into tears.

Roger immediately looked contrite. "Don't cry, Nattie."

"I'm sorry, Roger. I love you like a brother, you're the best friend I've ever had, and I was only trying to protect you. I'd hate to see you hurt."

Roger put his arms around her. "Ah, Nattie, it's okay."

Striker shook his head.

Roger left after Natasha agreed it would be best if she kept her nose out of his love life and maybe didn't come around the mansion for a few days till Misty calmed down.

Natasha bristled at this last part but kept her mouth shut. She walked Roger to the front door, hugged him goodbye, and hobbled back to the kitchen.

"Before you start yelling, can you give me a minute?" she said, limping over to the sink, picking up the makeshift ice pack.

Striker watched her with a suspicious look in his eyes. She placed the frozen bag against the side of her face and started moving around, trying to work the kinks out of her back, making sounds of discomfort and wincing.

Striker's face changed. "What's wrong? Did you hurt yourself?"

Natasha gave him a tearful look. "I fell on my back when I landed and it hurts like the devil."

"Let me see."

"Plus a limb whacked my eye," she added, trying to gain sympathy, raising her shirt and turning around so he could examine her back. "Everything's blurry. I can't see clearly out of that eye."

That did it. Striker took her upstairs to play doctor.

Chapter 30

Natasha woke up in a grouchy mood the morning of the dog show, irritated that she would be stuck inside all day guarding Chumley when it was supposed to be absolutely beautiful — perfect boating weather, perfect horseback riding weather, perfect making-love-with-Striker weather.

Striker, picking up on her mood and not sure what was going on with her, kept quiet. Wary of asking her, he wondered if she was back to all that resentment shit over his interfering with her case. It surprised him when she threw her napkin down at the breakfast bar and said, "I hate this."

"What?"

"Having to go guard Chumley. I'm really mad at Myrtle for doing this to me, you know."

Although he was glad she felt that way, he tried not to show it.

"So, what are you going to do today?" she asked.

"Scotty and I are meeting a realtor to look at a building we're thinking about buying."

Natasha nodded, glancing at the clock. "What time are you leaving?"

"Around ten."

Her eyes drifted back to the clock. "Any chance I can get in some playtime before I have to leave?"

Striker grinned.

Feeling much better, Natasha hopped in her jeep and left. She collected Myrtle and Chumley and drove to the arena. While Myrtle handled the paperwork, Natasha strolled around with Chumley, watching the other animals and their owners. The little Pug was in his environment, and she watched with amusement the way he strutted around. He actually did look like a champion.

Roger appeared in front of her, startling her.

"Hey, guy," she said, giving him a hug. "What brings you here?"

Roger shrugged, glancing around. "I've never been to one of these things and I thought it'd be fun to watch."

Natasha looked past him. "Where's Misty?"

His eyes drifted around the room. "She was right beside me a minute ago."

Natasha sighed. "Has she forgiven me yet?"

Roger gave her a small smile. "I don't know. She hasn't said."

"Is this going to affect our friendship?"

"Nattie, you know better than that."

She studied him for a moment. "Other than Misty, are you here by yourself?"

Roger hesitated before saying, "Why do you ask?"

"Let me guess. Striker sent you, Pit, and Bigun to keep an eye on me, right?"

Roger wouldn't look at her.

She leaned toward him. "Is he here?"

"He's coming later, after his meeting."

Natasha nodded, trying to determine whether or not this made her angry.

"He's worried about you, Nattie."

Deciding it was nice having someone that concerned for her, she smiled. "Yeah, I know."

Natasha glanced at her watch, noting that she had half an hour before she was scheduled to take Chumley to the room where they groomed the dogs. She glimpsed Pit and Bigun trying to hide from her and pretended that she didn't notice them.

Roger watched a Weimaraner being paraded around. He told Natasha he'd be right back and left to talk to the owner about the breed.

Intending to go to the grooming room a few minutes early in order to check the layout, Natasha headed in that direction. Misty stepped in front of her, halting her progress. Natasha stared at her, trying to gauge whether or not she was still angry.

"Hi," Misty said with a bright smile.

"Hey," Natasha answered. "Misty, about that picnic —"

Misty shook her head. "Don't worry about it. I completely understand, so let's forget the whole thing."

"Great," Natasha said, feeling relieved.

"Listen," Misty said, "there's a young woman outside who asked me to tell you she needs to talk to you."

"What about?"

"I'm not sure. She said something about some man who wrote a letter is here and that she thinks he's going to hurt the dog." Misty waved a hand toward Chumley.

Natasha glanced around. "Why didn't she come inside?"

"I think she's scared that guy will see her. She said to tell you she'd be in the back parking lot."

Natasha looked around for Myrtle so she could leave Chumley with her.

"I'll hold him if you want," Misty offered.

Natasha hesitated. She preferred to leave Chumley with his owner.

"I'll find Roger and we'll watch him together," Misty said.

"You're sure you don't mind?" Natasha asked, handing her the leash.

"Not at all. I love dogs."

"I'll be right back." Natasha hurried toward the exit and stood at the back entrance, surveying the parking lot.

"I was hoping you'd show up," a woman said, stepping close.

Natasha studied her, felt a tug of recognition. "Do we know each other?"

The young woman smiled, revealing blackened teeth.

"From the bikers' bar?"

The woman nodded. "My name's Kit."

"What do you want to talk to me about, Kit?" Natasha's gaze traveled the lot, concerned the biker she had kicked was lurking about, wanting revenge.

"Well, you was asking about a dog. Remember, you showed me his picture?"

"Yeah?"

"You wanted to know if I'd seen him?"

"Well, it doesn't matter now. We got him back."

"What you didn't ask me about was the letter that was sent."

Natasha gave Kit her full attention. "You know who sent the letter?"

"Yeah."

"Tell me the letter you're referring to."

"That he better not show up for this show or he'd be dead. *That* letter."

"Okay. So that was an actual threat?"

"Yeah. The guy's here who sent the letter. He means to harm that dog."

Natasha became alert. "Where?"

Kit suspiciously cast her eyes around. "Walk outside with me and I'll tell you."

"Why don't you tell me here?"

"'Cause like I said, he's here. If he sees me talking to you, I'm dead."

"You've talked to me now for what, two, three minutes? If he's gonna see you, he already has."

"No, man. He's in the grooming room. I don't want him to come outside and see me talking to you. Walk me to my car. I'll tell you there, then I'm gone."

Natasha thought about it. It didn't feel right, but if the man who had threatened Chumley was here, she needed to know.

"Come on," Kit said.

"Let's go."

Kit led her to a secluded corner in the back parking lot, next to a van that Natasha supposed was white underneath all that dirt and dust. Kit turned around and her eyes focused on something behind Natasha.

Natasha turned to see what Kit was looking at. "Okay, so who's —"

Everything went black.

Striker instructed Pit and Bigun to keep an eye on Natasha without letting her see them and to call him if anything happened. He told Roger to be visual, knowing Roger didn't have the skills the other two should possess to be present but not seen. He knew Natasha would be upset with him, but he'd deal with that later.

Striker had gotten tied up with the business he and Scott were attending to and was late arriving, Scott deciding to ride along in case Striker needed his help. When they stepped inside the building, Myrtle hurried toward them with a worried look on her face.

"Mr. Striker, have you seen Natasha and Chumley?" she said when she reached them.

Striker's stomach clenched. "No, but I just got here."

"I can't find them and I've looked everywhere," Myrtle said with a panicked look. "We're supposed to be ready in fifteen minutes."

Striker tried not to let his concern show. "Don't worry, Ms. Galbreath, I'll find her." He pulled out his cellphone and alerted Pit.

"Where's Natasha?" he said when Pit answered.

"Man, I was just trying to call you," Pit said. "I saw her leave a few minutes ago."

"Leave?"

"Yeah, man. She was standing at the back door, talking to that sheep from the biker bar. The girl that was with that biker that Nattie fought with."

"What? Was the biker with her?"

"No, man, the sheep was alone. Nattie walked into the parking lot with her. I was way across the room when I saw Nattie heading out, and by the time I got there, they were gone, man."

Striker didn't like Pit sounding this panicked. "Where are you?"

"Outside, man, in the parking lot in the back."

Striker and Scott raced outside. Myrtle watched them leave, and glanced helplessly around the room.

"You didn't see where they went?" Striker asked Pit when they joined him.

Pit shook his head with a sick look.

Bigun ran up to them. He nodded at Striker. "I've searched this whole lot, dude. She's not here," he said, gasping for breath.

"You're sure Natasha was with that girl from the biker bar?" Striker asked Pit.

"Yeah, man."

"Where's Chumley?"

"I saw Misty walk outside with him, right after Nattie left," Bigun said.

Striker considered this. Maybe some of the pieces were finally falling into place. "One of Natasha's suspects is Ned Peterson, the guy who owns that bar. You seen him around today?"

Pit and Bigun looked at one another.

"I don't know what he looks like, man," Pit said, turning back to Striker.

"Me either, dude," Bigun said.

"Get me a list showing the owners and their dogs," Striker said in a tight voice.

Bigun dashed away. He was back within moments, handing a catalog to Striker.

Striker studied it. "He's listed as an owner, but not as the one showing the dog. That could mean he's not here, which might mean he has Natasha. There could be a link between him, this sheep and the biker."

Roger joined them, looking worried. "I've searched all over the building but can't find her. I tried reaching Nattie on her phone, but she's not answering." He turned to Striker. "I'm sorry, Striker. I left her when I shouldn't have —"

"It's not your fault. If they wanted her bad enough, they would have found a way." Striker studied the ground for a moment. He glanced up. "Is Misty still here? Does she have Chumley?"

Roger gave him a confused look. "Misty has Chumley?"

"Bigun saw her walking outside with the dog."

"I haven't seen Misty since we got here," Roger said.

Striker's expression was glum. "Shit. She could be in on this too. Since the only place we have to start is at the bar, let's go there first. Maybe they're headed there."

Chapter 31

Natasha came to herself, lying on the floor in the back of a moving vehicle. She groggily struggled to sit up, fighting a dizzy sensation. Something warm and moist nuzzled her face. Chumley. "Hey, boy," she said, running her hands over his small body to make sure he hadn't been harmed.

She glanced toward the front of what she thought must be a cargo van. Her eyes widened. The biker, the one she had kicked, sat in the passenger seat, watching her. Misty occupied the driver's seat. Natasha picked up the Pug and held him against her chest.

"I thought there was something screwy about you," she said to Misty.

Misty gave her a smug smile in the rear-view mirror.

The biker swiveled around to face her. "Took you long enough to wake up, bitch," he said, in a mild voice.

Natasha tried to match her tone of voice to his. "Don't you think this is a little bit extreme?"

He grinned. "Extreme?"

"Hey, you didn't want Chumley to show today, you could have just asked."

He jabbed a finger at her. "This ain't about that dog. This is about you."

"So why bring the dog?"

"She wants the dog," the biker said, pointing at Misty. "Said I could have you as a bonus if I helped her grab the mutt."

"In retaliation for my kicking your ass, I suppose."

His eyes hardened. "You're one stupid bitch, talking to me like that."

"Do I look scared? 'Cause I got to tell you, I'm not scared. I took you out once, I can do it again."

"Yeah? Well, listen up, Sis, by the time I get through with you, you're gonna be begging me to kick your ass." He sat back, lit a cigarette, and took a puff. Expelling smoke, he said, "We gonna have us a train and you're gonna be the choo-choo." He threw his head back and laughed at this.

She had been raped once. It would not happen again; she'd die first. Natasha forced a sneer on her face. "Ain't gonna happen."

His face registered surprise at her response.

"Are you serious? You seek vengeance against me, a woman maybe half your weight, by getting your gang to rape me? You don't have balls enough to face me alone, *mano a mano*?"

His hand froze in midair, the cigarette inches from his lips.

"I mean, the way I see it, this is between you and me, not me and your whole gang. But hey, you're scared of me. I can understand that. But I got to tell you, man, you're wimping out here, letting others take care of your business."

He exploded out of his seat. Misty put her hand on his chest and pushed against him. "She's baiting you, you idiot," she said. "Trying to psych you out."

"I know that," the biker mumbled, straightening in his seat, facing forward, ignoring Natasha.

Natasha slid her hand down her pants leg, searching for her .22, which she usually wore tucked into an ankle holster. She silently cursed, remembering she had locked her guns in her jeep when told by security that no one was allowed inside the arena with weapons of any sort. Her cellphone, which she had clipped to her waist, was missing. What the hell was she going to do? *Okay,* she told herself, *think. Remember all the training with Striker, our matches on the mats.* She had bested Striker before and he was a skilled adversary. This guy should be easy; he looked like he lifted more beers than weights. But she needed to take him out before anyone else. Send a message.

She felt along the floor around her, aware that Misty was watching her in the rear-view mirror. She glanced at the windows in the back and along the sides, wondering if she could break one and signal for help.

"Where's Kit?" Natasha asked.

"Dropped her off at her mama's house," the biker said, with a sly grin at Misty.

Natasha looked around the van, searching for something that could be used as a weapon. "So I take it Peterson's the one behind that letter threatening Chumley's life."

Misty shook her head. "Peterson doesn't have anything to do with this."

"Then how'd you hook up with this idiot?" Natasha said, watching the biker's eyes flare.

"I overheard you telling Roger about the fracas at the bar. It wasn't hard finding this guy, the way you described him."

Natasha thought about it. "Let me guess. The man you introduced as Frank is in on this, right? And don't tell me he's your dad."

"Frank's my boyfriend," Misty said with a sneer.

Natasha nodded. "So Frank's busy showing while you're making sure Chumley stays out of the way."

Misty smiled. "You got it."

"Don't you think Frank's a little too old for you? Who is he, one of your former professors?"

"You don't shut up, I'm going to let him have a go at you right now," Misty said, tilting her head in the direction of the biker.

Natasha shook her head with disgust. "You got involved with Roger just to get to Chumley? What the hell?"

"Actually, it worked out perfect, practically dropped in our laps."

"You think?" Natasha said snidely.

Misty ignored that. "I'd been doing some preliminary research on Roger for my dissertation. After we sent that letter, we figured Myrtle would back off. But when she hired you to guard the Pug, I remembered reading about you being Roger's bodyguard at one point. I asked around and found out you two were close. So I decided to approach Roger. I mean, what better way to keep an eye on that damn dog than to actually be right next to the guy who hears all your secrets?"

"You did more than approach Roger," Natasha said, her eyes dark with anger.

"He didn't seem to mind," Misty said, smirking.

Natasha couldn't believe this. "Wouldn't it have been simpler to just take the dog rather than invest all that time in Roger?"

Misty shrugged. "Killing two birds with one stone. It allowed me to do the research I needed to while keeping an eye on the dog. And Roger was a very pleasant distraction, although Frank doesn't need to know that."

"I'll be sure not to tell him," Natasha said.

Misty glared at her in the rearview mirror. "Besides, the way you kept screwing up and getting fired, we figured Myrtle would give up on the cluster."

"So which one of you was stupid enough to send a letter to a dog?" Natasha asked.

Misty grinned. "That was Frank. He thought it was cute."

"Shit." Natasha shook her head. "And the picnic? You were there for Chumley, weren't you?"

Misty's shrug told Natasha she had guessed right. "I listened in on your conversation with Roger that morning. When you told him about running in Sequoyah Hills, Frank and I figured that'd be a good place to snatch the dog. Follow you into the woods and take him. Smuggle him out in the picnic basket we brought. Too bad you saw us before we saw you. We still would have grabbed him, but your mom was in the way and there were too many people around. Too much baggage to get rid of."

Natasha held Chumley close and kissed the top of his head. "I don't understand how in the hell this little dog could be any kind of threat to you."

"You apparently don't understand the dog show world," Misty said. "It's all about campaigning, building those breed points and best in show points, attaining championship status, and getting to Westminster."

"What's Frank's last name?" Natasha asked.

Misty gave her a suspicious look. "Anderson. Why do you want to know?"

"I don't remember that name on my list of participants in the prior clusters," Natasha said. "And I know your name wasn't in any of the rosters or catalogs."

Misty shook her head. "It wouldn't be. This is our first year at this cluster. But we need points and weren't about to take a chance on that runt winning Best in Show again." She glanced at the biker. "Where do you want me to drop you two?"

"The bar's good enough."

They exited the interstate and drove onto Clinton Highway, maybe ten or fifteen minutes from the bar. Natasha had to do something. Now. She put Chumley down, rose to her feet, and tried the side door. She wasn't surprised to find it locked. She pushed her weight against it, hearing the biker curse, watching him come up out of the seat. *Okay, here. Now. Take him.*

She turned to meet him, waited until he was close enough, and kicked out, aiming for his groin but misjudging the distance and catching him in the stomach. The breath exploded out of him and he staggered back.

"Watch her damn feet," Misty shouted. "That's how she got you last time."

Natasha moved on him before he had a chance to recover. She aimed better this time, connecting under the jaw. She watched him flail back, into the front of the van. Misty threw out one arm to stop him. The van swerved onto the shoulder of the road. Natasha grabbed Chumley with one hand, the door handle with the other, and hung on.

Misty put both hands on the wheel and barely managed to wrestle the van under control. She braked to a complete stop, resting partially in the grass.

The anger in the biker's eyes held Natasha's attention long enough to miss the draw of the gun. "Now you did it," he said, pointing a pistol at her.

~~~

In his great rush to the bar, Striker drove as fast as he dared, carelessly ignoring all traffic signals that would have required him to wait. He blew past a van sitting half on the shoulder and half on the grass and didn't even consider stopping to help. He brought the SUV to a shuddering stop in front of the bar and hurried out of the vehicle, followed by Roger, Pit, Bigun, and Scott.

The building looked vacant; there wasn't a soul in sight. The other four men stood in the empty gravel parking lot exchanging glances, waiting for instructions from Striker.

Striker held up his hand, meaning *listen*. They all grew silent, their ears straining for sound. Nothing. Striker tried the door, but it was locked. He pulled out his gun, screwed on a silencer, and replaced the knob with a ragged hole. He kicked the door open and entered the building.

The inside felt as vacant as the outside.

Striker motioned for Pit and Bigun to spread out. Each man hugged opposite walls, guns drawn, moving carefully. Striker headed straight to the room in the back, kicked the door in and entered, ready to kill anyone that got in his way. Empty.

The bar felt preternaturally quiet, as if the air had been sucked out of the building. Striker retraced his steps. He strode outside and jogged along the side of the building, the others following along behind.

Rounding the back, he moved close to the bar, his ear next to the outer wall. Every few feet, he stopped to listen before continuing on. The other men watched him, moving when he did, stopping with him.

Near the end of the edifice, Striker squatted down and put his ear close to the ground, next to a vent. "Nothing," he said in a low voice. "It's just a crawl space." He stood and began moving once more.

"Where the hell are they?" Scott said.

~~~

Natasha froze, her gaze riveted on the small hole at the end of the gun. She squatted down and gently placed Chumley on the floor. She rose to her feet, arms in the air. "Okay," she said in a low voice.

The biker gave her a manic grin. "You afraid of me now, Sis?" he said, his voice raspy.

"Oh, yeah, I'm scared all right."

Misty shoved the van into park. "Tie that bitch up. If you'd done that to start with, none of this would have happened."

Handing the gun off to Misty, the biker lunged forward and backhanded Natasha. The force of the impact slung her face to the right. Tears sprang to her eyes.

"You're gonna regret that," she said.

"Yeah? How about I do that again?" He hit her once more.

Chumley hovered close to Natasha, growling at the biker, snapping at his feet. The biker kicked out and caught Chumley in the side, hurling the Pug toward the back of the van.

"Chumley." Natasha turned to go to him, but the biker grasped her arm and pulled her back, forcing her to remain where she stood. Chumley lay in a limp heap in a corner of the van, making no sound. It was too dark to see if he was breathing.

"Okay, now you've made me mad," Natasha said, rounding on him. The gun stopped her once more.

The biker forced her to her knees. Using rope that Misty handed to him, he tied her hands behind her back and her ankles together. "Kick me now, bitch," he said, returning to the passenger seat. "Let's go," he told Misty.

When they neared the bar, the biker leaned forward in his seat. "Slow down but don't pull in just yet," he said.

Misty eased up on the accelerator. "What's wrong?"

"That SUV don't belong there," he muttered. He shook his head. "This don't feel right. Go on by."

Natasha stared out the window as Striker's SUV drifted by. Tears sprung to her eyes. He had figured it out, but he'd never find her if they took her to another location. In desperation, she charged the door, shoved her body against it, praying it would give and spill her out onto the tarmac. She became aware of the van picking up speed, the biker moving toward her before blackness descended once more.

Striker stepped from behind the bar and looked around, feeling more powerless than he had ever felt in his life. A dirty white van with darkly tinted windows slowed down as it passed the building and then sped up, but Striker barely registered it. He turned a panicked face to the others, which only served to frighten them. In tense situations, Striker was the one who didn't become alarmed, who kept his head; they depended on him for that.

"We'll find her," Scott said. "But you've got to stay focused, Striker."

Striker stared at the ground, fighting for control. He turned his head toward the roadway. "Wasn't that the van that was on the side of the road back there?"

"Yeah, man, looks it," Pit said, watching the van's exhaust dissipate as it disappeared over a hill.

Striker headed toward the SUV, snatching his cellphone out of its holder. He punched in a number and said, "Check Ned Peterson, owns a bar on Clinton Highway called Hells Bells. I need to know what vehicles he owns, what property he holds. And I need it now, no time wasted." He started the SUV and peeled out of the lot, ignoring Bigun, who just barely managed to get the door closed.

Natasha woke facedown on the greasy-smelling metal floor in the back of the van. She lifted her head and looked around, fighting dizziness. Her arms were behind her, her hands still bound with rope. Her eyes traveled down; her legs were tied as well. So this wasn't a nightmare after all.

Chumley remained inert in the corner of the van. She watched him for several seconds, praying, "Please breathe, please breathe, please breathe." She blinked at the tears of relief flooding her eyes when she saw his small side rise and fall.

Noises were filtering through the buzz in her brain. It sounded like Misty and the biker were discussing where to take her. She worked her mouth, trying to create saliva to soothe the cottony dryness. They had hit her in the head twice now. Shoot, during this whole investigation with Chumley, she'd gotten her brain rattled...what? Three times? She'd probably have brain damage after this was over, probably drool all over herself, laugh when she should cry and vice versa.

She tested the rope, tight against her skin, and moved her feet. *Damn.* If she had worn the sandals she first put on that morning, she could easily slip out of these ropes. But then again, her boots added more power to the kicks, offering protection to her feet. She slowly drew her knees up to her chest, trying not to attract their attention.

"Do you see that black SUV back there?" Misty said.

The biker turned around to look through the back windows. "Yeah."

"Looks like that SUV that was sitting at the bar when we went past. You think they're following us?"

"Only one way to find out." The biker cranked down his window, leaned out, and took a potshot at Striker's vehicle.

Natasha struggled to her knees, watching the windshield crack and the SUV swerve onto the shoulder.

"No!" She rose to her feet and hobbled forward, into the biker.

"Shit. Get off me!" he yelled, pushing her back.

She fell on her butt, but forced herself back up, this time hurling herself into Misty. The van swerved. "Fuck," Misty screamed.

The biker pulled Natasha off and shoved her away. She stumbled back, fell hard, and heard more pops.

The biker laughed with glee. "Got his tire," he crowed. "That fucker's gone." A loud booming sound infiltrated the van. "He just took out the guardrail. He's off the road, man, he's gonna lose it."

Natasha rose to her knees, with tears streaming down her face. She watched Striker's SUV drop off an embankment, out of sight.

Striker had been following the van only because of its suspicious actions back at the bar, waiting for his contact to get back to him with more information about Peterson. The first shot took him by surprise and he swerved in response to the broken windshield.

"Shit. Everybody get your seat belts on," he said, wrestling the vehicle back under control.

Pit drew his gun, powering his window down. "No," Striker said. Everyone looked at him. "If Natasha's in there, I don't want her hurt." With reluctance, Pit, Bigun, and Scott put their guns away. "Scott, call 911 —"

They heard the loud pop before the SUV reacted. Striker fought the vehicle, trying to maintain control, feeling a sickening sensation when they swayed into the guardrail, hearing the crunch of metal, watching in amazement as the guardrail separated from the macadam, seeing the empty space below them.

"Shit. Hang on."

The biker settled back in his seat and glanced at Natasha with a sneer. "Calvary's gone, Sis. Ain't nobody gonna rescue you from the long ride you're about to go on." He jabbed Misty. "Hell, man, I'm so horny, I'm calling first and last dibs."

Misty laughed.

Natasha forced her concern for Striker's welfare to the back of her mind. *Okay, quit acting like a timid girl and do something.* She had to get out of here; she had to go help Striker. She scooted away from the window, into the shadowed portion of the back. She turned her back to them and collapsed on her side. She began to wiggle her butt through her arms, trying to get her hands in front of her, trying not to listen to the biker discuss what he had planned for her. She felt a surge of adrenaline when her arms broke free of her legs.

She brought the rope up to her face and tore at it with her teeth, working it. Nothing. Struggling with the bondage, trying hard to control her rising panic, she could feel the skin tearing at her wrists. She rubbed them in the rope, back and forth, ignoring the slimy lubricant of blood.

She began to mouth a prayer, one Striker's grandmother had taught him, one she had asked him to teach her. She loved the way the Cherokee words sounded rolling off her tongue; it never sounded right in English. A prayer they would say together, of thanks to God for their lives and their love. She fought the tears that were hovering close now, tears of panic, tears of fear, tears of regret.

Natasha yanked hard on her right arm, feeling the flesh rip, the blood spurt, and then freedom as she pulled it through the tether. She didn't take time to remove it from her left wrist, leaving the rope to dangle instead. Without hesitating, she reached down, shoved her boots off, and unfettered her feet. She unbuckled her belt and pulled it free. Looping it, she rose to her feet and moved toward the front of the van. She placed the garrote around Misty's throat and jerked hard.

Misty's hands left the steering wheel and settled over the belt, trying to pull it away from her neck.

"Fuck!" The biker reached over and grabbed the steering wheel with one hand, using the other to push against Natasha in an effort to shove her away.

"Ain't gonna happen," she growled, placing one foot against the back of the seat for more leverage, leaning back, tugging with all her might.

"Ease up on the gas," the biker yelled at Misty.

Misty didn't respond; she was too busy trying to loosen the belt enough to get a whisper of breath into her lungs.

Keeping one hand on the wheel, the biker pulled his gun with the other, his eyes going from the road to Natasha. He pointed the firearm at her. "Let go of the belt, bitch, now."

"Make me," she replied, pulling with all her might. She felt the rush of air as the bullet flew by her head before she even heard the report of the gun. She took the time to gauge the distance, watched the biker glance toward the road, and kicked out, knocking the pistol out of his hands. She aimed another foot at his temple, but he caught it before it landed and twisted, trying to knock her off her feet. She resisted at first, but then gave into it, falling, feeling the belt tighten even further. They careened on the edge of the roadway; she could hear the gravel spitting up beneath the wheels, the sickening sound of metal against metal. Then they were tumbling. Natasha and Chumley were tossed around the vehicle like towels in a dryer as they crashed over the embankment.

The SUV settled at the bottom of the ravine, landing right side up, to Striker's amazement. He listened to muttered curses from the others, muffled by the airbags that had exploded all around them. He leaned his weight against the door and shoved, but it wouldn't budge. "Everybody okay?" he yelled, kicking out with his feet, and was relieved to hear the others answer in the affirmative.

They had to climb out the back of the SUV, after shooting the glass out. Each man had sustained cuts to the face and arms, but no one seemed to notice. The five men stood looking off in the distance, as if that could help them reach the van. Striker retrieved his cellphone and called 911. He told them about the kidnapping in progress and provided the direction in which the van had been traveling. He threw his cell down, walked away from the others, looked up at the sky, and screamed, "No!"

The other men knew not to approach him; there would be no comforting Striker. Roger fell to his knees, put his hands over his face, and tried to stifle his sobs. Scott limped around, shaking his head, feeling helpless. He pulled out his cellphone and called their men to the scene. Pit and Bigun looked at one another before taking off running. Striker didn't hesitate to follow.

The van landed on its top. Natasha rested at the very back corner for a few moments, listening to the engine ticking down as it cooled, the wheels turning, thinking it was a miracle she was still alive. She tried moving her body, beginning with her neck. Other than soreness, it felt okay. She attributed the burning sensation in her upper back to stiff muscles while trying to ignore the dull ache in her lower back. Her arms seemed all right, but her left leg was useless. She knew there was blood, could feel it running onto her foot, but she refused to look down to see how bad it was. It hurt to breathe; she supposed she had cracked a rib. She prayed it hadn't penetrated a lung.

Wiping blood out of her eyes, she searched the van for Chumley. He lay in a crumpled heap above the windshield, next to the biker's gun. She feathered her hands along his body, searching for blood, and was relieved to find him still breathing. Chumley raised his head and gave her a dazed look.

"That's my baby," she said in a soothing tone, picking him up and kissing him. Natasha peered over the back of the driver's seat at Misty. Collapsed over the steering wheel, blood seeped from her ears and nose. Natasha knew that to be a bad sign. The biker was lodged into the foot space beneath his seat. At best, he was unconscious, at worst, dead. She didn't really care.

She scanned the vehicle, searching for a way out. The side doors as well as the driver and passenger doors had caved in; the windshield was a melange of broken cracks. She crawled to the back door and pushed on the handle, but it was jammed, too. She maneuvered her way to the front of the van to retrieve the gun. She returned to the back and shot the handle. She sat down and kicked out with her good leg, shedding tears of relief when the door flew open.

She collected Chumley and dropped out of the van, crying out in pain when her leg gave way and falling to her knees. The van had landed next to a creek bed, and Natasha crawled over to put cold water on her face, fighting the black dots dancing in the air around her. Chumley whimpered to be free, so she placed him on the ground. She watched him lap up the water, thankful that the small dog hadn't been seriously injured. When the world stopped spinning around her, she called the Pug to her, picked him up, and struggled to her feet. She had to find Striker. He might be hurt; he might need her help. "Please, God, don't let him die," she prayed, heading off.

Striker recognized the sound of the crash in the distance as that of a vehicle colliding with earth. "Oh, God, no," he said, and ran in that direction.

After what seemed an eternity, he saw Natasha in the distance, limping badly, dragging one leg behind her and holding that damn dog against her chest. Everything about her seemed red, even her hair. All that blood. He hurried toward her, shouting her name. She glanced up and, seeing him, collapsed on her knees. As he ran, he watched her struggle to stand. Then she was moving again, trying to run toward him, but something was wrong with her leg; it wasn't moving with her body. He reached her, snatched her up into his arms, felt her wrap her good leg around him, and heard her say into his neck, "What took you so long?" before bursting into tears.

She felt so damn fragile in his arms. He choked on the sob that threatened to escape. "Oh, baby, I've never been so scared."

Then her mouth was on his.

Chapter 32

The doctor insisted Natasha remain in the hospital overnight for observation since she had been struck over the head twice and had been rendered unconscious both times. She resisted, but Striker sided with the doctor and refused to give Natasha her clothes. He didn't tell her he couldn't have even if he had wanted to; he didn't know what the emergency room techs had done with the bloody mess. The doctor agreed with her it was miraculous she had survived with only a mild concussion, a sprained ankle, two bruised ribs, a bruised kidney, numerous contusions and lacerations, and a deep gash in her left leg.

Natasha insisted Striker stay with her during the examination. While the police talked to her, she had trouble controlling her impulse to cling to him and never let go. When he was required to go to the admittance office to handle paperwork, it was all she could do to keep from calling after him, asking him to please not leave her.

Striker managed to obtain a private room for Natasha and sat on the bed beside her, holding her, constantly checking her bandaged wrists and leg for seepage. She alternately hugged him and pushed herself away. Striker couldn't figure out what that was about. She trembled so violently at times that the bed would shake.

He lay beside her on the bed, gathering her into his arms and pulling her against him. "Just let me hold you, baby. I need to hold you."

She relaxed against him and only then did the trembling begin to abate. She eventually drifted off to sleep, clutching his shirt in her hands.

Striker eased up from the bed, watching Natasha, trying not to wake her. He walked to the waiting room to let Roger, Scott, Pit, and Bigun know she was all right. The four men were huddled together, talking in low voices, when Striker approached them.

"She's going to be fine," he said, answering their unspoken questions when they looked at him. "The doctor's keeping her overnight for observation, but he thinks she'll do just fine. She's asleep now."

Scott left to meet with the detective investigating the case. Pit and Bigun told Roger they'd go get their vehicle and wait for him out front. Striker watched the two men walk away, thankful for them, knowing they would take care of Roger. He gave his friend's shoulder an affectionate squeeze.

"I'm really sorry about Misty, Roger," he said.

Roger shook his head with dismay. "I think I could have loved her." Tears gathered in his eyes. "She used me, Striker."

Striker didn't know how to console his friend. He put his arm around his shoulder and hugged him. "Anything I can do, let me know," he said.

Roger nodded, looking away. When he had himself under control, he returned his eyes to Striker's. "You're staying, I suppose," he said.

Striker nodded.

"What are you going to do about her?"

Striker knew Roger was talking about Natasha and the bodyguard business. He shook his head with a miserable look. "I don't know, Roger, but it's about to drive me out of my mind."

Roger thought a moment. "You want some advice?"

"God, yes."

"Call in the big gun," Roger said and left.

Striker watched him stroll away, then pulled out his cellphone and dialed Stevie.

When Natasha woke the next morning, Striker was slumped in a chair next to her bed, his head tilted back, his long legs stretched out in front of him. One arm rested on the bed, his fingers brushing hers. She smiled, thinking there was no better sight to wake up to than Striker's beautiful face and body.

Seeming to sense her scrutiny, Striker slitted his eyes open. "Well, hey," he said, straightening up.

"Hey." Natasha moved to sit, but stopped with a wince. "Ooh," she said.

Striker was beside her in an instant, easing her back onto the pillow. "Lay back. You're gonna be sore as hell for a few days." He levered the bed to a sitting position.

"Thanks, darlin'," Natasha said.

Striker sat beside her, took her hand. He brushed hair back from her face, tucking it behind her ears. "How are you feeling?"

"Fine." She shrugged. "A little weak, a little lightheaded, but okay."

Their eyes met and held for a long moment.

"Tell me," she said.

Striker knew better than to dance around issues with her, so he put it to her straight. "Misty's dead." He watched the tears spring to her eyes. "I'm sorry, baby. The paramedics tried to resuscitate her at the scene, but it was useless. They declared her dead on arrival when they arrived at the hospital."

"How's Roger handling this?" Natasha said, her face tight with concern.

"I think he'll be okay. I told Pit and Bigun to stay close, keep him company. They're good friends, they'll help him."

"I need to see him."

"We will. Soon."

She wiped away tears. "It's so useless, Striker. All over a friggin' dog show."

"I know."

"What about the biker?"

"He's in this same hospital, but from what I understand, his injuries aren't considered serious enough to keep him here for long. He's talking, trying to place the blame for this whole mess on Misty."

"I hope in the near future he ends up spending some quality time with others of like mind in a not-so-nice place," Natasha said.

"He will," Striker said with conviction. "I talked to the detective handling this case — which reminds me, he needs to take your statement as soon as you feel up to it."

"I'll give it today."

"Anyway, it looks like Misty's partner, Frank, has skipped. KPD hasn't been able to locate him so far."

Natasha's door brushed open and Myrtle stuck her head into the room. "Hello, dear," she said with a bright smile. "Is it all right if I come in?"

Natasha wiped tears from her face as Striker stood and crossed over to greet Myrtle. "Come on in, Ms. Galbreath," he said, holding the door for her.

Myrtle beamed at him as she passed by. She leaned over to kiss Natasha on the cheek. "He's such a nice-looking man," she whispered.

Natasha smiled her agreement.

Myrtle stepped back. "I am so sorry, Natasha, dear, that you were injured."

Natasha shrugged as if it were nothing. "It's okay, Myrtle. I'm fine. Really."

"Well, I had to come by and personally thank you, dear, for your brave efforts to save my Chumley."

"How is he?" Natasha asked. "Did you bring him? Can I see him?"

"He's fine. I left him at home with my sister. When you feel up to it, please come over and visit us."

"I will."

Myrtle reached into her pocketbook and withdrew an envelope. "I can't stay long, but I wanted to bring by a little thank-you gift. I suppose now that we know who was behind the letter, we can put all this behind us."

"Definitely," Natasha said, wondering if she would ever be able to.

"Well, I'll be going along, dear. I hope you get a chance to come by soon."

"I will, Myrtle, I promise," Natasha said, knowing her attachment to Chumley was too great to be ignored.

After the door closed behind her, Natasha opened the envelope. Inside was a folded check. She pulled it out and her eyes widened. "Wow."

"What?" Striker said, joining her on the bed.

"A check for five thousand dollars." She looked at him. "Where do you want to go? Where can I take you? You promised me a month, remember?"

She was busy kissing Striker when Stevie shoved open the door, followed by Jacob. Their faces were pale, their expressions strained. Natasha snuck an angry glance at Striker. She had told him not to tell her parents where she was or what had happened. Ignoring her, Striker rose from the bed to exchange kisses with Stevie and shake hands with Jacob.

Stevie leaned down, kissed her daughter's cheek, and smoothed back her hair. "Heard you tangled with some mean mothers."

"Yeah, well." Natasha returned the smile her dad was sending her before his arms went around her.

Stevie sat on the bed. "How are you feeling?"

"Fine, Mom, I'm just fine. I don't know why Striker had to call you," she said, looking at him long enough to convey her ire. "I'm going home this morning. It's no big deal."

Stevie turned to Striker and her husband. "Would you two excuse us? There's something I need to discuss with Nattie."

Natasha watched the men leave, fighting the inclination to plead with them not to leave her alone with her mother.

After they were gone, Stevie gave Natasha a look.

"What?" Natasha asked while simultaneously thinking, *You shit, why'd you ask her that?*

"I've been wondering about something and maybe you can help me out," Stevie said.

Uh-oh.

"Here you are, engaged to a nice man, Natasha, a man who loves you very much, by the way. Yet you can't seem to control that reckless inclination you have for getting yourself into trouble."

Natasha shrugged. "Go figure."

"Have you set a date yet?"

"You're talking about the wedding?"

Stevie's look answered her question.

"Probably a year or two."

"Why so far away?"

"Well, you know, I want to do more with my career before I settle down —"

"That's bullshit."

Natasha's mouth dropped open. "Mom."

"What the hell is so great about being a bodyguard anyway that you would choose that over being married to the man you love?"

"It's my career, Mom. It's what I want to do."

"What about babies? You going to be a bodyguard, get yourself knocked around, beat up, and shot at while you're pregnant or after you have kids?"

"Come on, Mom. It's not like that."

Stevie stared at her.

"Well, okay, maybe it has been so far, but that's only because I got involved with two really weird cases."

Stevie continued to give her daughter a disgruntled look.

"No, Mom. I give you my promise, the moment I find out I'm pregnant, if we decide to, you know, get pregnant, I'll retire."

"Why not now? You don't have to work, not with Striker around."

"I can't quit now."

"Why not?"

"Mom, I can't just sit on my butt all day and let Striker support me. At least not until we have kids, if ever. I mean, do I look like the housewife type to you?"

Stevie gave her an offended look. "What's wrong with it?"

"Well, if that's your thing, that's fine, but it's... you know, not *my* thing."

"Why not a nice, sensible job? One that doesn't involve guns and knives and people wanting to kill you?"

Natasha rolled her eyes.

"Natasha, as your mother, I'm telling you, get out of this field. It's too dangerous, especially if you're part of it. Do something else with your life, something more productive."

Natasha's eyes narrowed. "What's more productive than protecting someone else's life?"

"Have babies, start a family right off. That's productive."

"Not until I prove myself."

"Prove what?" Stevie asked, her voice rising.

Striker and Jacob, standing outside the door, trying to talk about fishing and the like but not having much luck, glanced at one another.

"That I can do what I want to do," Natasha said. "That I am an individual, that I'm independent, capable of accomplishing something on my own."

"I think you've already proven that, Nattie."

"How, pray tell? First you and Dad support my butt, then Striker wants to. Why can't I be responsible for myself, make my own way in the world? Why can't I do that?"

"What the hell is wrong with being married and having a family? What's so dependent about that?"

Natasha glared at her mother. "You have always told me, above all else, to be my own person, live my own life, be independent, do what makes me happy, don't depend on someone else for that happiness. Well, that's what I'm trying to do here."

"I thought Striker made you happy."

"He does. But, shoot, Mom, I can't let myself become dependent on him for that." At Stevie's look, she continued. "I need to know that I can do this, that I can have my own career, be my own person, live my own life first."

"Nattie, listen to me —"

"Let me ask you this, Mom. If I were still an office manager or engaged in a vocation you wouldn't consider dangerous, would we be having this talk?"

Stevie rose. "I give up. I've never been able to talk any sense into you. I don't know what the heck is wrong with you. You never could see things the way other people do. You always had to make them more complicated."

Natasha quietly watched her mother stalk out of the room. A moment later, her dad stepped through the doorway.

"Hey, Dad." Her bright smile quickly turned into a frown, seeing the look on his face. In Natasha's mind, this was the actual big gun.

Chapter 33

Two weeks later, grooming horses at her parents' barn, Natasha reflected on the conclusion of the Chumley case. The biker had been placed under arrest and was sitting in a jail cell, unable to make bail. So far, the police had not been able to find Frank, who seemed to have vanished into thin air. Kit never made it to her mom's house, and all efforts to locate her had proven futile. Natasha had spent a great deal of time with Roger the past two weeks, concerned about the effect Misty's betrayal and ultimate death would have on him. So far, he seemed to be handling it well enough, at least better than she would have if it had happened to her.

She shook her head. *All over a dog show.*

She placed her face against Ben's neck, breathing in his wonderfully warm, comfortable smell. When she led the horse out of the barn, Cherokee, Natasha's Quarter Horse, raised her head and nickered. Natasha watched the blind horse trot over to join the others grazing near the creek. It was interesting the way Ben so easily maneuvered their pasture, using his auditory senses to direct him. And the way the other horses seemed to understand this and directed him with their noises.

Natasha sat down on a bale of hay to rest before beginning the arduous task of mucking stalls, idly rubbing her swollen ankle. Although she wasn't fully recovered from her injuries, she was making rapid progress. She lay back and closed her eyes, breathing in the earthy smell of dried grass, feeling it prick her back through her tank top. It felt good to be alone. Her grandmother had paid a visit, staying at Natasha's cottage for the better part of a week. This time, at Striker's insistence, Natasha remained at his place so he could take care of her, something he was very good at. Although B.S had been welcome, her stay had been filled with tension. Every time she and Striker were together, they would circle one another like two bucks ready to butt horns, with Natasha anxiously watching on the sidelines. They eventually came to some sort of understanding, and by the time B.S. left to return to Atlanta, she was actually showing some civility toward Striker and calling him by his correct name. Once Natasha learned the reason why, it didn't surprise her: Striker had agreed to be a resource for her.

Natasha's mind turned to Striker and their life together. In a week, they planned to leave for his cabin in the Smokies to spend quality time together without interruption. There they would make their wedding and honeymoon plans. She smiled with happiness. Oh, to be Striker's wife. The thought gave her goose bumps. She had not expected their relationship to become so intense in such a short period of time, and she was still trying to get used to the depth of her love for this man.

He was not only her soul mate, but her life mate as well, and she vowed to herself to do everything in her power to make him as happy as he made her. She began to dwell on her choice of vocation, knowing Striker's fear for her safety, as well as that of her parents. She was thinking that maybe she ought to just keep playing house with Striker and not worry about having a career when her cellphone rang.

"Natasha Chamberlain?" a woman with a lilting British accent asked.

"Yes?" Natasha said, thinking she didn't know anyone from across the great pond.

"Hello, love, this is Giki," the voice said.

Natasha frowned. Where in the heck had she heard that name before? "Giki?"

"Yes, love."

"Bloody 'ell." Natasha sounded just as British as her caller.

Giki said, "Do you know who I am, love?"

"Omigosh. The rock star."

"That's right, love."

"I am so honored. But why in the world would you be calling me?"

"Well, love, my great-aunt is Myrtle Galbreath, and she highly recommends you."

"Bloody 'ell."

"I'm touring the Southern states beginning next month, and I'd like to hire you to accompany me as my bodyguard while I'm in America."

"Bloody 'ell." Natasha fell off the bale of hay.

Natasha handed Gloria heavily padded, plastic earmuffs.

"Uh-oh," Gloria said with a teasing glimmer in her eyes.

Natasha nodded in a solemn way. "I don't know if those will even help. Shoot, I doubt if the earplugs plus those will keep you from hearing, but you can try it."

She was right. It didn't.

A Note From the Author

Each year, millions of cats and dogs are euthanized in animal shelters throughout America.

Please, if you are the owner of a domesticated animal, have your pet spayed or neutered. If you cannot afford it, ask your local veterinarian about donations from other animal lovers to cover the cost.

I would also urge all pet owners to treat your pet with kindness and enjoy the enormous amount of love and enrichment they can bring to your life.

If you witness anyone abusing an animal, please call your local law enforcement agency or humane department. In many states now, there are laws protecting animals from abuse.

~Christy Tillery French